Caribbean Chill

Ron Smoak

A Dane Skoglund Adventure

This is a work of fiction. Certain real locations are included but names, characters, places, and incidents either are the product of the author's imagination or are used fictitiously. Any resemblance to actual persons, living or dead, businesses, companies, events, or locales is entirely coincidental.

Ron Smoak
Canton, Georgia, USA
www.smoakmediagroup.com

Smoak Media Group, LLC, P.O. Box 4326, Canton, GA 30114

Copyright ©2014 by Ronald A. Smoak

ISBN-10: 0985888229 (ebook)
ISBN-13: 978-0-9858882-2-0 (ebook)
ISBN-10: 0985888237 (Paperback)
ISBN-13: 978-0-9858882-3-7 (Paperback)

PS23456789909 2014
Printed in the United States of America

Cover Design by Richard K. Green

The author has made every effort to provide accurate telephone numbers and Internet addresses at the time of publication. Both the publisher, Smoak Media Group, LLC, and the author assume no responsibility for errors or changes that occur after publication. The publisher does not have any control over and does not assume any responsibility for the author or third party websites or their content.

DEDICATION

This book is dedicated to my parents, Tivie and Alfred Smoak and my son, Christopher, his wife Christina and my dearest granddaughter, Elise.

They were products of a long, extensive line of Smoaks in South Carolina dating back to 1740. Their lineage is still producing offspring who shall carry on the line and make us all proud.

Ron Smoak

Other Books by Ron Smoak

Alpha Threat

Ron Smoak

ACKNOWLEDGMENTS

As always I have to thank my editor, Sherry Ruschell. She reads and edits my writings over and over and over again; nothing but true strength and determination.

I also want to give a big shout-out to my second family, my friends at *Maxwell's Cigar Bar* in Woodstock, Georgia. They are always supportive, always ready with comments and always true friends.

Most of all, I must thank my dear wife, Lee, who puts up with me, edits my writing and manages most of the post production marketing and sales. Without her, there would be no books… Thank You!

.

By nature, men are similar… by practice men are wide apart.

- Confucius

PART ONE

1782

CHAPTER ONE

January 29, 1782

Brimstone Hill Fortress, St. Kitts, West Indies, 2:00 p.m.

Lieutenant Warren Ashley peered over the wall of Brimstone Hill fortress. The sky was crystal clear with a few drifting high white clouds. Off to the southwest of the island in the Caribbean Sea, Ashley spotted the French fleet. Out of range of the fortress' cannon, the fleet was completing its blockade, cutting the British off from replenishment. As the French continued to disembark significant land forces, the siege of Brimstone Hill was inevitable. The warm, stiff trade winds raked the lieutenant's face forcing him to place one hand upon his fore-and-aft bicorn to prevent it from blowing away. He forcefully turned away from the in-the-face wind.

"I believe the French now have us at a disadvantage," said Ashley stoically to his sergeant standing beside him. "They have a significant blockade set up. I do not see how anything might get to us from the sea without being intercepted."

Ashley had reason for his concern. It was clear to him the French intended to force the British garrison under General Thomas Shirley and General Thomas Fraser to relent, awarding the fortress to French Admiral Comte Francois Joseph Paul de Grasse.

"Yes, sir," answered Sergeant Harold Garrick, his eyes glued to the more than twenty ships down below. "A rather formidable force as well, I might say. Several of those ships are France's finest."

"Quite," snapped the lieutenant. The two continued to worriedly assess the armada laid before them. In the imitable British style, Ashley added, "But we shall retain our stance here and defeat this enemy." Garrick nodded in agreement even though inwardly he had his doubts.

The tall, slender British officer looked resplendent in his red uniform, his wavy black hair barely showing from underneath his bicorn.

Never had he seen so many enemy ships in one place. It was going to get very bad in the near future.

The Brimstone Hill fortress sat atop a steep, heavily wooded eight hundred foot hill about ten miles northwest of Basseterre. Designed by the British and built by island slave labor, the fortress loomed above the sea. Previous military groups hoped to build such a fort, but the British were the only group, through superior architecture and engineering, that succeeded. The fortress enjoyed a commanding view of the sea to the west and the mountain forests of the north, south and east. It was easily the clear focal point of military interest on the island of St. Kitts. If one was to capture the island, which was the intent of the French, Brimstone must fall.

The fortress itself was built of volcanic rock, harvested from the hill on which it sat. To military groups, it was a shining example of a new British architectural design known as the polygonal system. This profile relied on geometrically designed barriers for defense. Each face of the fort could be swept by fire against all attackers. The most significant item was the relatively low walls and abundance of underground tunnels, magazines and passages. Gone were the looming high walls of the forts of the medieval era castles. Brimstone Hill was one of the first fortresses of its kind in the Caribbean, much less in the entire world. It was thought to be impregnable.

"Mister Ashley!" They both turned urgently to see their captain approach. "The Admiral believes we are to expect shelling to begin within the hour. Place your men and make ready the defense of the fort. Inform General Fraser that we are ready in all respects."

"Yes, sir," answered Ashley, saluting smartly and nearly losing his bicorn. The captain quickly turned and moved on to another position to repeat his order to the next platoon.

"Sir, I will muster our full platoon and make ready," barked the sergeant even before Ashley could set the order.

"Very well, Sergeant. Make haste and tell the men to move smartly. We have little time before the fighting begins." Sergeant Garrick saluted and hurried off screaming at the men at the top of his voice. Lieutenant Ashley took one final look at the ships approximately eight hundred feet below and wondered if he would survive the day.

This was his first time in defending such a fortress. Fear filled his mind although he did not outwardly display his emotions. This day could be his last or the last for many of his men. He surmised that the men were scared as well.

"Steady, men," said Ashley in a surprisingly calm voice. "We have the best defenses provided by the Crown. We will repel any action against this fort." Several men reacted with a muted cheer while others seemed to be lost in their own thoughts; of death, no doubt. Ashley's thoughts turned to his home and his family. He wondered if he were to die here would his body be returned or relegated to a nondescript cemetery under a few trees thousands of miles from England.

Quickly he erased his worries from his mind and strode off to update the General and attend to the defense of the fort. He must carry on.

CHAPTER TWO

January 29, 1782

Aboard the Ship Ville de Paris, off St. Kitts, West Indies, 2:15 p.m.

Admiral Francois Joseph Paul de Grasse stood atop the afterdeck peering through a spyglass at the fortress high on the hill to his left. After a long perusal of the fort, he lowered the glass and handed it to his orderly standing behind him.

"Get me the map of the fort," he demanded to no one in particular. "Have we received the ready signal from the fleet?" he asked without emotion.

"No, sir," answered his orderly, Captain Jacques Bertrand, as he placed the spyglass into its protective case. "The *Auguste, Duc de Bourgogne* and *Languedoc* have answered but we are awaiting an answer from the *Couronne*."

Another seaman hurried over with a large leather map case, opening the top and handing it to Captain Bertrand. He removed the map and held it at arm's length in front of the Admiral. De Grasse stepped over and began to peruse the stiff map. After a few seconds he turned to Bertrand.

"The road from below curls around the mound and enters the fort here," he said, pointing to a spot on the map. "That will be their weakest point. Concentrate your fire on the battlements to the right where the fort entrance opens to the road. We may be able to damage the area and give our ground forces a soft spot to attack as they swarm up that side of the mount."

"Aye, sir," came the response from his orderly, who immediately rerolled the map and placed it back into the hands of the seaman who brought it.

"Captain, please signal Admiral Genouilly of our intention to commence firing. Tell him we await their readiness." The Admiral was perturbed at his subordinate Admiral's shortcomings but did his best to not show his disapproval to those around him.

"Aye, sir," answered Captain Bertrand, who looked to one of his lieutenants. "Signal the *Couronne* that the Admiral is awaiting their ready." The officer turned and ran to the high point of the afterdeck where the signalman stood. After a quick conversation, signals were flashed and the two men's eyes were trained on the *Couronne,* expecting a quick response.

Aboard the *Couronne*, the first officer saw the signal. He glanced over at Admiral Genouilly, who returned a look of disgust.

The first officer burst into action. "Make ready in all respects for battle!" he screamed to the crew. He began shouting multiple orders that were repeated throughout the ship. Within minutes, a deck officer reported to the first officer.

"All ready for action, sir."

"Very well! All hands stand ready," cried the first officer. The Admiral stepped over.

"Signal the Admiral of our readiness," commanded Genouilly, reaching into his breast coat and removing his snuff box. "I want a full report as to why we did not make ready when I ordered such fifteen minutes ago." At that the Admiral sniffed a pinch of snuff and stepped off of the afterdeck below to his quarters.

"I can tell you why," said the first officer under his breath. "You never issued such an order. And now you leave the deck while we are to begin an attack." The second officer stood quietly beside the first officer, nodding his agreement but not uttering a sound.

Captain Bertrand aboard the *Ville de Paris* received the signal from the *Couronne* with a slight smile. He knew of Genouilly's shortcomings and his loose command aboard his ship. Admiral Charles Genouilly was born into a family with naval connections. His father, a respected naval engineer, provided many friends in high places that rendered him an admiralship even though most in the Navy thought him not to be qualified. This incensed many in the Admiralty as well as many of the French naval officers under his command.

"All ships reporting ready, sir," said Bertrand, waiting for de Grasse's response.

"It's about time!" Admiral de Grasse said storming away from the rail. "That damned man will be the death of us all before this fight is out." Captain Bertrand fought back a smile, trying to maintain the necessary decorum in front of the fleet commander.

"Captain, you may begin your bombardment at will, sir. But make haste as the day is moving to an end soon," said the Admiral.

"Yes, sir," said Bertrand saluting. "Make ready to fire...port side!"

The command was repeated across the deck and down to the firing decks below. The Captain waited for a few seconds and then screamed FIRE at the top of his lungs.

Roughly half of the eighty cannons aboard the *Ville de Paris* began firing on the fort at the top of the hill. The ship shuddered as gun after gun spewed explosive cannon balls toward Brimstone. The siege had begun. A second volley from the guns roared as well flinging their presents of death toward the fort's walls.

Several of the other ships sailing with the Admiral's flagship also began firing. Officers lined the decks of the ships trying to determine the damage done. The time lag between the loud report of a cannon and the sound of the explosions on the fort were ten to fifteen seconds apart. Captain Bertrand was worried the range was too far even with the cannons' sharp upward aiming angle. However, the shells were indeed reaching the walls! Explosions were crawling across the top of the fort.

"Fire at will!" commanded Bertrand, hoping to unleash a withering barrage. An acrid haze of smoke was already surrounding the ship. The heavy smoke burned the eyes of Bertrand but he dared not let that keep him from his duty.

Bertrand turned and asked de Grasse's orderly for the spy glass from the case. He took the glass and trained it upon the fort. The shots were slamming into the rock walls, exploding mercilessly but merely marring the rock face. So far the bombardment was simply creating noise, which was enough to rattle the troops.

CHAPTER THREE

January 29, 1782

Brimstone Hill Fortress, St. Kitts, West Indies, 2:35 p.m.

"Stations!" screamed Lieutenant Ashley as the first sounds of cannons reached the fort walls. Several explosive shells burst against the fort's rock wall a few seconds before the deep bellowing of fire from the ships reached the top of the hilltop. At least sixteen hits slammed into the sturdy walls, causing little damage but flinging cannon ball shards and rock pieces everywhere. Several men fell with the first bursts. One unlucky soldier caught a cannon ball shard in the torso, slicing him in half instantly. The battle was on. A long dance with death had begun. Soldiers from other units were scurrying about on specific duties but to the uninformed it looked like total chaos. Medics assigned to the walls began to assess the wounded from the first volley. Still more cannons bellowed, some from down below from the ships while other shots seemed much closer and came from behind the fort.

"Sir, we have cannons behind us!" screamed a soldier ducking behind Ashley. "They are all around us!" The man was right. Unbeknownst to the brigade in the fort, French troops had managed to scale the lower hills at the rear of the fort and set up their cannons.

Ashley whirled around just as a volley from a landward cannon unleashed. "How in the blazes did they get to those positions?" he thought. The French must have worked miracles to get those cannons ashore, transported them around the fort and set them up at the rear...without anyone seeing them? What happened to their troops in the area?

Instantly another set of explosions burst against the wall in front of Lieutenant Ashley, nearly knocking him to the ground. Bits of rock and shell pelted him and the men around him. It felt like a thousand bee stings. Two more men fell with shrapnel wounds from the exploding cannon balls. He grimaced and wiped his face, already covered with rock dust.

For a week the British held out under the siege of the French. Of the nearly 1,500 men in the fort, they suffered the loss of about a hundred men with many more wounded or sick. Food was getting low as well as water. General Fraser stood at the far wall of the fortress. He knew the end was near. Especially since he heard the rations, ammunition and artillery sent from the governor to relieve them were intercepted by the French. That cache included several modern siege guns that would now be turned on Brimstone.

"Mister Ashley," called the General.

"Sir," answered the bedraggled lieutenant struggling to move up to the General's side. Ashley was not only exhausted but had sustained several small wounds which had festered in the heat and grime of war. He bore a fever but had not put himself on the sick list. His uniform was tattered and he had long lost his bicorn.

"Ashley, I regret to inform you that the supplies, guns and ammunition will not be arriving. It seems the locals commandeered the loads and turned them over to the French. Now it seems they have our guns and our ammunition to drive us off of Brimstone."

Ashley's heart sank. He was counting on those provisions, guns and ammunition to not only re-energize the fight in their favor but also boost the morale of the men. Now it was not to happen. For a second he showed his disheartenment but quickly recovered. But not before General Fraser saw his reaction.

"That is all right, my boy," General Fraser said calmly, trying mightily to assuage the young officer's fear. "As professional soldiers we all must learn to lose battles as much as we win them. We will be all right. I have asked Major Wills to determine the best way for us to surrender the garrison if it comes to that. We hope to march down to Sir Hood's ships and be off of this ragged island for good once we surrender." Ashley stood there quietly. Inside he felt like dying. He had never been in a losing battle and it hurt mightily.

"But before we go I need you to put together a group of eight men for a very special and secret mission for me."

"Of course, sir," answered the lieutenant, flashing back to the moment. "What would you have us to do, sir?"

"Step over here, Ashley. A word with you..." The General placed his arm around the shoulders of the young lieutenant and walked him over to an area away from the others. Single shells were still falling about but most men had little regard for them now. They figured if they were to die they would at least be off of this rock. Death? So be it.

"Ashley, have you ever been to level three below this fort?" asked General Fraser.

"Sir, that would be the dungeons, would it not? I have been there a few times with prisoners."

"Yes, it is the dungeons." Fraser looked at the young man intently. "This fortress does hold a secret. The Crown uses the hidden dungeons below the fort to safeguard treasures enabling us to sustain ourselves. For years it has been a concealed storage place for loot captured in these waters from Spanish and Dutch ships. I have orders directly from the First Lord of the Admiralty to remove and return the treasure to Admiral Hood."

The young lieutenant was astonished. He found the General to be a confident and respected officer. He was amazed the General hid such important information from him.

"I understand, sir," said Ashley even though he thought it mad to be worried about treasure at a time like this. "How much treasure is there, sir? Can eight men carry it out?"

"The amount is quite large. It will take several hours even with your men. Take these keys," said Fraser, handing Ashley two large iron keys on a ring. "Tonight after dark go to the far northern side of the dungeon and look for a carved eagle on the wall. Ten paces to the left of the eagle you will find a carved stone door with a double keyhole. Use these keys to unlock the door and push it open. This will not be easy as the door is of significant weight. It will take the force of several men to push it open. Once you enter the next room, follow the hallway, go down and retrieve the strongboxes. Your exit will be marked as well. There are several boats there to get you out to sea. Do you understand?"

"Yes, sir, I do," answered Ashley even though he did not. "Boats, sir? Under the dungeon?" What was he saying? The General simply looked at him with no answer. He decided not to ask any more questions and do what the General ordered. "I will go pick the men now if I have your permission," Ashley said quietly.

"By all means, Ashley, go at once and tell no one of this task. You are in complete command and answer only to me. Do you understand completely?" The General looked him square in the eyes.

"Yes, sir." At that Lieutenant Ashley strode off to gather his men.

CHAPTER FOUR

January 29, 1782

Deep below Brimstone Hill Fortress, St. Kitts, West Indies, 11:05 p.m.

"Men, follow me closely and make no noise," ordered Lieutenant Ashley. He had selected eight of his most trusted men for the mission. The men moved down several stone stairways, finally reaching the lowest level of the fort. The group walked through the empty dungeon toward the north side just as the General directed. Even though they were almost a hundred feet below the top of the hill, they continued to hear and feel the dull vibrations of explosions against the fort's walls.

Ashley led the men with a burning oil lantern in his hand, squinting intently, searching for the eagle carving on the wall. There was a strong musty smell like that of a tomb. If not for the lanterns the men carried, they would have been in a complete blackness known only to the dead.

"Look for a carved eagle in the wall," said Ashley to the men as they spread out. They all took a few steps toward the walls, their lamps lighting the darkness.

I found it, sir," cried one of the men. Ashley quickly stepped over. He used his hand to wipe much of the dirt and dust off of the carving. Yes, that was it. The dust was heavy. No one had been here in a long while. He turned to his left and marked off ten paces. He spied the stone coping around an area of wall. It looked like solid stone. Ashley looked for the two keyholes. They were hidden beneath the dirt and dust. He finally found them just to the right of the coping thickly covered with dust. He used his fingers to attempt to clean the keyhole, reverting to the key to make the final opening. The key in the keyhole, he turned the key unlocking the door. There was a heavy click. He ordered several men to push. They struggled mightily until the door finally budged. Once there was room enough for a man to pass, Ashley pulled the men back and, again leading with his lantern, stepped into the interior.

Ashley expected a room with a box of jewels, silver and gold, but what he found was an empty room. As two other men entered, he stood in amazement to face another door on the wall to his right, this one made of heavy ship's wood. He stepped over to the door and pulled the latch. It moved slightly. There was no lock.

"You there! Lend your backs and open this door," commanded Ashley.

The two soldiers pried open the door, pulling against the cast-iron latch and working their fingers into the slight opening. Cobwebs and more dust covered the old door, which he wiped away with his free hand. Once broken free, it opened with little effort. Ashley stepped through into a much larger room with a wooden floor.

Facing him was a massive set of multiple stairways leading down deep into the hill under the fort. Looking about, he realized he stood on a square platform ten feet square. He gingerly stepped over to the railing and looked down. He saw nothing but blackness. But he could hear and smell a most extraordinary thing, the sea. It finally dawned on him that this was a cave!

Was this his way out? General Fraser told him he would know it when he saw it. He glanced over to the head of the stairs leading down. There was a plaque with a simple message... "To the Sea..."

"You," he said pointing to one of the soldiers, "take three men and go back and close the stone door. I don't want anyone to follow us."

"Yes, sir," the men replied and they were off.

"How many lanterns do we have?" asked Ashley. The men checked. They had six in all.

"Six lanterns, sir," reported one man.

On the walls Ashley spotted several unlit torches. "Take a few of those torches with us. We may need them later."

The men gathered the torches and looked to Ashley for orders.

"Stand close," commanded Ashley.

"Very well. As soon as they close the stone door and return, we will venture down, complete our mission and make our way out of here." In the glowing orange light of the lanterns Ashley could see a mixture of smiles and puzzlement on the men's faces. They had no idea about the mission but knew this may be their only chance for living through the bombardment above. The men were happy to find an escape route under the fort to the sea. Within a minute the four men returned to the group.

Ashley walked over to the stairway and noticed about ten heavy ropes attached to several pulleys mounted on a formidable wooden structure above the platform. All were covered in cobwebs and dust. Only the relatively fresh open air from below allowed their breathing without strain. In the dim light he realized the ropes were attached to something deep below them. They had found an elevator to bring goods in and out from underneath the fortress! Ashley stepped to his right and saw the railing was not attached to the platform. It could be removed to access the lift as it rose to the top level.

"Look for ropes tied off... probably over there," he said pointing over to the dark corner. A few men moved toward the darkened area.

15

"I have it, sir. There are at least ten ropes engaged here. I believe them to be lift control ropes."

"Yes, indeed, I believe they are as well," said Ashley happily, stepping over. Now they would be able to ride down rather than walk. But they still had no idea how far down they would go. "Release the ropes and mechanism and raise the platform."

Six of the men manned the ropes as Ashley and two others looked over the railing down into the abyss below. All they could see was darkness.

As the men pulled the ropes there was a heavy creaking sound and dust began to fall from the mechanism above their heads. The men looked down to keep the dirt and dust from falling into their eyes. Several were coughing.

"Take care, lads. Make fast your ropes and pull together. Our lives depend on it." Ashley intently watched as the ropes pulled against pulleys attached to heavy counterweights over to their right. Ah, he thought. Now he saw what was happening. The ropes the men were pulling simply unlatched the counterweights and released them to ride the tracks down. This action in turn caused the lift below to steadily rise.

The noise of the mechanism multiplied with each creak and groan inside the cavern, sounding as if the wooden structure was coming apart. Two of the men stood back from the railing over by the door. There were squeals of wood rubbing tightly on wood. Dust fell through the flickering light of the lanterns looking like clouds of reddish smoke. A musty odor permeated the room. Ashley reached into his jacket and retrieved a handkerchief to hold over his nose and mouth to repel the dusty cloud. He wondered if the ropes and mechanisms were too badly deteriorated to be safe. He knew there was no turning back. There was no other way out now and he would most certainly be shot if he disobeyed orders and abandoned his duty.

"Careful, lads," he spoke calmly trying to disguise his own fear and bolster the men.

It took less than five minutes but seemed an eternity for the lift to rise until it was flush with the platform on which they stood. Ashley could feel a cool breeze coming from the depths of the cavern now. And he could hear a lapping sound of water against a hard surface. Yes, this had to be the way out to the sea. "All right, men. Tie the ropes off and make ready to lower the lift." Ashley walked over to the railing, opened the gate portion of the rail and stepped gingerly onto the lift platform. He half expected to plummet to the depths below. But it was much more solid than he expected. He stomped his foot on the platform. It did not budge. It was evidently built very well to enable heavy loads to be brought up and down at will. He smiled to himself. "You men come with me," he ordered pointing to four men with lanterns. "The rest of you stay here."

They boarded the lift. Ashley looked considerably more confident the lift would work. The other men with him looked scared but followed Ashley's lead.

"Don't worry, lads," Ashley spoke boldly. "I assure you this is perfectly safe. Look how well it is constructed." Ashley pounded on the lift structure with his right hand. As he expected, nothing moved. It was solid. The four men riding with Ashley didn't seem to be swayed. They were still not certain this contraption would work. Here they were in a cavern under the dungeon in a large shaft that seemed to have no bottom, riding some sort of elevator that went to God knows where in the darkness. Ashley smiled and gave the order to lower. The lift floor creaked loudly, so loudly that the riders were startled, one man jumping off back onto the platform.

"Here you," yelled Ashley. "Get back on board. We have much work to do!" The man stepped back aboard and Ashley nodded to the men working the ropes. Again there was a heavy creaking sound and the floor of the lift began to go down. Ashley was excited. While hell was breaking loose above, he and his men would be able to retrieve the General's treasure and escape to the sea. No one would ever expect them to be able to get out of the fort this way. He began to think as to how he would move up the coast and find a ship to ferry them away.

Suddenly there was a loud pop and the lift stopped abruptly.

"What's the matter?" yelled Ashley back up at the men above.

An answer came swiftly. "No problem we can see, sir. It must have just been something under strain that loosened. Everything seems fine here."

"Very well. Continue to lower us." Within seconds the lift returned to its smooth, slow downward trek.

It took a full ten minutes for the lift to get to the lowest level. Once the group was near the bottom, Ashley slowly waved his lantern, trying to get a better view of the area around them. It was clear they were still a few feet above the bottom. Now the smell of the sea was much more prominent. At times under the lantern light he could see glistening waves below. The lift slowly stopped, aligning itself with another wooden platform built onto the rock wall.

"We are about five feet above the water," said Ashley quietly. "Step over to the platform and try to find the way out." The four men moved off of the lift onto the platform. There was a wide rocky ledge leading off to one side of the cavern. "Careful, men. Move to your left. I believe I hear the water lapping."

The men moved slowly into the darkness along the ledge. They followed the wall around a corner. Now they were out of sight around the corner. "Sir, we are in a cave," one of the men called back. "It looks to be an opening several yards away."

"Very well!" yelled Ashley. "Move ahead and report back."

"Yes, sir," replied one of the men.

As they moved ahead the men began to see a widening of the cavern. Further to their right another wooden platform began to appear in the darkness. However, unlike the previous platforms, this one was huge. This was the main operations area of the cavern. There was a wooden building built against the wall about thirty feet from the water's edge of the platform. An inscription was hewn into the rock on the right side of the building... 1699.

Several more lanterns were hanging from the outside wall of the building evidently to provide lighting to the work area. Moving ever forward, the men could now see two large rowboats tied to the dock. Just past the building a larger boat of nearly forty feet loomed in the darkness. The men lit the lanterns mounted on the outside of the building and out on the deck, bathing the entire area with a dim but widely spread light. One man turned and noticed the inscription.

"Look at this!" the man exclaimed. "1699. That's a long time ago, mate."

Another soldier ran his hand over the carving. "Somebody carved that here. Right into the rock, it is!"

"I'll bet it was those who built this," replied another.

"Built the dock maybe but not this here cave. It must have been a volcano that made this cave."

"Go back and report this to the lieutenant," said one of the men to another. The man turned and hustled back down the ledge. The other three began to look about the building.

As the returning man turned the corner of the cave, he saw Ashley standing at the edge of the lift talking to the two men with him.

CHAPTER FIVE

January 29, 1782

Deep Below Brimstone Hill Fortress, St. Kitts, West Indies, 3:30 a.m.

All of the men were now together again on the dock in front of the building. The lanterns they carried pierced through the darkness creating an aura of light around them.
"You three men check the building. See if you can find a storage area with large boxes," ordered Lieutenant Ashley in a monotone voice. His orders echoed throughout the cave causing an eerie feeling in the dark. "Sergeant, take the rest of the men and check out these boats. I want them ready so we can load them and get out of here as soon as we are able."
"Yes, sir," replied one of the three as they turned and gingerly entered the building carrying their lanterns. The other five men scrambled aboard the forty foot small sailing ship tied to the dock. Even they surmised that the larger boat would serve a better escape rather than the other two smaller skiffs. Ashley stood there in the weak light and began to look around. He saw the inscription carved into the rock. Even he had to reach out and touch it to believe it.
The actual cave was immense. He was amazed at its size. The dark granite walls rose to a height of more than sixty feet and at least thirty-five feet wide at the dock. The interior rock was shiny, wet from the large amount of water held in the mountain. As his eyes moved down the rock toward the channel to the sea, there was no light to be seen at the end, just a jet black cavern leading away. He noticed the cave retained its height but narrowed to just a mere fifteen feet in width. It would be a tight fit to get the small ship out of the cave. But he knew it came in so it should be able to leave.

He ambled over to the edge of the dock and turned, holding his lantern high above his head in order to see above the small building. In the fading light he noticed a wooden perch built above the building. The perch was set back into the rocks and was slightly hidden from below. Ashley noticed a pair of swivel guns mounted to the railing. He deduced this provided protection to the entire cave area in case of attack. He took his lantern and walked over to the left side of the building finding a narrow, steep stairway hewn into the rock leading up to the next level. When he got atop the perch, he was amazed at the clear view of the waterway below as the view dissolved into the darkness of the other side. He also noticed a heavy wooden crane mounted against the rock wall to his right. The base was equipped with a swivel system enabling the boom to swing out about the dock below. So that was how the boats were loaded! He stepped over and inspected the device. It looked in good condition.

He turned his exploration to the darkened stone wall behind him. He saw nothing surprising, but in stepping over from the swivel guns his boot caught on something on the deck. Looking down he saw a steel rail of an imbedded railway ending there on the platform. This was very interesting, Ashley thought. Whoever had worked here must have been moving something very heavy. Could it be treasure? He followed the tracks back around a bend in the cave until he came to a heavy oaken door. Success! That must be the vault.

"Sergeant, come up here immediately. Bring one of your men," yelled Ashley. He could hear the men scurrying around below but with the echo in the cave they could not find Ashley. "Up here, you dimwits," barked the lieutenant looking down on top of the men below. "There is a way up over here," Ashley said pointing to the once hidden stairs.

The men ran around to the stairway and climbed up. As they reached the top the other men came out of the building below. "Sir! Lieutenant Ashley?" cried one of the men leading the group coming out of the building. Ashley strode back around the bend and met the men coming up the stairs. He stepped over to the rail and looked down on the other men below.

"What did you find?" Ashley asked.

"Nothing really, sir, merely the normal shipping tools and supplies. We did find a store of powder and shot, though," reported one soldier.

"We also found several other rooms as well, sir," continued the other soldier. "There are several bunk rooms, a kitchen and two large common rooms. It looks as though there were dozens of men stationed here. The pantry is still packed with bags of food and goods. Behind all of this we found another cave. It is as though some of the men were tasked with enlarging the area by digging a cave directly through the mountain..."

Ashley turned to the soldier who was speaking.

"How far does the cave go?" he interrupted.

"Not far, sir. I walked about forty feet back and saw its end," answered the soldier.

"There were no branches off of the main cave?"

"No, sir."

"Very well," said Ashley. "Did you happen to see an axe or any other hand tools?"

"Yes, sir, we did, sir, several. Picks and shovels as well."

"Good. Bring a few axes up here. We have a door to break down." Ashley turned and led the men around the corner. Within a minute the men with axes joined them all in front of the door.

"Take down this door, Sergeant," commanded Ashley.

With that order, one of the burliest of the men stepped forward and removed his tunic top, handing it to another soldier.

"Here, hold this while I tear this door down," the sergeant said.

He took up the axe and began his task. The first blow struck the heavy door with a huge thud that echoed throughout the cave. The noise startled several men on the dock below. Yet the strike only yielded a small chip of wood. The door stood defiant. The sergeant released his grip and spit on his palms, rubbing his hands together. He lifted the axe again and set to work on the door.

Everyone else stepped back as wood chips and dust flew everywhere. Ashley stepped back against the rail and took out his handkerchief, holding it over his mouth and nose. The noise was deafening as it echoed throughout the cave.

It was slow going. The door was much more substantial than it looked on the surface. It was several layers of hard oak nailed and glued together with pitch. Together the sandwich of wood stood more like iron. Each blow of the axe chipped off only a small sliver of wood. After an hour and several men, the door finally released its secrets.

As the men pulled away the final remnants, Ashley came forward with his lantern and stepped into the ruined doorway. Looking down he saw iron rails continuing on the floor leading back into the darkness. He was elated! This was clearly an old mine where the treasure was held. He noticed the rails disappeared back into the darkness. The walls were hewn rock. It was clearly dug by hand. The pick and chisel marks proved that point.

"Sergeant, take two men and find out what's back there."

The sergeant looked at two men, motioned to them and the three entered the darkness, each with a lantern. One carried an axe as some sort of defense. He was evidently scared of what or who he might find deep in the darkness. Ashley followed the men's progress.

The tunnel was about five feet high and a mere foot wider on each side than the rails on the floor. The area was surprisingly clean. It looked as though it was swept regularly. After twenty feet, the mine curved right and then abruptly to the left. Once around the first bend, Ashley noted the light dimmed. At the next turn, the light from the lanterns the men carried was gone.

All of the men stepped back onto the decking above the dock. Ashley glanced down, noticing the rest of his men continuing the work on the large boat below. He turned to his men around him.

"We will wait here until they return," said Ashley. "But I believe what we seek is in there somewhere."

After five minutes the sergeant and his men returned. "We went to the end and the tracks stopped. But over to one side we found several rail cars and at least thirty to forty iron strongboxes," reported the sergeant.

"We've found it!" cried Ashley smiling widely. "Everyone down to the end and let's get the boxes loaded."

As the men scrambled down the mine, Ashley stepped back to the perch over the boats. He saw the remainder of his men working below. "Is the boat ready?" he yelled to the two men still down on the dock.

"Yes, sir, she's ready, sir," came the reply from one of the men. Ashley spun on his heels and walked rapidly back to his men. He had a good feeling about this. As he reached the back of the mine, the men placed several of the small rail cars on the tracks and were loading each one with the strongboxes. About half of the boxes were loaded.

"Bring a box to me, Sergeant," Ashley bellowed with a huge grin. "Let's have a look at what we are to carry."

One of the boxes was manhandled over in front of the lieutenant. The sergeant placed the blade of one axe on the lock and held it there while another soldier used his axe to strike. There was a large spark as the lock burst open and fell away. The sergeant pulled the latch back and opened the lid.

Even in the poor light of the lanterns, the bright sheen of pure gold shone like the sun. Intermixed were glorious jewels of several colors. All of the men were speechless. Ashley reached down and ran his hand through jewels, silver and gold, hundreds of Spanish gold coins looking as new as the day they were minted. This was part of a Spanish treasure trove that never made it back to Spain.

"God in heaven..." slipped one of the men. The sergeant gave him a stern look. "I am sorry, sir. It just slipped out. I couldn't help it."

"That's all right," said Ashley. "I was about to say the same thing. Look smart. Let's get this onboard now. I want to leave within the hour."

It took much longer than they thought. The heavy strongboxes were a bear to move about. But finally the loading was complete. It was nearly ten in the morning.

In all they counted forty-eight boxes of treasure. All were stowed away below deck on the large boat. They were ready to leave.

"Is everyone aboard?" he asked.

"All are aboard. Our cargo is held fast and we are ready to sail, sir," answered the sergeant crisply.

Ashley took his place as the captain of the ship even though he never sailed a ship before.

"Get a man on the bow there with a lantern to find the way. Tie the lantern to a long pole and hang it out in front of us. We don't know if we have a clear way or not. When we get to the sea, douse all lanterns. We have to get past the French in broad daylight unnoticed."

They eased the large boat from the dock. Using several large paddles, they began to row the ship down the cave. When the cave narrowed, the men used the paddles to push against the walls moving the ship along. She seemed to travel well but was laboring under the added weight of the loot.

Still, Ashley felt elated. They were underway and with a bit of luck they would be away from the island long before dawn. After fifteen minutes of pushing the ship Ashley felt the cool rush of wind in his face. They were nearing the cave entrance to the sea! They could hear waves crashing. Ashley worried if the waves would be too much for the heavily laden ship. But he had nowhere else to go.

"Douse the lanterns," ordered Ashley. "Get ready to raise the sails. We are coming out of the cave."

With the lanterns out, they could see the mouth of the cave. It was covered with vines and undergrowth but they should be able to get through. The morning sun shone brightly, lighting the way out. Unbeknownst to Ashley, the cave entrance was over one mile north of Brimstone Hill, far away from the French ships laying south. They were going to make it!

The men used the oars to clear back the vines and the ship eased into the sea. Even amidst the rolling waves the ship moved steadily out of the cave.

"Raise your sails, Sergeant," commanded Ashley as if he were a grizzled old sea captain himself. With the sails raised the ship took off as if it were being pulled to the sea. "Now we are moving." Ashley grabbed an eyeglass from a small cabinet at his knees beside the tiller. He scanned the horizon in all directions looking for sails in the distance. There were none. "And not a French ship to be seen!" remarked Ashley. "Let's go, lads."

The men wore grins from ear to ear. They made it! Now all they must do is sail to a nearby British held island and they were heroes.

CHAPTER SIX

January 29, 1782

At Sea off of St. Kitts, West Indies, 3:45 p.m.

After several hours of sailing to the north, one could see darkening clouds back toward the east. An early evening storm was brewing. The breeze was growing, moving the small ship faster toward their goal. Behind them they could no longer see St. Kitts.

"Good morning, Lieutenant Ashley," grinned the sergeant as Ashley stepped up on deck after a few hours of sleep. "We are in great shape, sir. The sky is clear and there are no French ships anywhere. A storm could be coming, though," he said, motioning eastward.

The lieutenant retired below earlier feigning exhaustion but was really nursing a bad case of seasickness. He was no sailor. The sergeant reached into a basket beside the wheel and pulled out some crusty bread and cheese. "A bit of lunch for you, sir?"

Ashley's eyes bulged and he caught himself before he puked. He took a long breath. "No, thank you, Sergeant. I'm quite well without. Do you have any idea where we are?"

"Not exactly, sir, but we should be getting close to a few isles that are held by the Crown. If I did my navigating correctly, we should see islands very soon."

"So you know how to navigate a ship?" asked Ashley.

"Well, no, sir, but I've seen it done and I think I did a reasonable job at it. The sun rises in the east and sets in the west. We are headed north."

Ashley closed his eyes. He didn't know which bothered him more, a sergeant that was navigating or seasickness. Neither was much fun. Their ship was moving well but was beginning to struggle against the growing waves.

Suddenly one of the men burst up the ladder from below.

"We are sinking!" he screamed.

Ashley looked at the sergeant. Both the men's eyes were wide with fear. They could take a battle but a sinking ship? Most of them could not even swim!

Ashley jumped down to the main deck. "What do you mean we are sinking?"

"It must be the weight of the strongboxes, sir. The water is coming from cracks in the hull around the boxes."

"Show me," screamed Ashley. They both bound down the ladder and into the forward hold. Other men on the deck were watching intently. The water was two feet deep and rising fast. The weight of the boxes caused immense strain on the aged hull causing leaks. Water was coming in and could not be stopped. Ashley took one look and realized there was no way to stop the water. It was coming in too rapidly. He ran aft and leapt back upon the deck.

"Sergeant, how far are we from land?" he screamed.

"I don't know, sir. I think we should see an island very soon, maybe an hour or so."

"We don't have an hour," Ashley said morosely. "We are sinking fast by the bow." He quickly looked about the deck. "Where are the lifeboats?"

"Lifeboats, sir? There are no lifeboats. This is a small sailing bark used to ferry cargo to and from larger ships."

"Well, what are we to do, Sergeant?" Fear was again beginning to take over Ashley.

"I don't know, sir. I don't know," replied the sergeant morbidly.

The two men looked at each other. What was a complete success a few minutes ago was now a disaster. There was little they could do.

Within twenty minutes the ship slowed to a crawl and the forward decks were awash. They would sink within minutes.

One of the men screamed, "I don't want to die!" The others moved aft to be near Lieutenant Ashley.

In a strange calmness, Ashley looked at his men. He was horrified but accepted their fate. The men looked to him for hope. But there was none.

"Come, men. We all thought we would die in battle at Brimstone Hill, but we survived. Now it is certain we will die in the depths of the sea. Our families will not have the honor of our bodies. But it does not lessen the fact we did our duty to the Crown by making certain the treasure did not fall into the hands of the French. I am supremely proud of each and every one of you. May God bless you all."

The men quietly awaited their fate. In minutes the bow dipped under the water. Thirty seconds later the treasure-laden ship passed beneath the waves, leaving the men bobbing in the sea. None lasted more than fifteen minutes as the sharks began their feeding frenzy. Soon the sea was at peace again. Only a few remnants from the boat floated in the sea. The ship, the treasure and the men were gone. So was the underground secret of Brimstone Hill Fortress.

CHAPTER SEVEN

February 9, 1782

Brimstone Hill Fortress, St. Kitts, West Indies, 9:00 a.m.

General Fraser paced the floor in his dank office within the fort. More than a week had passed. He could still hear the bombardment continuing outside. A relatively cool breeze blew into the office, exiting through a small window port above the desk. Being that the fort was in the Caribbean; its design was altered slightly to ensure that the omnipresent sea breezes were harnessed as much as possible to help cool the fort. If not for this natural air conditioning, the interior of the fort would be an unbearable oven.

He sat down behind his grand desk. He had brought it along with him from England. It was present at all of his posts. It gave him a feeling of consistency that most military officers could not afford. Its wood was a rich mahogany, hand carved by his uncle back in London. It was a gift to him from his family upon his becoming a General. The desk was greatly admired by his fellow officers and the admirals who stopped by in port every now and then. He was very proud of it.

But alas, his mind was slowly rewinding the events of the last several days. His once plum command was now in tatters. Many of his men were dead and his fort was sure to fall. He looked down at his spit-shined boots. He could actually see himself in them. His orderly did a fine job last evening polishing his boots. But what for, he thought. His men were dirty, tired and hungry and most of all so tired of the incessant barrage the French batteries served upon them.

The General changed his thoughts to Lieutenant Ashley. There was no word of the man. He smiled. That was good, he thought. Ashley must have successfully found the route and secretly removed the treasure to safety. Otherwise the lieutenant would have returned.

Realizing his fate was certain; General Fraser stood and stepped over to the cabinet that held his safe. He began to turn the tumblers to open it.

"Orderly," he bellowed.

Within seconds the door flew open and a young, haggard lieutenant burst through the opening. His uniform was dirty, torn and reeked of old sweat.

"Yes, sir," he chirped, wiping his sleeve across the right side of his face to remove some dirt. He stood at attention.

"Be at ease, Johnson," the General said quietly, looking over this young man. How his men had suffered. Once the lieutenant was in perfect form; he looked sharp and correct in every way. Now look at him. Barely able to carry on, he was a beaten soldier, simply doing his duty to his beloved General.

"Come in, son. We must prepare for the inevitable." He returned to opening his safe.

The young orderly was shocked. "Son?" The General had never called him that. The General looked back at the orderly.

"Have someone ready a fire so that I may burn my official papers and orders. They must not fall into the enemy's hands."

"Right away, sir," answered the orderly. As he turned, he hesitated for just a second. "Sir, forgive me, but am I to understand that we will be surrendering?"

General Fraser stopped opening the safe, staring straight ahead. The orderly knew he had upset the General and rushed to atone for his comment.

"I am sorry, sir. I didn't mean…"

The General smiled. He felt genuinely ashamed. He looked down for a few seconds. Then Fraser calmly stepped away from the safe and looked directly at the orderly.

"Yes, Johnson, I will be surrendering the garrison in order to save the lives of my men. I do not like it, but I am astute enough to know when a cause is lost. Our only recourse is to surrender like soldiers and make terms to leave the island immediately."

Lieutenant Johnson eyed the General with a sheepish look. "Thank you, sir. I mean, this will save our lives. Thank you for saving our lives, sir." With that he turned and strode out of the door.

General Fraser returned to his safe, taking out the contents and piling them on his desk. He also opened a side cabinet and began removing the files. Lieutenant Johnson returned.

"I have prepared a fire, sir," he reported. "Are you ready for me to take care of the burning?"

"Yes, Lieutenant, I am ready. Take these first." He handed the documents from the safe to the orderly. "Make absolutely certain these are destroyed with no way to revive them."

"I will personally take care of burning these documents, sir."

"Thank you, Lieutenant Johnson. Thank you."

It took no longer than an hour to completely clear out and burn the documents in the General's office. Now the orderly returned.

"Sir, what are we to do with your desk?"

The General ran his hand across the desktop. He clearly did not want to give it up. "Take the desk out and throw it from the wall. If I cannot have it, I cannot fathom anyone else having it." With that he turned and walked methodically out of the office, leaving the orderly standing there stunned. Throw it off of the fort's wall?

Lieutenant Johnson left the room to enlist several men to carry out the General's bidding. What a waste, he thought.

Several days of continued bombardment sealed the fate of the British. But in that time a pact was made between the French and the British to surrender the fort. In return for the surrender, the British were accorded the right to march out of the fort with their heads held high with their weapons and their flag. It had taken several days to work out a suitable result, but nevertheless an acceptable agreement was signed.

Lieutenant Ashley and his men were never accounted for after the siege. General Fraser was the only one who knew of their mission and he did not divulge that information to anyone. It was thought that Ashley and his men perished defending the fort and their bodies not recovered. With the death of General Fraser years later, the fate of Lieutenant Warren Ashley, his men and their secret task died as well.

PART TWO

Present Day

CHAPTER EIGHT

May 15, 2013

At Sea, South of St. Maarten, Netherlands Antilles, 5:30 p.m.

"Honey, get me a drink, will ya?" yelled Kirk Jones to his wife, Ann, who was below deck. They were on a southeast course of 120 degrees on the way to Nevis. Their Beneteau Oceanis 54 was knifing through the blue sea. The sun was beginning its slow dip below the waves in the west. The hiss of the waves was the only sound except for the groaning of a few stays, a soft fluffing of the sail.

"You want juice, water or a beer?" Ann shouted back out to the cockpit.

"Juice is fine for now. I want to get in some calmer seas before I get a real drink."

Kirk readjusted his faded orange Clemson tiger paw cap to ensure it covered his balding head out here in the brilliant Caribbean sun. His closely cropped graying hair needed a trim. Maybe Ann would do it for him when they got to Nevis.

At fifty-eight, Kirk removed himself from the daily grind of managing his fortune a year ago, leaving the job to his son Wade. Ann turned fifty-five two weeks ago when they were in Tortola. Both considered themselves full-blown young senior citizens. They always dreamed of sailing away together so when Kirk, the consummate sailor, came across the sparsely used Beneteau ocean cruiser, they jumped at the chance. They immediately named her *"Sea Ya"* and within a week sailed directly from Charleston to the Caribbean for the adventure of their lives.

Ann and Kirk Jones were on the third month of an open-ended cruise around the Caribbean Sea. Kirk was an information technology guru who parlayed a small nest egg left to him by his father into a massive fortune with some very adept investments on a few web companies. Kirk graduated from Clemson University with an electrical engineering degree and later returned for a Master's in business administration and a Ph.D. in computer engineering from Georgia Tech. That was the gateway to his IT fortune.

Ann and Kirk were part of the social elite in Charleston. Kirk's family had lived in Charleston for decades and his inheritance not only included a small fortune but their beautiful pastel colored home downtown on the Battery.

Ann was a Charlestonian, born and bred. Her ancestry spanned back to the original Charles Towne in 1670 over on the west side of the Ashley River at Albemarle Point. Her ancestors included several mayors of Charleston and a few state representatives and senators as well as two South Carolina governors. Ann's pedigree was as credible as any original Carolinian. She received her degree in environmental studies from Davidson College in North Carolina. Her mother grieved briefly about her going "North" for an education, passing up several scholarships at South Carolina universities. But in the end, her family was very pleased at her accomplishments.

Both Ann and Kirk loved the south. Both relished the refined life of living in Charleston, its food and the social amenities. And both loved to sail.

Ann Jones popped up from below and into the now setting sun. "Here's your juice. All we have is pineapple so we need to re-provision when we get to Nevis."

"I figured that as well," said Kirk, sitting on the port side of the sailboat steering the wheel with his bare foot. "We are out of M&M's too."

"Oh, horrors!" cried Ann, mocking her husband. "No M&M's... how can we survive?"

Kirk laughed. He was world famous for loving those little bits of chocolate. He even invested in the maker of M&M's candy. His favorite was the peanut M&M's but they were harder to come by down here. And they were pricy. So he settled for the originals.

Ann passed the juice to Kirk and sat across from him on the transom. The moderate sea breeze blew her dark hair off of her face. "It looks like it's going to be a beautiful evening. Anything going on with the weather?"

"Nope. Clear as a bell for the next several days. It's just a bit windy. But it won't be long before we start hurricane season. This neck of the woods will get pretty nasty."

"Will we be back in Charleston by then?" asked Ann, looking up at the sails above her head.

"Depends," said Kirk. "If we leave Nevis within a few weeks and head back home, we should be able to make it easily. But if you want to stay longer, we can scout out a weather port or two and ride out any storms as long as we stay way out of its path. We also could sail down to Aruba or Curacao. Hurricanes don't generally track that far south."

"What a hard decision," remarked Ann. "I so love it down here but at the same time I yearn to be back in Charleston with our friends."

"Well, we have a few weeks to decide so don't fret about it. We'll figure it out in due time." Kirk was always the calmer head when decisions were needed. Ann loved it.

Kirk could see a few clouds growing off to the northeast over near St. Barts. While not overly concerned, he decided to keep an eye on the possible storm. Small storms came up quickly in this region and could give their boat a harsh buffering. He was a stickler for safety and did not want to get caught out in the open sea with any storm brewing. He would rather bring the boat into port and ride it out there. Ann saw him checking the sky and wondered what he was thinking.

"See something you don't like?" she asked quietly.

"Well, I may have jinxed us by saying the weather was nice. I'm watching those clouds over there near St. Barts. They could be brewing a storm." Ann reached into a bin and pulled out a pair of binoculars and took a look.

"Hmmm, it does look like some rain over there but maybe it's just a shower."

"Just the same, I'm going to keep watch in case it decides to explode on us." Ann smiled. She so appreciated Kirk's carefulness, especially here out at sea. She found herself staring at her husband, her man. Life was good.

CHAPTER NINE

May 15, 2013

At Sea, South of St. Maarten, Netherland Antilles, 6:20 p.m.

The old fishing trawler chugged along, moving slowly but surely through the darkening waters. She purposely did not carry any lights and the bridge lighting was suppressed as to not shine as a beacon in the night. She flew no flag and to the casual viewer looked like any of a number of fishing vessels in and around the islands.

She was dirtier than most boats in the area but her engine sounded strong due to a recent overhaul that generally reconditioned this forty-five foot boat into a thoroughbred. Her top speed was now nearly 30 knots. It was much like a Volkswagen with a Porsche supercharged engine. Now she was a predator. The rework had improved nearly every system on the boat except its overall appearance. The *May Pop* was pure pirate boat, nasty and deadly in a fight. It still looked old and dirty. Inside she was shiny and new. She could run circles around all of the boats in the Caribbean except possibly two or three U. S. Coast Guard fast attack ships.

"Sighting anything?" asked the first mate, stepping into the bridge. He looked at the open charts on the desk behind the wheel to see their location and course. He checked the GPS and radar.

"There are a few sailboats out there. Nothing too large, though," announced the swarthy man steering the boat.

"Bates, keep your eyes peeled for anything out near us without other ships around," said the first officer to the helmsman.

"Aye, sir."

"Is the captain in his cabin?"

"Yes, sir. He left the bridge about five minutes ago," answered Bates. With that the first officer left the bridge and went down the stairs below.

The *May Pop* was out of Guadeloupe, one of the small fishing villages on the north side of the island near Saint-Jacques. Captain Maurice de Terr had sailed these waters for more than forty years. His grizzled look and rough ways made him the perfect captain of the *May Pop*. He was as mean as a trapped rattlesnake and generally only looked out for himself. But he knew the seas around the islands from Anguilla south to Dominica.

A generally gruff man, his hard life left him a hard man. Fishing was the base of his life but through his contacts in the islands he had also been introduced to more lucrative but illegal business options. That's where the first officer came into the picture.

Dante Brees was the first officer of the *May Pop* for the last five years. It was through his contacts that de Terr delved into a dark world of smuggling, piracy and kidnapping. They seemed to be getting deeper and deeper into illegal activities, but in return, they were all making substantially more money.

At the soft knock on the cabin hatch the captain turned. "Come in." Brees stepped in.

"Hey, are we going to do anything tonight?"

"What do you have in mind?" answered the captain with another question.

"I have a lookout watching for any smaller boats out by themselves. There's some weather coming in from the northeast but the seas are pretty calm. The moon is obscured as well. We could safely grab a boat and not be seen.

The captain looked up at Brees and bit his lower lip. "You see anything interesting out there?"

"There are a few sailboats but no target yet. We should know within the hour," said Brees as he sat down in a chair and began picking the dirt from under his fingernails.

"Call me when and if you see anything," said the captain, standing up. "That will be all, Mr. Brees." Brees took the hint.

"Yes, sir," answered Brees as he left for the bridge.

An hour later, after checking their radar, they spotted a sail. Brees was on the bridge. He took the binoculars to check out the sailboat in the failing light.

"She's about a mile and a half in front of us," said the mate steering the *May Pop*.

"Can we take her?" asked Brees. "Do we have the speed?"

"Yes, Mr. Brees. We can take her at will. It would be best for us to take her at night."

Brees thought for a second. It would be easier at night when most sailors are tired and not as sharp, especially if the sailboat slows after dark. "Let's get ready. But we must make certain she does not have a chance to make any radio calls," ordered Brees. "We'll board the sailboat about 2:00 a.m. and take anything of value and get rid of the crew. I will tell the captain."

"Very well, sir," answered Bates.

CHAPTER TEN

May 16, 2013

Two nautical miles off Philipsburg, St. Maarten, Netherland Antilles,

1:00 p.m.

The pristine Sanya 57 catamaran sliced through the deep blue water sending a fine spray giving the air the freshness of the sea. In the sunshine the spray looked like millions of diamonds flying in all directions. Flying fish whizzed out of the bow wake, flying in the wind and then back into the dark blue waters.

Hugo Winsor was at the helm sporting his raggedy University of Texas cap that looked as though it had been worn to hell and back three times. The sun fell warmly on Hugo's face on a gorgeous day as he steered the boat into the wind. There were a few high clouds and a westerly wind that sustained the huge sails of the ocean-going catamaran.

The smell of the Caribbean Sea was crisp and clean. With not another boat in sight, the looming hills of an island seemed close enough to touch. Life could not be better. Hugo had just taken delivery of his new toy two days ago in Tortola, immediately naming her *Sweet Texas*, a nod to his Texan background.

"Yo, Dane," yelled Hugo. "That's Philipsburg on the port bow!"

Dane Skoglund opened his eyes from his catnap on the salon seat. His chiseled looks, short blond hair and six foot two bronzed body made him look like a god. He was the kind of guy for which women would swoon. But Dane was no ladies' man. In fact, Hugo would force him into blind dates when they were back in Miami.

Dane's shyness made him wanted by women even more. He had a quiet, all business demeanor causing him to look aloof in most situations. Aloof he was not. Keenly focused on something else was the most likely cause. Anyway, women loved him for it. He was hard to get, so to speak.

He strolled over to the helm station on the starboard side of the huge catamaran and stuck his head up to see Hugo.

"St. Maarten already?" he asked. "That was a fast traverse. It seems like we just left Tortola."

"Yeah," answered Hugo with a massive smile, "this baby can fly. I can't believe we waited this long to buy one of these. She literally guides herself through the water." Dane smiled broadly. He could not remember the last time he saw his buddy Hugo so happy…at least without a female present.

"How far do you think we are from port?" asked Dane, frankly not even caring if they made port at all. Dane was thoroughly enjoying sailing around the Caribbean. The events surrounding the past several months were still clear in his mind. The capture and rescue of his sister, Dana, and her husband, Randall, still bothered him. Since the incident, he had wondered many times what might have happened if things did not go their way. In many ways he believed that both he and Hugo were living on borrowed time. Hence, he was determined to live this vacation to the hilt.

Dana and Randall were planning another trek, this time to Peru. When he last talked to them about a week ago, Dana was excited to be able to have their entire trip fully funded by the United States government, another perk earned from their experiences in Brazil. So with his sister and her husband at ease, Dane and Hugo had embarked upon a six-month cruise around and about the Caribbean, with Hugo furnishing the boat.

Hugo turned his head toward Dane. "It shouldn't be more than twenty minutes. Why, Boss? You gotta be somewhere?" Hugo grinned.

"Oh, hell, no, not that," answered Dane. "We just need a few provisions before we take off again." Hugo nodded his head in agreement and returned his attention to their course.

"I think a cold one is in order as well," added Hugo, adjusting his trim and steering toward the wide harbor.

Hugo handled the huge catamaran like it was a toy. The ease of sailing such a beautiful, seaworthy boat and Hugo's natural affinity to the sea made the job almost simple. Even though he was from Texas, Hugo had taken to the water like a fish throughout his life. That was the reason he and Dane hooked up in the Navy and moved along through SEAL training together. Although not brothers, they were inseparable. Hugo adjusted his ragged University of Texas ball cap covering his close cropped, jet black hair. His Texas roots were back into Mexico before the Mexican War. Throughout his early life and high school he worked hard at his father's garage and a short stint in the Texas oil fields. That had made him a man, beholding to no one and very able to take care of himself. All this before he joined the U.S. Navy; all this in a compact five foot nine inch man.

Now with his family riches and the gold he and Dane split from their Amazon adventure, both were set for life. In fact, one would have to literally work hard to spend all of the money these two guys now possessed. Even so, they were unchanged, except for this new boat Hugo had bought.

The fifty-seven foot cat was entering the wide port of Philipsburg. Off to starboard, two large cruise ships were docked at the A.C. Wathey Pier and Port Facility. Royal Caribbean's *Allure of the Seas* was tied up on its starboard side or northeast side of the long pier. The sheer size of the ship amazed Dane. It looked like a giant floating building, sparkling white in the bright afternoon sun.

"Good Lord, look at the size of that cruise ship! We must look like a flea against those behemoths."

Hugo began loosening his sails, slowing the large catamaran significantly. The automatic sail reefing system on the cat made lowering the sails a thing of the past. "Yeah, that puppy is pretty damned big," he said, returning his attention to the cruise ship. "In fact, that's the *Allure of the Seas*, the largest cruise ship in the world."

Dane had seen some large ships back at home in Miami, but this was the first time he had actually seen the *Allure* since Ft. Lauderdale, Florida was her home port. "Man, I have seen pictures of her but the pictures do not depict how HUGE she actually is!" said Dane without taking his eyes off of the massive ship.

"We can come in right behind her, I think," said Hugo, "depending on the security layout." Within a minute, the marine radio in the cockpit crackled and the voice of the harbor master came through loud and crystal clear.

"Large sailing cat to the southwest, this is the Philipsburg harbor master. Please adhere to standard security distances from the cruise pier. Please acknowledge…"

"Oh, crap, now I've done it. My first port of call and I've pissed off the harbor master," Hugo said smiling and steering the catamaran to give a wide berth to the cruise pier. Hugo pressed the microphone key. "Ah, Philipsburg harbor master, this is the *Sweet Texas*, out of Tortola. We will, of course, comply with all security regulations. We will be mooring in your fair bay and would like to get mooring instructions and location."

"*Sweet Texas*, not a problem. Please set your course to 015 degrees and proceed at harbor speed. I have dispatched a pilot dingy to intercept and lead you to a mooring site."

"Understand and will comply," answered Hugo with his nicest Texas drawl. "We are very happy to be visiting your fine island. I will watch for the pilot."

"Very good," said the voice of the harbor master. "Welcome to beautiful Philipsburg, St. Maarten!"

"Sounds like nice folks," grinned Dane, "even though you may have gotten off to a bit of a rough start."

"Aw, everyone's nice down here," smiled Hugo, "especially when I turn on my charm."

Dane burst out laughing. "Oh, my God, it's going to be one of those trips. I guess I should alert the women."

Hugo spotted the small pilot dingy racing out to the cat. In a few minutes they should be tied up to a mooring buoy and set to roam the streets of Philipsburg like all of the tourists.

Dane was enamored with the size of the *Allure*, which was now only about a hundred yards from them. He could see people walking about the great ship like ants. He could also hear the lilting sounds of a Caribbean steel drum band playing on one of the open decks about fifteen stories above their heads. He sat back letting the sun flow over his tanned body. This was paradise!

CHAPTER ELEVEN

May 16, 2013

Philipsburg, St. Maarten, Netherland Antilles, 3:00 p.m.

Great Bay Beach is the front door to Philipsburg. Lined with many shops, bars, restaurants and hotels, the pristine, gloriously white sandy beach is a picture postcard of the Caribbean. Dane and Hugo tied off their dingy at the small pier across from Wathey Square and took in the show as they walked toward the south. The beach was covered with beautiful women lying in the sun. The bars advertised their special deal; two beach chairs and an umbrella for twenty dollars plus a free bucket of five beers.

"Man, this is beautiful!" cried Hugo, waving his arms out across the beach. "Just look at the ladies."

Dane couldn't help but laugh. "Hugo, this is exactly like the beach back in Miami. How can this be any better?"

"Because I don't work here," laughed Hugo, tipping his beat-up Texas cap to a group of bikini-clad blondes.

"I see," said Dane. His scrutiny was down the beach toward a big sign, Bobby's Marina. Beside the marina were a number of folks standing around a small outdoor bar to the left of the marina. Since people were milling around the dock, this must be the place to get a beer in Philipsburg. "That place looks good for a brew, Hugo. What do you think?"

"Sure, I'll buy ya a cold one, or six."

"Can't argue with that," grinned Dane as they quickened their pace down the beach toward the bar. Again the huge *Allure of the Seas* caught their eye at the pier just beyond Bobby's.

"Just think, Dane," started Hugo. "That gorgeous ship is full of fine ladies. It's a captive environment when they are at sea. They can't get off and I could have a ball." Dane smiled. Here was Hugo with a multimillion dollar luxury catamaran moored in the bay and he wanted to go off sailing on a cruise ship! The man was incorrigible.

The two were greeted with loud music from the bar long before they got to the door. The huge deck in front of the bar was covered with party folk. Hugo was dancing a jig and tipping his cap to all of the ladies. He was definitely in his element. Dane, on the other hand, was a little uncomfortable. He was a quiet man that normally did not enjoy such partying. He was not a "stick in the mud" but didn't care for loud music and dancing. To him, music was Frank Sinatra or Tony Bennett. Hugo's music was all out rock and roll.

They walked up the low stairway to the deck and in through the door. They were immediately hit in the face with air conditioning. It felt great after the four block long walk they had just completed in the hot sun. The two surveyed the large room and found a place at the far end of the bar, ordering two ice-cold Heinekens. Hugo took his beer and ran the bottle across his face, savoring the icy feeling on his hot skin. Each took a long draw and turned in unison to view the dance floor filled with young folks, mostly from the cruise ship.

These folks knew how to party. To their left was a large group of young people, mostly girls in bikini tops and shorts. They were facing an eight-foot board with eighteen holes drilled in it holding eighteen glasses of a reddish liquid. Following a short count, each person grasped the board together and brought the board and glass up to their mouths, drinking the contents like a shot. Most were able to drink their glass but several were already drunk and did little more than pour the libation all over them. The crowd roared with their approval. Hugo looked at Dane and grinned.

"My kind of place," said Hugo. "I think I need to try that."

"Whoa, Tex. Let's hold off a bit until we can acclimate to this party. Drink your beer first."

In Hugo's mind this was going to be a great day. He was already scoping out which of the beautiful girls he wanted to take back to the *Sweet Texas*. There was the sweet young blonde who was thoroughly enjoying herself with four other ladies. Hugo reasoned they were from one of the cruise ships since she was wearing a cutoff Royal Caribbean t-shirt with nothing underneath. Being a breast man at heart and seeing her nubile chest bouncing around under her shirt nearly set him afire.

"Damn, Dane. You see that?"

Dane calmly took a look, took a drink and smiled. "That is pretty fine but she's got to be no more than twenty-one. A little too young for you, buddy."

"Well, she's over 18 and that dainty chest of hers is just driving me wild. Look at those titties waggle!"

Dane knew from experience what was coming next. Hugo would place her in his sights and the poor girl wouldn't have a chance. Hugo was great at getting the girls, especially when he set his mind to it.

Hugo ran his hands through his hair. He didn't have a comb. He straightened his collar and set out on his self-appointed charge.

"Hey, buddy," said Hugo as he turned on his bar stool, "watch my beer."

A booming voice came out of the crowd. At first Hugo thought it was God telling him to back off.

"Oh, my God! Dane Skoglund! What the hell are you doing here?" The loud voice came from over to their right. Both Dane and Hugo turned to see a tall, skinny guy wearing a brightly colored floral shirt wading through the crowd headed their way. He wore a wide grin that nearly cut his head in half. "And Hugo too!"

Both were stunned at the sight of one of their oldest and trusted comrades from the SEALS, Robert Rand. "Damnation, Hugo, it's Bob!" blurted Dane. "I can't believe it! What the hell are you doing here?"

"Hell, I live here," cried Rand, first grasping Dane's hand and then pulling him close for a bear hug. Hugo stood grinning as well, awaiting his turn.

Bob Rand was a dear friend and colleague that had served with Dane and Hugo over in the Middle East. They all shared secret missions and other covert actions that had put the men in dire danger. Some were so dangerous that several times they thought they were not going to make it out alive. That type of closeness begat a loyalty and trust that lasts forever.

"What am I doing here; what the hell are you two doing here? You come in on a cruise ship?" asked Bob. "Oh, hell, guys, who cares. I'm so glad to see you!"

"How long has it been?" asked Hugo. "It's got to be eight or more years."

"More like ten," interjected Dane. "We last saw you in 2003 at the start of the Iraq war. We did those covert ops behind the lines for the amphibious assault on Basra. That was in March of 2003."

"Seems like a lifetime ago," said Bob, pounding Hugo on the back. "How are you guys?"

"Great until I got beat up here in Philipsburg," grinned Hugo as he sidled away from Bob's back slaps.

"Hey, come with me. I have a quieter place back over here." Bob led the threesome to a far corner of the bar. The music was still loud but it did seem a bit quieter back away from the bar and the dance floor. A large open window overlooking the beach provided a cooling breeze. Even though, Hugo's neck was craning trying to catch a glimpse of a sweet little brunette standing at the end of the bar with two of her friends. Dane appreciated the quieter corner of the bar.

As they sat down, a waitress came over immediately to get their order. "Your money's no good here, guys," said Bob. "I'm buying and I don't care if the tab is a millions bucks! What'll ya have?"

"Another one of these," ordered Dane, waving his now empty Heiney. "I think I may stay for a while."

"Me too," added Hugo. "Hey, make it six cold ones. I have a powerful Texas thirst!"

Bob reeled back laughing. "Damn, Hugo, you haven't changed a bit. Uglier but still the same hard drinking Texan."

"Hey, hard to change perfection," cried Hugo at the top of his lungs. Dane and Bob roared laughing.

"Wow, Dane and Hugo down here in St. Maarten at my home base. I can't believe it."

"Believe it, baby, we are here!" said Dane. "We just picked up Hugo's boat and we decided a great way to christen her was to sail over to St. Maarten. So here we are."

"A new boat?" asked Bob. "Where? What kind?"

"I bought me a nice catamaran so I can woo all of the ladies down here in paradise."

"How big?"

"Fifty-seven feet," answered Hugo.

"Fifty-seven feet! Good God almighty that must have set you back a few dinars. Is that where all that Iraqi gold went back in the desert?" Bob said smiling.

"I wish," said Hugo, trying to move past the cost of the boat. Talking money always made him uneasy. "You look like you have a nice setup down here. What are you up to?"

"I have five, count 'em, five high-end jewelry and electronics stores that make me a mint," bellowed Bob holding up five fingers. I swear tourists buy anything from diamonds and emeralds to grey market cameras and electronics. Business comes to us almost daily in the form of these cruise ships," he continued as he waved a hand toward the pier. "They bring in thousands of folks that are just itching to spend money. And we make a killing!"

"Hell, I'll bet you do," said Dane, slogging down his second beer and beginning to feel more relaxed.

"Bob, where does a guy get a good Cuban cigar down here?"

"Hugo, I have tons of them in my warehouse. How many boxes do you need, twenty…thirty? I have Cohibas, Juan Lopez, Upmans and the cream of the Cuban crop, the Montecristo No. 2; God's cigar, the finest cigar known to man."

"My, my, this is heaven," said Hugo, leaning his chair back against the wall. "I could get used to this place."

CHAPTER TWELVE

May 16, 2013

A Bar, St. Maarten, Netherland Antilles, 7:00 p.m.

The guys sat and talked for hours rehashing some of their unclassified exploits throughout the world. Laughter was abundant interspersed with shrieks that sounded like a group of little girls. They were having a ball.

"Hey, I'm getting hungry. Who's up for a big steak?" bellowed Bob.

"Sounds great to me," said Dane. Hugo lifted the last of his beers and slammed the bottle down on the table.

"Count me in!" Hugo added. "I'm sure you got a favorite place?"

"Hell, yeah, I do…best in the Caribbean!" barked Bob. "But first I need to let my daughter know I won't be home for a while."

"Daughter? You have a daughter?" asked Dane with a puzzled look.

"Yeah. You know the girl I married about the time I joined the Navy? Well, that was years ago. She left me a short time after but not before she and I had a little girl. My ex-wife died several years ago and my daughter came here to live with me. Erin is now twenty-one and an absolute doll," explained Bob, showing his pride in his daughter. Dane wondered why Bob did not mention her when they worked together back in 2003.

"She's a doll?" asked Hugo, his eyes widening.

"Damn you, Winsor, you stay away from my daughter or I will personally slice you up into little pieces!"

Dane roared in laughter. "Damn, Hugo, he's got you pegged." Hugo just sat there smiling.

"Aww, I'll have to find me another then," answered Hugo meekly, glancing around the bar. The cruise ships had sailed at 5:00 p.m. and only the locals and a few hotel guests remained in the bar. He realized Bob was half kidding but the half serious part truly scared him. Bob was a master with a knife.

"Hey, sweetie," said Bob into his cell phone. "Listen, I'm going to be a bit late. Two dear friends from my SEAL days are down here and I want to show 'em the island. We might be a while so don't wait up."

Hugo could hear a sweet sounding voice on the other end of the line laughing. I guess Bob does the night life thing often.

"Okay, I will see you later," closed Bob as he plopped his iPhone in his pocket. "You guys ready?"

"Lead on!" blurted Hugo, catching a burp halfway through his answer.

As the trio left the bar, Dane asked Bob, "So your daughter lives here with you?"

"Yep. She manages several of my stores and she's my right-hand man, so to speak."

"And her mother?" asked Dane.

"Well, she died several years ago back in the States. Cancer. She was a very nice and kind person that really didn't deserve a schmuck like me."

"Sorry to hear that," said Dane. "She must have been a great lady."

"Yes, she was. And Erin is a dead ringer for her. I swear if I close my eyes I can see Brit in Erin."

"She sounds like a beautiful young lady. When do we get to properly meet her?" asked Dane.

"Soon, very soon. First let's get some food!"

"Yeah, let's eat!" said Hugo bringing up the rear. "I'm starving."

CHAPTER THIRTEEN

May 18, 2013

Philipsburg, St. Maarten, Netherland Antilles, 3:30 p.m.

Dane Skoglund leaned over to answer his ringing iPhone. Set on vibrate, it was skittering across the back sun deck on the *Sweet Texas* moored in the harbor. He picked it up and answered, wondering who in the world would be calling him.

"Hello?"

"Hey, stranger," came a woman's lilting voice. "What ya doin'? I see ya out sittin' in the sun."

Dane pulled the phone down from his ear and looked at it. The number being shown on the screen said Sherrie Knowlton. But she was back in Miami.

"Ah…who is this?" he asked sheepishly.

"It's me, Sherrie!"

Dane sat up and adjusted his cap. "What in the world are you calling for?"

"Thought I would give you a heads-up that you are going to have company in a few seconds," Sherrie answered in a sultry voice.

"I…" stammered Dane.

"Look back over your bow."

Dane adjusted his sunglasses and moved over to the port side of the back deck. He could see a small Sea Eagle inflatable runabout bearing down on the *Sweet Texas*. On the bow of the boat was a beautiful blonde with a bikini top and shorts waving frantically at him.

"Sherrie! What are you doing here?" said Dane into his phone as he terminated the call and stood up. The boat was slowing down. All he could see was Sherrie's wide grin under a Miami lifeguard cap. The boat pulled behind, the driver tossing a line to Dane. He wrapped the line around a cleat at the rear and pulled the boat close behind the big catamaran's rear stairway.

"What in the world...?" smiled Dane. Before he could finish Hugo came bounding up from below.

"Hey, Sher! Ya got my message, huh?" cried Hugo, ambling over to help Dane get Sherrie aboard.

"I sure did!" said Sherrie loudly. "I also brought my brother Greg with me too."

"Great! We need an extra hand."

"Now, this is a nice boat!" said Greg Knowlton, passing their luggage aboard to a speechless Dane.

"Don't look so surprised, Dane," said Sherrie. "Hugo sent for us a few days ago. He said if we wanted the vacation of a lifetime for free, now was our chance."

"Surprised, Boss?" asked Hugo smiling.

"Well, yeah, but sure. Ya'll come aboard. I mean welcome aboard!" said Dane, giving a hand to Greg with one hand and untying the line to the runabout with the other.

"Have a great vacation," the driver yelled as he turned his boat and gave it some gas. The eighteen-footer leaped through the water and headed back to the shore. Sherrie and Greg plopped down at the table in the shade.

"We finally made it," said Sherrie.

"Wait a second. I'm a bit flabbergasted," huffed Dane, parking his rear beside Sherrie. She grabbed his arm and planted a kiss on his cheek.

"You happy to see me, Dane?" she cooed.

"Well, yeah, but how..." Dane was a bit shy. With his military background as such, he sometimes found it hard to express feelings.

"That was my part," said Hugo, reaching into a cooler and pulling out four ice cold Red Stripes. "I thought we shouldn't be the only ones having a great time down here so I called Sherrie and told her to come on down. Greg was available so I told her to bring him along too. So here we are in St. Maarten, chillin' on my cat and not a care in the world!"

Greg was still enamored with the *Sweet Texas*. "Hugo, how big is this catamaran?"

"Fifty-seven feet of beauty and mirth," replied the Texan. "And it's all ours until we say it ain't."

"Wow," was all that Greg could muster.

"We have beds for all, food and drink for all and plenty of sunshine and places to go," announced Hugo, standing at the aft of the catamaran. "It's all fun and games for us!" Hugo raised his Red Stripe high. "Let us drink to friends and family, and the *Sweet Texas!*"

"Yes!" the group agreed as they all held their beers up in a toast.

"So where do we sleep on this boat?" asked Sherrie, winking at Dane. He hurriedly took a sip of beer.

"We have five double bedrooms and one single, and another two crew singles in the bow. So if we all take a double we still have two cabins left!" explained Hugo. "Now, if anyone doubles up with someone else…" Hugo looked at Dane and then at Sherrie… "Then we have more room for others." Dane began to turn red.

"What is going on here?" he blurted.

"Not a thing, my brother, not a thing," said Hugo, grinning and glancing at Sherrie. Greg was grinning ear to ear. Everyone knew Sherrie had a thing for Dane. Dane, being the big Swedish lug, took the comments in stride, too shy to make his move quickly.

"So we each get a bedroom?" asked Greg.

"If you want it," answered Hugo. "Yours to do whatever you want."

Greg beamed. "Wow."

"I gotta get him to stop saying wow," laughed Hugo. They roared.

"This, my friends, is going to be fun!" said Dane. "Hey, Hugo, where are we off to next?"

"I thought we would run down to St. Kitts and Nevis. You know, Mick Jagger sometimes hangs out down there."

"Then Nevis and St. Kitts it is!" cried Dane, "at least first thing tomorrow morning. Let's go ashore and do some shopping for our trip. We need more Snickers and more beer!"

"Oh, and some prime steaks," added Hugo. "And maybe Greg and I can find a sweet young thing to join us for the trip. Whatcha say, Greg?"

"Lead on, brother, lead on!"

"Oh, hell, this is going to be one wild vacation," blurted Dane, raising his Red Stripe. He was glad Hugo had invited Sherrie. Hugo was a great wingman, especially with women.

"Yes, it is!" yelled Sherrie, raising her beer to toast with the rest. There was no happier bunch of people in the world than those on the *Sweet Texas*.

CHAPTER FOURTEEN

May 19, 2013

Philipsburg, St. Maarten, Netherland Antilles, 7:00 a.m.

Sherrie was the first one up and had the coffee brewing. It took a few minutes to figure out how to get the damn thing started but soon she had it going like gangbusters. The smell of freshly brewed coffee filled the air. She poured her first cup and added sugar and cream and walked to the back deck. Barefoot and wearing a halter top, at twenty-eight, she was simply gorgeous. Her lithe body was perfect for the Caribbean. Her golden tan from Miami and that blonde hair set her apart from thousands of other girls down here.

The catamaran was moored in the harbor and she could see the sun peeking over the hills to the east. Inwardly she wondered what she was doing here. Had she acted too much on a whim when Hugo called and invited her to join them? She had very strong feelings for Dane and she truly thought Dane had the same toward her. But she was not certain. Not yet. Maybe this cruise would give her the answer she craved. She heard a footstep.

"Hey there, cutie," came a voice behind her. Dane stepped up the stairway into the salon.

"Well, good morning, Dane," smiled Sherrie. "Coffee's ready. Can I pour you some?"

"Sure. That would be nice. You sleep all right?"

"Like a baby."

"Some folks have a hard time sleeping in a boat on the water. She moves and rolls with all of the traffic in the harbor. It makes some folks sick."

"Not me. I loved it. Like being rocked to sleep."

Dane took his cup. Sherrie knew he liked his coffee black so she didn't offer anything else. She just poured him a cup.

"Dane, you aren't mad because I came down here, are you?"

"No, no, not at all. We needed a female to keep us out of trouble," smiled Dane, taking another sip. The harbor was calm this time of the morning. The water was as smooth as a mirror. A very slight fog seemed to lie over the boats giving the air a chilly feel. Sherrie took her coffee and sat on the salon sofa, placing her cup on the deck beside her. She wrapped her arms around her chest, her toes wiggling like a child's.

"You cold?" asked Dane.

"Not really. Just a chill in the air until the sun rises some more. Then I'll bet it will be hot."

"Yeah, it can get a bit warm down here but the sea breezes do keep you cool."

"So how are you doing after the Amazon thing and all?"

"Actually, Sherrie, I feel really well. Granted I would not want to go through that again but I don't regret it a bit. Dana and Randall are safe and Hugo and I got out relatively unscathed. It could have been a lot worse."

Dane walked over and stood beside Sherrie and looked out over the water. "It was kinda like Iraq. We did some bad things but we did them to bad people. I guess that makes it good."

Sherrie looked at Dane. "I swear I don't know what I would have done if you guys had not made it, especially you."

Dane smiled. "You would have carried on just like everything else would have. The one thing I learned in Iraq was time goes on, like it or not."

Sherrie reached out and squeezed Dane's hand. "No, I don't think so. Back at home you are my boss. But here you are a great looking, sweet man that I care for big time. I like this man down here."

Dane smiled. "I didn't know you felt that way."

Shyly Sherrie looked up at Dane and said, "Well, I do. I like you a lot. And I would never want to lose you."

"Well, good morning, you two!" bellowed Hugo, prancing up the stairs into the salon. "What's for breakfast?"

Dane looked at Sherrie and smiled sweetly. He squeezed her hand reassuringly. "Let's see what we can rustle up, Texas! I know we got eggs, bacon and pancake mix." He turned, released Sherrie's hand and headed to the kitchen. "You start the bacon and I'll start the pancakes."

"Ah, I didn't crash a little cookin' already, did I?" asked Hugo sheepishly, realizing he had busted in on their quiet time.

Sherrie smiled. "We got a long time to continue cookin', Hugo."

Dane shot a glance at Hugo but couldn't refrain from a huge grin. "This is going to be the greatest vacation of all time."

CHAPTER FIFTEEN

May 19, 2013

At Sea, South of St. Maarten, Netherland Antilles, 5:35 p.m.

"This is the most fun I have had in years!" yelled Sherrie over the din of waves breaking over the bow of the *Sweet Texas*. The spray was flying in the winds as the large catamaran knifed through the water directly on course toward St. Kitts. The smell of the sea was clean and refreshing. The deep blue waters gave up their darkness to a bright coral blue as they neared the islands.

Gulls were swooping over the deck. Maybe that was because Greg and Dane were taking turns tossing crackers into the air and watching the gulls catch them in midair. Sherrie smiled as she watched Dane. His tall, svelte figure was dashing clad in the cut-off jean shorts and his deepening tan. He and Hugo had only been in the Caribbean a week and a half but both were getting darker each day. Dane's Swedish background yielded the blond hair which she watched flying outside of his cap. A rugged man, Dane was the consummate SEAL. Fit and ready for anything. Sherrie liked that. She liked that a lot.

"Hugo, how far out from St. Kitts?" yelled Dane. Hugo, sitting at the helm, checked his watch and turned around.

"We should be there before dark," he said grinning. "Why? You got somewhere to go?"

"Hell, no! Not me!" answered Dane with a big grin. "Suits me we sail on until we get to Africa."

Dane and Hugo had been through much together. Before the Amazon and the rescuing of Dane's sister and her husband, they were together in the Navy. Their SEAL team was deployed behind the lines during the Iraq war and later during the opening days of Afghanistan. They worked and lived so close they were like brothers, maybe even closer.

With the funds the two gained from the Amazon affair along with Hugo's family fortune, these two would never have to work again. But they were not all about spending money, far from it. Before they left, the two had set up a foundation to care for those who served in battle that returned wounded or maimed. They had close friends who did not come back. They felt doing something for those that did return was the least they could do.

Now they were in the Caribbean on an extended vacation. But both knew they would never return to their lifeguard jobs in Miami. They couldn't. There was too much world out there to explore. One only gets this kind of opportunity once in life and they decided to embrace it. Thus, the catamaran was purchased and the sea became their home.

The sun was beginning to wane in the west. Another day was passing in paradise.

Greg stood on the port fore hull grasping a halyard. He looked like a pirate, shading his eyes with one hand and hanging on with his other. He jumped down on the trampoline and made his way back to the cockpit on the starboard side. "Hey, is that St. Kitts I see on the horizon?" he asked.

Hugo stood in his perch and raised a pair of binoculars. "Yeah, that should be it. We should be in port in a couple or three hours if all goes well."

"I've never been there," said Greg standing beside the cockpit. "It looks beautiful from here."

"It is beautiful," said Dane, climbing the steps to the cockpit to join them. Sherrie was on the back sun deck. She was in a dynamite white bikini. "I was there a few years ago. It's one of the most beautiful Caribbean islands I know. Green and lush with a few rolling hills. It reminds me a lot of Hawaii."

Greg stepped past Dane and back down into the salon under the shade of the awning. He immediately reached for a cold one. "Anyone need a beer?"

"I'll take one," yelled Hugo. "Driving this baby causes a huge thirst."

Greg laughed and pulled a second beer from the cooler. "Dane? Sherrie?"

"I'm fine," said Sherrie, working on her tan.

"Throw one my way," said Dane. Greg grabbed two and climbed back up into the cockpit with Hugo and Dane. He sat down and perused the controls.

"Ever sailed anything like this?" asked Hugo.

"Nothing this big. I had a Prindle 18 back in Miami."

"Me too!" said Hugo grinning. "This baby handles just like my Prindle but the reaction time is a slight bit slower due to her size. You want to sail her?"

"Hell, yes, I want to sail her!"

"Here, take over. You and Sherrie need to learn to sail her and get to feel comfortable with her. We never know when you may have to take over as captain sometime."

Greg's grin was so large it looked as though his face was going to fall off. He was in heaven behind the wheel of this fine catamaran. "Damn, she's nice!"

"Yes, sir, she is," beamed Hugo.

Their course was now 130 degrees southeast. At a speed of fourteen knots they were still several hours from Basseterre on the southern side of the island near where the island forms a long, thin piece of land ending at Nag's Head. Hugo had toyed with trying to make port in Charlestown, Nevis, but now decided St. Kitts was far enough for today.

The sun was beginning to set and it would be dark very soon. While sailing at night was not a problem in these waters, Hugo did not want to take any chances with a boat he was largely still unfamiliar with. He hoped to make his final turn into port right at dark. That is if the wind held out. It was becoming calmer with each hour.

"Hang on to her for a minute. I need to hit the head," said Hugo, heading down to the salon. "Think you can handle her?"

"Hell, yes!" beamed Greg, his smile wide. "You don't know how I have dreamed for this day." Hugo tipped his hat and disappeared below.

Greg Knowlton was two years younger than his sister Sherrie but they were very close. When their parents were killed, the two bonded even more. Greg watched out for his big sister, although in size his six foot two frame towered over Sherrie at five foot five.

"So Greggie, you like sailing this boat, huh?" asked Sherrie as she climbed the steps up to the cockpit. She joined her brother's side on the bench seat. Greg was sailing the boat with his feet just like he always saw the old salts do with their big sailboats. He raised his arm and wrapped it around Sherrie.

"I swear we have died and gone to heaven. I never thought things could be this great."

"It is pretty damn good, isn't it?" Sherrie looked off into the darkening sky. The Caribbean was so beautiful.

CHAPTER SIXTEEN

May 19, 2013

At Sea, South of St. Kitts, 7:20 p.m.

"Something big on the horizon, sir," reported the lookout aboard the *May Pop*. Since plundering the sailboat a few nights ago off St. Maarten, the old fishing trawler ran south to claim they were nowhere in the area. Again she purposely did not carry any lights and the bridge lighting was suppressed. She also flew no flag.

The first mate reached for a pair of binoculars and took a look himself. Captain de Terr stepped into the cabin and took off his cap. Even with the sea breeze it was still hot.

"We've sighted a large sailing vessel off our starboard side on a parallel course. She may be trying to make Basseterre or even Nevis tonight," said Dante Brees, the first officer.

"Does she look promising?" asked de Terr.

"Can't tell yet but she's pretty big. I'd say fifty foot or more," answered Brees.

"Well, let's get closer and check it out. The bigger the boat, the better the haul," smiled de Terr, showing his dark yellowed teeth. "And we are always on the lookout for nice things."

The *May Pop's* motors began to churn louder as the captain ordered their speed increased. They were now in pursuit of prey.

The *May Pop* was very well armed. Tucked inside a small wooden hut at the center of the ship was a twenty-millimeter cannon. Under normal conditions the hefty gun rode well below decks. When put into action, it rose hydraulically with the top of the hut folding in two to open, giving the gun a clear shot. It was the same principle of the old World War II British merchant raiders known as Q-Ships. They disguised themselves as private merchant ships but changed into deadly fighting ships within minutes to attack U-boats or other attacking ships.

Also aboard were several jet skis. These were heavily modified enabling them to outrun most watercraft known with minimal noise. They were speedy and were used to pounce upon unprepared watercraft so the pirates could overwhelm a crew before they knew they were under attack.

The *May Pop* was rapidly gaining on the *Sweet Texas* and would have her in their clutches within the hour.

CHAPTER SEVENTEEN

May 19, 2013

At Sea, South of St. Kitts, 8:15 p.m.

The *Sweet Texas* was slowing slightly. Hugo let out some sail in order to begin a long tortoise-like turn into the Basseterre area. It was dark now and the sea looked like ink. They were about two miles off shore but could clearly see the myriad of lights in Basseterre and the townships close by.

"God, it's so damn beautiful," said Sherrie quietly. "I had no idea."

"Yeah, it does kinda take your breath away," said Dane. He looked up at Hugo, who was at the helm. Greg was right beside him. "If you think this place is mesmerizing during the day, at night it takes on a whole new aspect of beauty."

"It sure does," said Sherrie, sideling up and taking Dane's arm in hers and squeezing it.

Suddenly there was a whirring sound that could be heard above the rushing sounds of the waves and water. Dane's trained ears picked up on it immediately. His head popped up and began to turn to and fro trying to ascertain the direction from which the noise came. He glanced up at Hugo, who also picked up on it.

There was a loud crack that sounded like something hit the boat just above Dane's head. He looked up and saw a bullet hole. He jerked around to see a pair of jet skis bearing down in the dark on their boat from astern. A second crack yielded another hole in the fiberglass top above their heads. He grabbed Sherrie and shoved her to the deck.

"Someone's shooting at us!" Dane screamed loudly. "They're behind us!"

Hugo whirled around, saw the jet skis and tightened the sails. It felt as though someone stepped on the gas. The large catamaran increased its speed by five knots within seconds. But even that was no match for the fast, agile jet skis.

Dane screamed at Sherrie. "Get down to a lower deck and stay there." He did not look to see if she complied. He simply bolted across the deck and up to the pilot cockpit.

"The bastards are shooting at us!" he yelled at Hugo.

"Who are they? Where did they come from?"

"Don't know! Get us out of here! Now!" cried Dane.

"Trying my best, Boss, but I don't think we can outrun jet skis," answered Hugo.

That was not the answer Dane was looking for. "I'm going down to get a weapon," he said as he turned to Greg. "Stay down or come with me."

"I'm with you," said Greg. They both bound down the stairs to the salon level. Almost immediately Greg spun around and blood spattered across Dane's chest.

"I'm hit!" screamed Greg. "Oh, my God, I'm shot!"

Dane grabbed Greg's arm and literally shoved him into the enclosed area of the salon. Sherrie was peering up from the lower level. She heard Greg's cry of pain.

"Oh, no!" she screamed. She saw the blood smeared across the floor of the salon area left by Greg. "Greg! Dane, what's happening?"

Dane leapt over Sherrie as she knelt beside her brother. He was bleeding profusely from not one but two wounds, one a mere flesh wound on the side of his head and the other in his upper shoulder. The head wound, although not serious, was bleeding profusely.

"Oh, my God!" cried Sherrie reaching around, grabbing several white napkins to hold on Greg's wounds.

Bounding through the lower level, Dane ducked into his cabin and returned with two remnants of his past, a pair of H&K MP5 submachine guns with silencers. He quickly checked the magazines and pulled back the bolt on one gun. He was ready to strike!

Dane came up from the lower deck in two bounds of his long legs. At the top of the stairs he paused a second to glance at Greg and Sherrie on the salon floor. Greg was alert and scared but his face grimaced in pain. Sherrie was crying and had Greg's blood all over her chest where she wiped the blood on her hands from the now red-soaked napkins. She had almost stopped the bleeding. Another round smashed into the fiberglass above their heads. The guys on the jet skis were still shooting!

Not a word was said as Dane stood and turned quickly to look up into the cockpit.

"You okay?" he yelled.

"Yeah, but this is serious!" answered Hugo in his own way of downplaying a dangerous situation.

"Got something for you," said Dane as he tossed one of the H&Ks up to Hugo. Before there was an answer, Dane turned and leveled his submachine gun at the lead jet ski. He fired off a burst in full automatic mode. It sounded like a short, muffled duck quack. At a firing rate of 800+ rounds per minute it took only a few seconds to spray the pursuers with thirty 9 mm rounds.

The two skis veered off in opposite directions. Dane's burst of fire hit one of the attackers, who flew off the jet ski into the water. The other attacker stopped dead in the water, amazed that his cohort had been hit by gunfire. They had not expected someone to fight back, especially with automatic weapons. Dane looked back to check on Sherrie and Greg while Hugo fired a burst of his own. The riderless jet ski exploded in a ball of fire. Hugo's shots shredded the jet ski's gas tank and caused the explosion.

Hugo turned his attention back to the boat. They were now screaming through the water headed toward shore.

Dane scanned the water for the second jet ski. He could still hear it but that was because it was hightailing it away from the *Sweet Texas*. He flipped the safety on, ejected his magazine and checked that he still had ammo. The pursuit was over. The remaining jet ski vanished into the darkness while the other's burning carcass slowly sank quickly in the waves.

"Oh, Dane, Greg's shot," screamed Sherrie, bringing him back to focus on Greg. "Help him, please!"

Dane laid the gun down and with one hand ripped Greg's t-shirt off. He could now see an oozing bullet wound in his upper shoulder. That was not too bad, he thought to himself. He turned his attention to the head wound. Miraculously that shot had merely grazed Greg's head but had left a hefty scalp wound that was still bleeding profusely.

"Will he live?" squeaked Sherrie, almost overcome with grief. "Is he going to die?" Her sobbing was increasing.

Dane smiled and placed his hand gently on her shoulder. "Sher, he's going to be fine but we have to get him to a doctor. His head wound is only superficial but it's bleeding like a son-of-a-bitch." He reached up on the salon side table and pulled down a small bar towel. Removing the napkins, he placed the towel over Greg's head wound. "Hold this here. It will slow the bleeding." He turned to the chest wound. It was actually worse although it was bleeding very little. "Looks like he caught one here as well but it is so high the bullet may have missed bone. Leave that one alone for now. He's a very lucky man."

Hugo jumped down from his cockpit perch. "They're gone. One blew up and the other hightailed it outta here." He looked at Greg with a frown. "How bad?"

"Not as bad as it looks," answered Dane. "He caught one in the upper chest/shoulder. He got a nasty scalp wound where most of the blood is coming from. We need to get him to shore as quickly as possible and report this."

"And leave out the part that we have machine guns?"

"Bingo!"

"I'll have us in Basseterre harbor in a few. Y'all sit tight and leave the driving to me," said Hugo as he leapt back up into the cockpit and began turning the catamaran toward shore.

Dane turned to Sherrie. She was a mess. Still crying and holding her dear brother, she could not believe what had just happened. "What was that all about? Why were they shooting at us?" she sobbed.

"I don't know, Sher. If I had to guess, I would say they were pirates of some kind. They saw the big new catamaran and figured we were a pushover. Guess they were as surprised as we were," explained Dane. "We are on the way in to Basseterre. We will go to the police and report all of this and see what they can tell us. But right now, I'm very thankful we are all still here, albeit one of us decided to stop a few bullets." He turned to Greg, who was now managing a thin smile.

"Damn, this getting shot hurts like hell," Greg said meekly.

"Don't worry," said Dane. "You are going to be okay. You have a scratch on your head and a hole in your shoulder that you can tell your kids about some day." Sherrie laughed softly and Greg smiled. Once again everything was all right again, thanks to Dane and Hugo.

CHAPTER EIGHTEEN

May 19, 2013

At Sea, South of St. Kitts, 9:25 p.m.

The *May Pop* slowed to pluck the jet ski from the water.

"Where's Pappy?" asked Brees.

"He's gone…dead."

"What? What the hell happened?"

"They had guns, machine guns. They fired on Pappy and his jet ski blew up. I never saw his body. I just took off. They were firing at me as I got away. It was a miracle that I got back in one piece."

Brees chomped down on his cigar in disgust. His men had failed. Not only had they failed but this put the *May Pop* in a bad situation. She was one of a few boats in the area and would surely come under scrutiny when the attack was reported on shore. He had to remove the evidence.

"Sink the jet ski," ordered Brees. One of the deck hands motioned to another to give him a hand sinking the small craft. As buoyant as they were, the jet ski was not easy to purposely sink. The two hands were trying to figure out the best way to accomplish their order.

"You," Brees said pointing to the sailor from the returned jet ski, "come with me." The two men walked briskly through a hatch and down below.

Brees led the man to a cabin on the lowest deck. The first officer stepped through the hatch and waited. The sailor entered the cabin, not sure of what was to happen. Brees turned around and cold-cocked the man, sending him sprawling across the floor. He closed the heavy hatch and pulled a lever on the wall. Brees glanced at his hand. His knuckles were bloody from the strike. There was a hissing sound. The compartment was now under pressure.

"You friggin' dumbass! You got Pappy killed and bungled this entire operation. Now they are going to come after us," screamed Brees. The man was shaking his head slowly, holding his mouth. His jaw was broken.

The sailor tried to sit up but was still dazed. In one quick motion Brees attached manacles to the man's legs and wrists. At the end of a chain was an iron anchor which must have weighed a hundred pounds or more. "You screwed up. Now you must pay." Brees stepped back close to the cabin hatch and pulled another lever. The deck under the sailor opened and the anchor dropped into the sea below, seconds later dragging the sailor across the deck and into the dark sea. Brees' eyes and the sailor's eyes locked briefly as the man tried desperately to grab a handhold on a bulkhead to no avail. The sailor's face was one of horror as he sank swiftly to the bottom of the sea, a thousand feet below the ship.

Brees released the lever and the deck opening closed tightly. He pulled the other lever and a hissing noise signaled the pressure releasing. He switched his cigar butt to the other side of his mouth and smiled. "That dumbass will tell no tales." He grinned and opened the hatch and returned to the bridge to inform the captain of the situation.

The captain was on the bridge. He was seething. When Brees stepped in he stared at his first officer. "And what excuse do you have?"

"It seems our men were met with an armed defense. Pappy was lost when his jet ski blew up and the other man decided to go for a swim with an anchor." The eyes of the sailor at the helm widened. Brees looked at him. "As we all know, dead men tell no tales." The helmsman decided that he had heard nothing.

"Armed defense?" asked the captain.

"Yes, sir. They had automatic weapons."

The captain stared at Brees. Automatic weapons, he thought. These weren't just the run-of-the-mill sailors out of Tortola on a sightseeing cruise. He had no idea who these folks were but he did know they were a serious threat. De Terr rubbed the razor stubble on his chin. Yes, this was a serious threat.

"Very well, Brees," said Captain de Terr looking out to sea. "You have covered our tracks?"

"Yes, sir. The remaining jet ski was sunk. There is nothing to tie us to the incident."

The captain leered at Brees. "You were lucky this time," he hissed. With that comment the captain stepped through the hatch down toward his cabin. The first officer returned to the captain's chair and sat down. It was time for another cigar.

CHAPTER NINETEEN

May 21, 2013

Basseterre, St. Kitts, 10:05 a.m.

It had been two days since they were fired upon. Greg was still in the hospital but was due to get out in the afternoon. His scalp wound was healing nicely. His shaved head was going to need a cap in this baking Caribbean sun. His shoulder wound was not as awful as thought. The bullet had traveled through with minimal damage. While his arm was in a sling, most of the pain had passed. Sherrie was thrilled.

The police, however, were not. They were wary of Dane and Hugo's version of the story. It seemed the authorities were tipped off by someone that a large catamaran with four Americans aboard was plying the water off of St. Kitts and St. Maarten buying and selling drugs. A search of the *Sweet Texas* had turned up no evidence of drugs, drug residue or weapons. The secret weapons bin Hugo had specifically made to hide their guns had worked as planned.

At Dane and Hugo's insistence, the St. Kitts police had spoken with the police in Philipsburg and compared notes. It seems that in addition to the disappearance of Ann and Kirk Jones and their sailboat there were several other 'disappearances' that had come to light throughout the area; too many to now ignore. But with the *Sweet Texas* being the only survivor of these so-called calamities, she was the one under scrutiny.

After two days of off-and-on questioning, the Basseterre police finally granted Dane and Hugo their leave.

Sherrie, Dane and Hugo sat on the back deck of the *Sweet Texas* eating a lunch of sandwiches, fruit and Hugo's famous chili. They chased their food with cold beer.

"You know how much I had to pay for the beef in this chili?" complained Hugo. "Hell, I paid almost ten dollars a pound! Can you believe that? With beef costing that much down here, we need to bring down a bunch of steers from Texas and set us up a cattle ranch to sell to the locals."

"Not a bad idea," said Dane. "We could become full-time cowboys."

"Sounds like a lot of hard work to me," added Sherrie. "I for one want to travel and see all there is to see in this wide, wide world. Life's too short to stick around in one place too long."

"I hear ya, sister," grinned Hugo, raising his Red Stripe. "Here's to enjoying life, not working through life."

"Yeah, and not getting your ass shot up out there on the water," added Dane.

"That was a fluke, I tell ya. That kind of thing just doesn't happen all the time," said Hugo, munching on a ham sandwich.

"Well, I guess you're right. The authorities will handle the bad guys," Dane lamented. "It's just that when it happens to you..."

"Hey, we have to go get Greg in an hour. Are we going to leave then?" asked Sherrie, trying to get the boys' minds off of events of the past few days.

"Hey, we do need to talk about that. I think we need to run back up to St. Maarten, grab some more supplies and then tool up toward Tortola and hang out with all of the tourists up there," Hugo said.

"Ha ha," laughed Dane. "You want to get your hands on some of those pretty lady tourists around Tortola, St. John and St. Thomas!"

"Oh, yes, I do," answered Hugo. "A man has to play sometime."

Sherrie laughed out loud. "So this is what guys talk about when they are together. Where to find women?"

"Yes, ma'am," replied Hugo. "It's what we do so well."

"Well, some of us do better than most," smiled Dane, pointing to a beaming Hugo.

Sherrie smiled. The way these guys approached life was exactly why she loved working with them in Miami. When Hugo asked her to join them, she jumped at the chance. Both were fantastic, but Dane was the love of her life.

Once the trio bailed Greg out of the hospital, they decided it was too late in the evening to sail for St. Maarten. Besides, there was a thunderstorm approaching from the east. Now near 9:00 p.m. Greg had turned in. Hugo, Dane and Sherrie sat on the upper lounge deck watching the approaching storm.

"Look at that lightning!" said Sherrie.

"It is beautiful, isn't it?" replied Dane.

"Yeah, but it's a bit scary knowing you are sitting out here in the water with all of that headed our way."

Hugo grinned. "Not a problem, m'lady. We are as safe as can be."

Sherrie moved closer to Dane. "Even so, it freaks me out. Lightning and thunder always have, even as a kid. Once when I was three lightning struck a tree outside my bedroom window. It scared me so bad I still vividly remember the entire incident. Even though, I was so young."

"Nothing but a bit of noise and light," assured Dane. "Now, the wind can cause us some trouble, but we are safe here at anchor. Settle back and enjoy the show." Dane placed his left arm around Sherrie. As Hugo watched, his eyebrows rose. Hugo could see this relationship was finally getting some traction.

The three of them sat there nursing their drinks for another fifteen minutes as the breeze began to cool the air. Not to be one to crowd a guy's moment, Hugo stood up and stretched.

"Think I'll turn in early tonight. Enjoy the thunderstorm from my nice, soft bed. If it's all right with everyone, we'll leave tomorrow morning so we can get to St. Maarten by the afternoon."

"Sounds good to me," said Sherrie with a grin, not moving from under Dane's arm.

"Me too," answered Dane with a slight smile. He winked at Hugo, who took the hint, and off to his cabin he went. On one side of the boat there was a half-moon shining brightly. On the other side the brewing storm. A tepid breeze blew across the boat. Rain was surely on its way. In the distance was the sound of low rolling thunder over the hills. The mixture made for a romantic atmosphere. Sherrie snuggled up to Dane as the rumble of thunder came closer.

"Scared?" asked Dane.

"Not when I'm with you," she answered coyly, laying her head on his shoulder. "I really want to thank you for saving our lives the other night. I was so scared but you just took control and got us out of a terrible situation."

"We were very lucky," answered Dane, being a bit coy himself.

"No, I mean it. You saved us all, especially Greg."

"Well, Hugo did have a big part in the whole thing. He's the one that got the jet ski."

Sherrie ran her hand across Dane's chest. "You are the best a girl could ever have. Think we should turn in?"

"Yeah, it's getting late and the rain will be here in a minute. Why don't you go on down. I have a few things to check up on before we turn in."

Sherrie looked at Dane. "Before 'we' turn in?" she asked.

Dane looked at her shyly. "I'd like that."

"I'd like that very much," Sherrie said softly. "I'll wait for you below." She stretched her neck and gave him a kiss on his lips. "See ya in a minute." She stood up and slowly walked into the salon and down the stairs below, relishing what was to come.

Dane stood still savoring the moment. He had wanted this for a long time. Now, today, it was perfect. He checked the deck and moorings and went down below. He passed Sherrie's cabin. The door was open and the light out. He turned to his cabin. He opened the door to a soft light and Sherrie lying ready in the bed. Her sweet smile told him all he needed to know. He entered and closed the door. He was right. Everything was as he hoped.

CHAPTER TWENTY

May 22, 2013

At Sea off St. Maarten, Netherland Antilles, 2:00 p.m.

"There's St. Maarten!" shouted Hugo, pointing off to the north. They had made great sailing time from Basseterre to St. Maarten. However, they were still about forty-five minutes from entering Philipsburg harbor where they would moor.

The crossing was uneventful. The *Sweet Texas* sailed a northwest course toward Philipsburg. After a quick brunch, everyone aboard was happy and enjoying the trip. Even Greg had taken off his sling and sat in the sunshine on the back deck. Sherrie had on one of her patented white string bikinis and was sprawled across the forward trampoline lying beside Dane.

Hugo was at the helm, of course, in his own world. Normally to have a scantily clad beauty lying on the boat before him would have made him go mad. But Sherrie was like a sister.

A catamaran this roomy was too small to completely hide the amorous goings on between two people enjoying their sexuality. Sherrie and Dane had kept him awaken most of the night. Now they were catching up on their sleep while he sailed them all to St. Maarten.

"Hey, need a break?" asked Greg, stepping up to the cockpit.

"Sure. You okay?"

"Actually, I'm feeling better all the time. I swear taking the sling off has cured me."

Hugo chuckled. "I've seen many a gunshot wound and believe me, they don't heal in a few days. More like a few weeks than days."

"Yeah, I know I'm pushing it but I don't want to waste my time aboard over just a scratch. And I don't want to be aboard if I can't contribute."

Hugo looked at Greg. "Man, you have contributed every day you have been here. Do not worry about that." He looked forward to Sherrie and Dane. "Now, those two are pushing the envelope today. They kept me awake last night and now they sleep while I drive." Hugo smiled broadly at Greg. "He's one helluva man, Greg. I've seen this coming for a long while and I'm so very happy they finally found each other. It couldn't happen to a finer pair."

"Yeah, I know. Dane's all Sherrie's talked about since you called and asked us to come along. I have never seen her so happy," explained Greg. "Oh and since we are on the subject, I don't think I thanked you for what you did back there when those guys jumped us. If you and Dane had not been there, well, we wouldn't be here. Thank you." Greg held out his hand. Hugo took it and gave Greg a bear hug.

"You haven't figured this out yet, have ya," said Hugo grinning, stepping back.

Greg looked at Hugo, puzzled. He didn't understand Hugo's question.

"You are my family!" declared Hugo. "You are the only family I have. You never need to say thank you. You never need to ask permission. As trite as it sounds, we are family. We have each other's back and we will protect each other until we die."

Greg smiled from ear to ear. "Well, brother, that is so okay by me!"

Thirty minutes later they moored in Philipsburg harbor. They all piled into the *Sweet Texas'* zodiac and hit the grocery store. Three big guys and one petite girl tore through the store like there was no tomorrow. It only took three hours to replenish their food and drink stores and they were ready to bug out to Tortola.

They decided to hit a bar, get something to drink and have a steak. All four dropped into the place Dane and Hugo had found on their earlier stop and grabbed a table.

"Beer, my good barkeep, we need ice cold beer," said Hugo as the smiling waitress came over.

"We have plenty of beer and it's as cold as a witch's tit in the dead of winter in Minnesota," she said, laying four napkins on the table.

"My kind of girl!" cried Hugo, looking up at the waitress. "Sweetheart, you look mighty fine!"

"Oh, don't mind him," explained Sherrie. "He thinks he is God's gift to the world."

"Oh, I am, I am," answered Hugo, beaming his patented grin.

"We'll just have beer for now," said Dane. "Red Stripe, okay?"

"Fine with me," said Greg.

"Me too," added Sherrie.

After thirty minutes worth of beer the group was ready to go when in walked Bob Rand.

"Damn, it's the dynamic duo again! Where you guys been?" he asked as he pulled a chair up to the table beside Sherrie. "And who are you, beautiful?"

"Down boy," smiled Dane. "She's with me."

"Aww, Dane, you always get the pretty ones. Hi. I'm Bob Rand. It's very nice to meet you."

"I'm Sherrie Knowlton. Glad to meet you Bob. This is my brother, Greg."

"Hi, Greg. Oh, Dane, she is a good one," smiled Rand.

"How do you know Dane?" Sherrie asked.

"We all met in the SEALS. Shared the same BUDS class and served together in the Middle East. Dane and Hugo are two of the finest human beings on this earth. They saved my ass many times over."

"And he saved ours too," chimed in Hugo.

Rand noticed Greg's sling. "Hey, Greg, you fall off a horse or something?"

"It's nothing; just a scratch."

"Hell, this guy took two slugs from some pirates a few days ago. He ain't a slouch," said Hugo, patting Greg on the back.

"Pirates?" asked Rand, looking concerned. His eyes narrowed. "Around here?"

"No, down off of St. Kitts. They jumped us at night while we were at sea. If it weren't for deadeye Hugo here, we might be sleeping with the fish right now," answered Dane.

"Son-of-a-bitch," said Rand. "Really? And they shot at you? Sounds like you were lucky to get out of that in one piece."

Greg smiled. "Yeah, some of us almost didn't. Have there been many attacks like this lately?" asked Greg.

"A few, but that's just conjecture. We did have a nice couple from South Carolina disappear several days ago. They vanished without a trace. Usually if it is pirates the boat shows up again, just renamed," explained Rand. "But this couple just vanished."

"Are we close to the Devil's Triangle?" asked Sherrie, remembering the stories from television.

Rand laughed. "No, my dear, that's a good bit north of here, but even so, we don't really believe in that stuff."

"Well, I didn't believe in pirates until I had to take one out," said Dane. "These guys were playing for keeps."

"Damn. Pirates, you say," said Rand thoughtfully.

CHAPTER TWENTY-ONE

May 1, 2013

Across the Sea, in the Desert, Iraq, 4:00 p.m.

Even out in the Iraqi desert the call to prayers was heard. The lilting singing reverberated throughout the small village. The devout Iraqis were scurrying though the streets to the local mosque or regular prayer places.

Mahmoud El-Gahazi stood at the doorway of a mud hut smoking a Turkish cigarette, his eyes squinting due to the smoke. He watched the faithful dash to their prayers as he kept an eye out for the man he was waiting to meet. There was business to be done. As important as it was, religion must take a back seat for now.

The desert wind kicked up, blowing fine sand into his face. The hot wind cooled him strangely as it blew against his brilliant white robes. He had arranged this encounter a week before. He had made several phone calls to verify the man he would be meeting and he checked out. He fingered the Glock 33 under his robes, knowing nothing in this world was truly safe.

Hamza Al-Bari bounced in the Land Rover as it skimmed through the desert toward town about two miles away. The engine roared as a large dust cloud spewed from the tires. Al-Bari scanned the road in front of him. Years after the war, the road could still yield an unexploded bomb or improvised explosive device (IED). Some of the locals were crazy enough to continue fooling with them. Every few days there were lone explosions in the desert; another person trying to abscond with an unexploded shell or bomb and sell it for a profit. Alas, one slip and not only their profit but their life was gone.

"When we get to the town, I want you to keep a very sharp eye," ordered Al-Bari. "These men we are dealing with have no fear of us. They are only swayed by money; nothing else. If they see an opportunity to take our funds, they will. They will kill us all and bury us in the sand. Only Allah will know our resting place."

The driver and the two armed men in the back nodded their understanding. Between the legs of Al-Bari was a satchel. It contained a small token of goodwill, five hundred thousand United States dollars. A bribe, if you will, to lay the groundwork for the purchase Al-Bari was planning.

"Hamza, the town is ahead," said the driver. "Tell me where I should turn."

Al-Bari pulled a small piece of paper from the breast pocket of his shirt and scanned it. He read a bit and then gazed ahead. He surveyed the town now coming up fast.

"Everyone get ready and stay on your toes," warned Al-Bari. "This has a chance of turning very nasty very fast."

He was worried for good reason. He had done transactions like this many times. Several went bad, to the effect of someone dying. His luck kept him alive although he chalked his luck up to being prepared and vigilant.

The two men in back checked their weapons and equipment. They were hired mercenaries, or mercs, as they were commonly called. They fought for anyone with the ability to pay them. If they had any political agenda, they hid it well. Killing was their business and they did it well. Al-Bari turned to the men. "You are here for our protection. We are counting on you."

One of the mercs gave Al-Bari a stone-faced look. "That's what we are here for."

The other merc chimed in, "And paid for."

"Paid well," Al-Bari said under his breath. He hated mercs but they were a necessary evil in this game. He especially hated westerners. These two guys were infidels in his mind and could not be trusted. He was as wary of the mercs as he was the folks they were meeting.

"Slow down," Al-Bari said softly, turning his attention back to the driver. "We go into the town, take the first left and go through the archway. Everyone will be at prayers. We should be able to get in unseen. We go in, do our deal and get out." He turned to the men in back. "Understand?" The two looked perturbed but nodded in agreement anyway.

They entered the town and the Land Rover slowed to make the turn. There about 20 yards ahead was the archway. They slowed even more and drove through. Suddenly they found themselves in a dead end with only one way out. The Land Rover stopped.

"I don't like this," said one of the mercs under his breath. "Nowhere to escape." The other man grunted his acknowledgement.

"Stay with the car," said Al-Bari. He was clearly wary of the situation as well. Had he known this was a dead end, he would not have driven through the arch. This had all of the makings of a trap. Damn!

Mahmoud El-Gahazi watched the Land Rover approach and come to a stop. He flipped his cigarette to the side. He smiled widely and stepped out of the doorway, slowly walking over to meet the man getting out of the passenger side door.

"*Asalaam walaikum*," said El-Gahazi, touching his forehead with his right hand and bowing ever so slightly

"*Walaikum asalaam*," answered Al-Bari, his eyes darting about but returning to El-Gahazi. He watched intently for El-Gahazi's hands.

"I am honored at your presence, Hamza Al-Bari. You are very punctual. I trust you have the token of your sincerity?" asked El-Gahazi, still smiling like a Cheshire cat.

Al-Bari nodded his affirmation but did not speak. He turned back to the vehicle and nodded at the two men in the Land Rover.

"Very good," smiled El-Gahazi, stepping toward Al-Bari.

Al-Bari raised his hand slightly. "Let us go inside away from prying eyes."

"Why, yes, I agree," said El-Gahazi, still smiling. What struck Al-Bari was the dark yellow, rotting teeth of the man before him. The man looked like Mahmoud El-Gahazi but the real El-Gahazi had excellent teeth. They had previously met several months ago when the deal was first discussed. Al-Bari turned his head slightly and winked at the driver. El-Gahazi led the way to the door.

"Are you going to bring in the money?" asked El-Gahazi, turning to look at Al-Bari.

"My man will bring it when I see the merchandise," he answered, running his hand past his jacket making certain his pistol was still there.

"I would be more comfortable if we kept this transaction to ourselves. There is no need for your man to get involved. Bring the money with you. We are all friends here."

Al-Bari smiled but did not say anything. He simply reached into his jacket and pulled out his Glock.

As he leveled his gun a volley of machine gun fire riddled Al-Bari and the Land Rover from two directions. The two armed men in the rear of the vehicle tumbled out of the back and began firing in return. One moved around to the side of the Land Rover and glanced down at Al-Bari. Three head shots had ripped through his face, which now looked like goo. He was definitely dead.

The second man began firing at the door of the house. Dust and pieces of clay and dirt flew in all directions. But the bullets hit nothing but the walls. Another burst of gunfire came from El-Gahazi's men, hitting one of Al-Bari's men in the shoulder at the edge of his body armor. He spun around, looking up to spy his attacker. The wounded man raised his weapon and fired a killing burst. The Arab on the roof fell to the ground, bouncing off of the Land Rover and resting in the dusty street.

"Let's get out of here," screamed the wounded man as the Land Rover roared to life. Miraculously, the driver was unharmed in the hail of gunfire. The second man leapt into the back while the wounded man got into the passenger side and reached for the door. The vehicle surged backwards through the archway; ripping the passenger door off before he could close it. One of El-Gahazi's men ran out into the courtyard but before he could get off a shot he was cut down.

"What about Al-Bari?" the driver shouted.

"He's dead as hell. Don't worry about him. We have to inform Danson," said the wounded man, wincing in pain. "Damn, this is the first time I've ever been shot. It hurts like hell!" The vehicle's engine roared as they spun around and headed back out of town.

"They're not following us!" yelled the man in the back, replacing the magazine on his Uzi submachine gun. "Just keep going."

"You won't see me stopping for any red lights," joked the driver as the vehicle passed 70 miles per hour. The men breathed a sigh of relief. Yes, they had lost Al-Bari but they were still alive. And they had the money. Such were the thoughts of mercenaries.

The Range Rover sped away out of town, finally slowing after ten miles. The car stopped just off the road behind two house-sized boulders. The driver jumped out and began running back toward the town. The wounded merc sat there tending his bleeding. The second merc leapt from the car and took aim at the fleeing man. Two shots rang out. The running man stumbled and fell into the dust. In the distance another car could be seen speeding down the road.

"We gotta get the hell out of here now!" he screamed to the wounded man. "Someone's following us! Guess they want the money too!"

The uninjured merc jumped into the driver's seat and sped away with his cohort covering their escape from the rear of the car.

"So long, towelheads!" yelled the driver as the two drove away. "We'll tell Danson they took the cash and we were barely able to get away with our lives."

The wounded man smiled. "Sounds like a good story to me! We deserve a good payday regardless of the botched job."

CHAPTER TWENTY-TWO

May 2, 2013

Damascus, Syria, 10:25 a.m.

Winston Danson sat his coffee cup down on the table in front of him. His administrative assistant walked into the conference room and handed him a small sheet of paper folded in half.

"Thank you, Jennifer," said Danson smiling. He opened the paper and read its contents. His smile evaporated. He turned to his right to look out the window. It was another hot day in Damascus. Just like the previous hundred or so days. It was the same thing each day; hot, sunny and dusty. The smog was bad but the dust in the smog made it even worse. He arose and walked over to the window.

Danson was a wanted man back in the United States. His dealings with arms dealers across the world made him a pariah back home. Syria was about the only place in the world he could safely run his business. And business was good, very good. Generous payoffs to the government assured his customers and his shipments were safe. His business made him a very wealthy man. While some aspire to possess power over people, Danson merely wanted a soft, cushy life away from prying eyes. Syria had provided that. But today was a bit different.

"Amed, we have a problem. It looks like they decided to renege on our deal and steal our earnest money. In the melee, Al-Bari was killed and one of his guards wounded." Danson spoke softly without a hint of anger. Amed Zawari sat at the table, his hands folded in front of him.

"The pig Bashir lied to us to get our money," Zawari retorted. "We cannot trust him. And he killed a fellow Muslim, Hamza Al-Bari; that I cannot condone."

The door to the conference room opened and Danson's administrative assistant entered again. She walked over to Danson and whispered something into his ear. Danson immediately turned from the window.

"Send him in," he said sternly. "I want to talk to him." Jennifer left the room and within moments Qudamah Bashir entered the conference room. Before he could speak, the conference room door closed and locked. Both Danson and Zawari stared at him. If looks could kill...

"My brothers, we have been betrayed," blurted Bashir without any pleasantries normally extended in this part of the world. "Mahmoud El-Gahazi has been killed and replaced by someone else. We have just found his body."

The two men at the table looked at each other. They did not believe Bashir.

"You mean that was not your man, Mahmoud El-Gahazi, which killed Hamza Al-Bari?" asked Danson. Zawari was staring a hole in Bashir and planning his death in his mind.

"No. El-Gahazi was murdered four days ago. We found his body last evening after prayers. His throat was cut." Then it hit him. "Al-Bari is dead?"

There was no answer from either Danson or Zawari.

Bashir quickly recovered. "Then it seems that your man, Al-Bari, met with an imposter who wanted only the money."

"I see," said Danson, still not completely convinced. "An imposter, you say?"

"Yes, of course. I would not think of going against our agreement," said Bashir, sweat now beading about his brow.

"So we still have an agreement?" asked Zawari, showing his anger.

"Yes. Yes. We have always had an agreement," said Bashir nervously. "I have the package and we still agree on the price. It's just that someone else tried to step in between us and steal your money. That person will pay with his life, I swear."

Zawari looked at Danson. "I still do not believe him." Danson arose and walked over to Bashir.

Looking Bashir directly in the eyes, Danson said, "We still have an agreement. We will transfer two million US dollars to your offshore accounts when we get our package, not before. Is that clear?"

Bashir looked a bit puzzled. "But that was not our agreement. We agreed you would pay me five hundred thousand US dollars up front and the remaining three and a half million would be transferred upon your acceptance of the package."

"The deal has changed with the death of my brother, Al-Bari," snarled Zawari. "His death will only cost you two million unless you decide to back out and I kill you right now. We will get what we want from a source we can trust." Bashir knew Zawari's threat was very real.

Bashir thought for a moment. There was really nothing he could do. He could agree or die here in this room. He chose to agree.

"Gentlemen, we have a deal. I will direct my people to deliver the nerve gas to you today at a place of your choosing." Bashir beamed. Neither Danson nor Zawari were smiling.

"Agreed," stated Danson. "Deliver the package to our contacts in Nebal at 4:00 p.m. today. If the package is not there or the package is not to our liking, I will slit your throat myself. Do we have an understanding?"

Bashir swallowed hard. "Yes, we have an understanding." At that Bashir turned, opened the conference room door and left, closing it behind him.

Zawari looked at Danson, who was now looking out the window again.

"Alert our people in Nebal to the arrival of the nerve gas. We have worked for years to get our hands on some of Saddam Hussein's nerve gas cache. While we won't have all of it, we will have part of it to offer to our client," said Danson.

"Yes, sir, I will tell them the gas is coming," said Zawari. "I will also tell them to take it and kill every one of Bashir's men. Then we will kill Bashir."

Danson smiled deviously. "I knew I could trust you to take care of everything. Care for a cigar? I have a new stash of Cohibas from our client in the Caribbean."

"Why, yes, that would be nice."

"Amed, my dear friend, our future is looking very bright."

"Yes," replied Zawari, "and very lucrative."

Danson laughed. "Oh, my friend, you have no concept as to how rich we will be!" The two men sat back and enjoyed their cigars.

CHAPTER TWENTY-THREE

May 17, 2013

In a Cove, St. Maarten, Netherland Antilles, 1:00 p.m.

The cell phone rang twice before the man answered it.

"Yes?" was his unobtrusive answer to those on the call. "Then we have a deal?" There was a pause, then "Very good. I will arrange payment as we discussed."

The man hung up his phone and sat back to tend to his fishing rod. The small cove held hundreds of fish and he was determined to take a few of them home for dinner. Through the azure colored water he could see his prey. It was a far cry from his real prey out at sea.

He sat back, removed his hat and ran his hand through his thinning hair. He thought about the deal. If all went as planned, he would have his purchase within a few days. Things would be easier then, at least for his men. Killing was such a messy job when left to amateurs.

"I can expect delivery by next Wednesday then; right?" Battee Cook waited for his answer. "That is good. We can put it to use immediately. I will be expecting your final delivery message as we discussed." Cook hung up his phone and turned to look out the window of the small shack near the beach on Pointe Blanche. A shrewd but dangerous man, Cook, who recently turned forty, still had a head full of jet black hair. That with his two-day-old heavy beard gave him a dangerous, swarthy look, the look of someone that you did not want to cross. At six feet five inches tall, he towered over many men. He learned early to use that height advantage to intimidate.

He was born and raised in the islands. For many years he ran a gang of thugs. They stole, robbed and cheated everyone out of anything worth a dime or more. Then the smuggling, drugs and arms began. Battee was a bad man by anyone's reckoning.

He looked for his number one man, Ernesto. After a few seconds of scanning the beach he saw him walking out from behind a tree. He must have taken a piss, he thought. Cook stood and walked out of the door, across the wood-floored porch and down onto the thick white sand.

"Ernesto!" he shouted as he waved his hand. Ernesto David turned his head back toward the shack and immediately began walking over. He was a slight man of about fifty-five but looked years older. David never amounted to anything. He merely lived off of what he could steal or make doing meager jobs around the island. Cook used him as everything from a gofer to an enforcer. He did whatever Cook told him to do.

It was hot in May. For that matter, it was hot here most of the time except for when the hurricanes stormed through.

Cook walked to meet him under a tree with a nice shady spot away from anyone's prying eyes or ears.

"The shipment will be Wednesday very early in the morning, 2:30 a.m. It will arrive by boat on this beach. Take it to storage and call me immediately. I want to inspect the purchase personally. Do not try to open the package. If I see it has been opened, there will be hell to pay," he warned. Ernesto's eyes widened but he understood.

"Yes sir. I will call you. No one will open it. I will guard it myself," said Ernesto quietly, all the time his eyes scanning for anyone within hearing distance.

"Good. I cannot stress the importance of the package and how dangerous it is. Who will be with you?" asked Cook.

"I have two other men," he answered. Ernesto looked at Cook. "This is that important? What's in it?"

Cook took the small butt end of the well-chewed cigar from his mouth and threw it to the ground. "It is not your concern. But understand this. If you botch it, I will personally kill you and your men." Cook stared a hole through Ernesto. "I may even kill your wife and kids as well."

Ernesto's eyes widened. Yes, this was serious if he was threatening me and my family. Before he could answer, Cook ordered him away to make ready for the shipment.

As Cook walked away, he began to worry about Ernesto. Sure the man was good. He was also loyal. But his brain was as big as a pea. He wondered if it was a good idea to rely on Ernesto's completing the job without issues. He also thought about the additional two men. No, hell no, he thought. He could not risk having anyone else involved. Cook stopped in his tracks and turned.

"Ernesto!"

Ernesto was walking down the beach. He turned back toward Cook. He smiled and waved.

Dumbass, thought Cook. "Ernesto, come here, you moron," he said gesturing for him to come back. Seeing and hearing this, Ernesto trotted back.

"Yes, Mr. Cook?"

"Forget what I said earlier. You and I will pick up the cargo. It is too important to me and to you to have any screw-ups. Meet me here under that tree at 2:15 a.m. We will both take the cargo together and move it to storage."

"Yes sir, Mr. Cook. "I will be here as you ask."

The two men parted ways, both going different ways up and down the beach. But two beady eyes were watching with mini binoculars from behind a stand of large oleander bushes at the edge of the beach, about twenty-five feet from the men. He also carried a listening device. He had heard everything.

CHAPTER TWENTY-FOUR

May 22, 2013

In a Cove, St. Maarten, Netherland Antilles, 2:35 a.m.

It was the dead of night, dark as hell. The clouds from the earlier storm still covered the sky. With no visible stars and moon, it was as if a colossal wet blanket was being laid over the island. A cool sea breeze blew. All one could hear was the lapping of the waves and the occasional squawking of a sea gull.

Battee Cook and Ernesto David crouched under a palm tree at the back of the small, narrow beach. They watched. They were patiently waiting for a delivery boat that would arrive soon.

Ernesto reached for a cigarette. Battee slapped his hand away, knocking the cigarette into the sand.

"No smoking you idiot! You can see a lit cigarette for a mile. We don't want to show ourselves until we know the boat is here."

Ernesto nodded his head meekly and began stroking the sandy ground for the unlit cigarette. He could smoke it later. No use in wasting a good cigarette. These things cost real money.

The two men waited another ten minutes when Battee heard a splashing sound. It was the boat! Finally!

Battee looked at Ernesto. "When they get to the beach, go out and get the goods."

As the boat made the beach, Ernesto walked out to greet the two men exiting the boat. "Who are you?" asked one of the men cautiously.

"Ernesto," he answered quietly.

"Very good, we are to deliver this to you and leave." With that the two men hefted a four foot by two foot wooden box out of the boat and onto the wet sand. "It is all yours," said one of the men and they hurriedly scrambled back into their boat and paddled off into the surf. Within minutes they disappeared into the darkness.

"Ernesto. Bring the box to me," a call came from the back of the beach. He tried but could barely lift the box himself. "It's too heavy. Come help me. I can't lift it by myself."

Suddenly three men surrounded Ernesto. "We'll take it from here." They pushed him away. One man stood over in the shadows and the other two men grabbed the box and carried it away.

Ernesto felt like he had been punched in the chest. There was a stinging pain. He looked down and saw a hunting arrow embedded deep into his chest. It didn't hurt; it just stung like a bee. Before he could look up again he became lightheaded and fell to the ground. This always happens when a razor-sharp hunting arrow slices through the bottom of a heart, dumping the entire body's blood supply into the chest cavity. Ernesto was dead before he hit the ground.

Back under the palms the three men lifted the box into the back of an electric golf cart and drove away. Their last duty was to bid goodbye to Battee, who still sat at the base of the palm by the beach. But he didn't return the goodbye. His throat was cut from ear to ear. Now there were no witnesses.

The men in the golf cart drove down the beach road until they came to a small dilapidated shack with several wrecked cars and trucks in the yard beyond. The area around the shack was overgrown with weeds. They wheeled around the back of the building and stopped. Two men unloaded the box and the third drove away. As the golf cart pulled away the two men carried the box beside a wrecked two-toned 1951 Buick Super four-door Deluxe Sedan surrounded by weeds. It looked like this car had been there for years. Rust was overtaking the colors and the windshield had long been smashed. Placing the box on the ground, they left the area. All was quiet except for the chirping of the incessant insects.

Twenty minutes later the sedan slowly lifted on the driver's side until it stood at a forty-five degree angle to the ground resting on the passenger side. A soft red light came from under the car. A single head peered from under the car to ensure no one was around. The head dropped down again. Within seconds two men dressed in dark green fatigues appeared out of the opening and stepped out onto the ground.

The old car concealed an entrance to a tunnel deep in the ground below the shack. The men looked around, checking again for trespassers. Finding no one else in the area, they took the box and stepped back into the opening under the Buick and down the stairs. Seconds later the car slowly sank back to the ground closing the clandestine entrance and concealing their getaway.

Inside the dim red light shone more brightly. It guided the men down the long stairway to a steel door. One man opened a small cover mounted on the wall and entered an eight-digit code. The door slid open and the two entered a short hall leading to a twelve-by-twelve room also bathed in a dim red light. As they sat the box down, the door behind them closed and the red light was replaced by bright fluorescent lighting.

Mounted in the wall to one side was a tiny surveillance camera, its red activity light ablaze. Someone was watching. Leading away from the open room was an exposed hallway. The two men placed the box on a stainless steel cart much like you might find in a morgue standing against the wall. Together they pushed the load down the hall into a room that looked like a laboratory. No one spoke a word.

"Place the box over here," ordered the small, bony man in the white doctor's coat who stepped out from behind a desk across the room. "Thank you, gentlemen. You may leave now."

The two men left the room and closed the door. It locked automatically.

"Well, what have we here," said Dr. Stephan Malicio. "Nils, get me a crowbar and hammer so we can open this box. You know how much I like surprises. Then get me two more boxes. I want to split this cargo up."

Nils, Dr. Malicio's assistant, returned from a storage room with the necessary tools and began opening the box. His beady eyes gleamed.

"We must be very, very careful," said Dr. Malicio quietly. "This is a very special cargo."

"Yes, Doctor. I understand."

"One slip and you might break the contents. That would be very bad, Nils. In fact, I doubt we would have time enough to tell each other goodbye before we died."

They pried the box open only to find four smaller boxes. All were marked with Iraqi seals and profuse warnings printed on every side of each box.

Nils stared at Malicio, his face showing real fear.

"Doctor, what is this?"

"Death, my dear Nils…Death."

CHAPTER TWENTY-FIVE

May 22, 2013

Damascus, Syria, 8:00 a.m.

"Mr. Danson, the shipment was delivered to Dr. Malicio last night in St. Maarten," said Amed Zawari. "Payment has also been made."

"Very good, Amed," said Winston Danson. "Have you spoken with Hawk?"

"Yes sir. He is pleased as well."

"It is imperative that we keep Hawk very happy. After all, he is our boss and benefactor. I don't know about you but I sincerely love the life he has provided for me here in Damascus."

"I understand completely," answered Zawari.

"Excellent. Then we are ready to move on to our next deal."

"Yes, we are ready but I have some unfinished business to attend to," hissed Amed Zawari. "There are some debts outside of the deal to be paid."

"Ah, yes. I understand. One must do what one must."

"It is as Allah wills it."

"Meanwhile I will be traveling to Singapore tomorrow. Can you satisfy your debt by the time I return in ten days?" asked Danson.

"Yes. Ten days is plenty of time," answered Zawari.

"When I return I expect to have negotiated a rather large arms deal where I will again need your fine assistance."

"I will be at your service, Mr. Danson." Zawari stood up and bowed slightly. "May Allah bless you, my friend."

"And you too," Danson answered.

Zawari turned and left the room. His target was the scum Bashir who killed his friend in Iraq. Nothing would stand in his way.

Qudamah Bashir returned to his home outside of Damascus with the money he'd earned from his most recent deal. Sure it was not exactly what he wanted, but the alternative was to die. He did not want to die; especially at the hands of Zawari. His decision to take the offer of two million rather than the first agreed upon figure of four million dollars saved his life.

His home was enormous even by Damascus standards. It sat on a hill overlooking a vast plain, part of which was irrigated. In this part of the world water is life and Bashir had plenty. He had invested his wealth mainly in Swiss banks but he reserved a large chunk to build and maintain a veritable oasis in the desert. The irrigation brought lush vegetation, plentiful vegetable and fruit gardens and his pride and joy, his horse farm. He raised fine Arabian horses and sold them all over the world. All told, Qudamah Bashir's estate covered more than a thousand acres.

As he sat at the fine oak table on the terrace, his beautiful wife, Amineh, came into the room with their daughter, Rabab.

"Come, come, my daughter and wife. See what your husband has provided for you." Bashir poured out several thousand dollars out of a bag onto the table.

"Oh, my husband, your earnings are great. This will keep the household running for a very long time," cried Amineh. "Allah has blessed this family! Look at the bounty we have," she said, waving her hand across the vista from the wide terrace spanning the entire rear of the house.

"Yes, he has blessed us. He blessed me with a loving wife and a beautiful daughter and son. He also blesses me with a myriad of friends and business associates."

"Husband, it is time for lunch. Shall I have lunch served out here on the terrace?" asked Amineh.

"Yes, that would be nice."

Bashir's wife motioned to a servant, who disappeared into the house.

"Did I hear you say that our son Naseem will be here later today?" asked Bashir.

"Why, yes. He called this morning and said he will be passing through and would like to stop by to visit us this afternoon. I told him we would love to see him," said Amineh.

"Yes, of course! My son comes to visit us," said Bashir. "This is a very fine day!"

A servant entered the terrace and began cleaning the table. Two more servants brought in two trays, one piled with various meats and vegetables and the other with fruit. A carafe of cold water and a pitcher of milk were also placed on the table. The family began their meal happily enjoying themselves.

Back in the kitchen the servants sat around a table and ate their meal. There was a knock on the door. One of the servants answered the door and invited a middle-aged man into the kitchen. He was delivering a large basket of bread.

"I have bread for the Bashir family," the man said quietly.

"Very well, please place it on the far table. Would you like something to eat?"

"No. That will not be necessary," the man answered. With that he stepped back, reached into the basket and pulled out a silenced Glock 9mm pistol. "I am sorry but you all must die." The man methodically shot each one of the servants in the head. Most of them never left their seats. He paused momentarily to peruse the bodies and walked casually down the hall to the terrace. As he entered the terrace Qudamah Bashir froze. He saw the gun.

"No, you cannot..." he sputtered.

"You have failed in your promises. For that you and your family will be killed. It is to be," said the man quietly. His first shot killed the daughter instantly. She slumped in her chair.

"My God..." said Amineh as the second shot blew off her nose. Hands flew to her face and she fell to the floor. The third shot caught her in the stomach. She rolled over and moaned.

"You are to watch your family die, Qudamah. Those are my orders from Amed Zawari, who claims the lives of you and your family." The assassin leveled his pistol at Bashir. "You were warned..."

The assassin fired the first shot into Bashir's left knee. His knee exploded as he collapsed to the floor screaming and writhing in pain. Bashir looked over at his wife and child. The child was dead, her brains literally blown out. His wife's face was shot away, a bloody mess. Her stomach wound was bleeding badly and she was grimacing in pain.

"Your daughter was innocent. Her death was swift. However, you and your wife are involved in these dealings."

The assassin fired again into the right knee of Bashir, ripping through his kneecap and destroying his knee joint. He screamed again in agony but with no one else in the household alive, no one heard his cries. Bashir lay on his back, both knees shattered. He looked up at the assassin with tears in his eyes as if to ask for mercy for his wife. The assassin merely stepped over, stood over Bashir's wife and calmly fired four shots into her head. The bullets split open her skull like a melon. Bashir closed his eyes and made peace with Allah, who he was now ready to meet.

The assassin stepped back over to Bashir and fired two shots into his crotch, destroying his manhood. "You must suffer for those who were killed by you." He cried out in torment, his eyes bulging with pain. Blood was everywhere and pouring from his wounds. Through the intense pain Bashir heard someone walk onto the terrace. He opened his eyes and looked up at the man above him. It was Zawari!

"Bashir, you pig, I told you I would kill you and your family. I have killed them all. Now it is my turn to kill you."

Bashir's brain registered an instant flash but no sound. The bullet crashed into his brain, immediately destroying his brain stem. He never felt pain again.

Zawari and the assassin calmly walked through the house, out the back door and drove away. Their work was done.

CHAPTER TWENTY-SIX

May 22, 2013

The Cave beneath Brimstone Hill, St. Kitts, 1:30 p.m.

The bright mercury-iodide lights spread an almost daylight hue across the entire cave. The cave entrance was about one mile away from the sea, ensuring protection from the outside. A small team of men were quickly moving several wooden boxes from a twenty-eight foot runabout that had arrived earlier in the morning from Dr. Malicio in St. Maarten. They placed each box on a pallet and strapped them down so they would not fall. Later they were to be moved to the upper level by a crane. At the same time, another man rolled over a powered pallet jack beside the pallet on the deck.

"Pick it up from this side," said the short, barrel-chested man. He adjusted his cap and watched as the men steadied the boxes on the pallet for the jack to lift the load. He chewed on his cigar, showing his nervousness regarding this cargo.

"Dammit, be careful, you fool," he screamed as the load accidentally nudged another pile of boxes. Even though the cave was at least fifteen degrees cooler than the outside air, Levi Smith was sweating profusely. He knew what was concealed in the boxes. His men did not.

"This is very important and expensive cargo," said Smith commandingly. "Take care of it!" He was right. It was important and cost millions. In fact, several people had died for this cargo. And now it was handed over to him for special care. He did not want to disappoint Hawk. Smith had seen what happened to those who failed in past endeavors. They merely vanished along with their families.

The load was now being lifted by crane to the upper level where the high-priced cargo was stored. Once the crates were safely in place, Smith's instructions were to open one box, removing only one item. That item was to be picked up and delivered to another destination that same evening.

"You men up there," yelled Smith, "get ready to take the crates."

"Yes, sir, Mr. Smith," said a young man who was overseeing the cargo transfer above. "I'll take good care."

"You damn well better or I will be the least of your worries," Smith said softly to himself, releasing the cigar from his teeth. It had gone out. He reached into his pocket for a match. He had none. "Who has a light?" he asked, turning to a small group of men standing beside the now empty pallet jack. Two men jumped forward to light the stubby cigar. Smith took a long draw, smoke swirling about his head, and stepped back to see the progress above. The small crane set the load down.

Smith took another long draw, its end glowing bright red, then removed the cigar stub from his mouth and flicked it over into the water. "I'm coming up."

On the top level the crates were moved back in the vault area nestled back in the tunnel. The men wrestled the boxes off of the squatty cart and laid them one atop the other against one wall. As Smith entered, the men moved aside.

"Here, you open this box," said Smith, pointing to the top of the stack. "The rest of you clear out."

The other men left the two men to do their work. Smith was still sweating. He knew that one slip and the whole lot of them would be dead in seconds. Smith watched as the top came off revealing two silver canisters, each about a foot to a foot and a half long. They looked like small SCUBA diving air tanks. The other man stepped back, allowing Smith to move in closer. He reached into the box and lifted a canister. He was absolutely amazed at how light it was. This was partly due to the gaseous nature of the contents. But the tank was also made of carbon fiber. The tank was extremely strong with only a small label with Persian script.

Smith hand carried the canister down to the lower level and placed it in a cardboard box. Then he balled up newspaper around the canister to provide cushioning. His final step was to tape the box shut. An old UPS shipping sticker was on the outside on one side and a large FRAGILE sticker on the other. The package had the appearance of an ordinary delivery box.

"I want you to keep this box right in your sight at all times until they come to get it tonight. Nobody, and I do mean nobody, touches it until then," warned Smith, speaking to the two men normally assigned to the office area on the dock. "Take it inside and wait for my orders. I mean it when I say protect it with your lives...literally."

At 10:00 p.m. a small motorboat slowly entered the cave coming in from the sea. Smith leisurely walked over to the rail. He could see two men in the boat, Captain de Terr of the *May Pop* and his first officer, Dante Brees. As the boat slowed, Brees threw out a line to the men on the dock.

"Welcome back, Captain," beamed Smith. "It is good to see you again."

Captain de Terr glanced at Smith smiling widely. His bright white teeth glistened. "Smith, you pig. How are you?"

Smith's smile vanished by his insult; his attempt at being cordial was nastily dashed. "Yeah, I'm fine," he grumbled, "just fine."

"You have our box ready?" snarled Brees without any cordiality. He hated Smith. To him Smith was nothing more than a stock boy who provided the *May Pop* with a place to bring their plunder and pick up important cargo like this box.

"Yes, yes, the box is ready for you," snapped Smith, beginning to sweat again. "It is under the strictest guard." Smith turned and motioned to one of his men to bring out the box.

Brees hopped up onto the dock. Captain de Terr remained in the boat, looking sternly at Smith. Once the box was brought out, Brees inspected his cargo and handed it to de Terr.

"There, you see? We had it all ready for you. Do you want to check it?" asked Smith.

Captain de Terr laughed loudly, drawing everyone's attention. "Smith, if there is something wrong with the package, I will gut you myself and feed your entrails to the fish!" Brees gave a quick thin smile and stepped back into the boat.

Smith looked stunned. His men had never witnessed him being spoken to that way. Smith decided he best offer a retort.

"Look, de Terr..." he began. Instantly Brees produced a pistol and aimed it at Smith's face.

"So little fat man... you want to die?" asked Brees. He grinned at the opportunity to blow Smith's head off and be rid of him once and for all. Smith stepped back quickly.

"Oh, no, no," he blubbered. "Everything is fine...very fine."

Brees' gun returned to its holster but his eyes remained fixed on Smith.

"You forget who you are dealing with, Mr. Smith. I am a reasonable man. You do your job. I do mine. Your job is to service me and my crew. If you don't want to do that anymore, I can accept your resignation or I can give it to the boss. Either way the resignation will be permanent."

Fear nearly overwhelmed Smith. "Oh, no, that is not what I meant... I mean, no, I do not want to resign," sputtered Smith.

"Very well then," a calm de Terr said. "Then act like your job and your life mean something to you." With that Brees pushed the boat away from the dock and started the motor.

"Oh, by the way, send out a couple more jet skis. We had to ditch the last one a few days ago. We will need them on this job."

"Yes, certainly," answered Smith. "I will have them sent out in five minutes."

"Good. We want to leave immediately," said Brees with a sneer. "Now get to it!"

Smith turned and ordered the delivery. He wiped his forehead and watched the small boat head into the darkness of the cave.

A minute later de Terr and Brees were out of sight, headed back to the sea and the *May Pop*. Smith could relax.

CHAPTER TWENTY-SEVEN

May 23, 2013

St. Maarten, Netherland Antilles, 11:00 a.m.

"I have received confirmation that Captain de Terr has picked up the box. I have also received confirmation that Mr. Smith has the remaining cargo safely stored in our unit at St. Kitts," reported James Doss.

"Excellent," said the Hawk. "This is very good news indeed. Also Bashir and his entire family and house staff were executed in Damascus yesterday as well." Hawk sat back in his fine leather desk chair and reached for a Cuban cigar. "James, you do exceptionally good work. By the way, have the results of your independent test of the shipment come back yet?"

Doss smiled. "Yes sir. I received them about ten minutes ago. Dr. Malicio has confirmed we are the proud owners of eight cylinders of the most deadly nerve agent known to man."

The boss beamed. "Damn, that's nice to hear. I guess, as with any other item, if you pay for the best you get the best. Now, do we have any more coming?"

"Yes sir. We have been able to procure twenty-four more cylinders. More than enough for our plans with some left over to sell for profit."

Hawk grinned widely.

Doss was Hawk's right-hand man in St. Maarten. Only he knew the true identity of Hawk and he protected that information fiercely. Doss was a short man, built like a fireplug but strong as a bull. He carried no fat at all. When his shirt came off, his ripped body was a mecca to women. And with his current employer he used that ability to run through women like water. There was a different one each day. Some were merely cast off. Several just disappeared. A few had been so brutally tortured that their remains made the authorities vomit. He was as deadly as a cobra but immensely loyal to the boss. Why not? Hawk made it possible for him to enjoy life in his own hideous way.

"The shipment was expensive, but no one other than the United States, Chinese or Russian military has the capability to counteract its use. We have the ultimate weapon in our hands thanks to the dumbass Americans and British," agreed Doss.

"And how's that?" asked Hawk.

Doss grinned. "This is one of Saddam Hussein's weapons of mass destruction the world was so worried about during the Gulf War of 1990 and 1991."

"Really?" queried Hawk, interested.

"Absolutely," continued Doss. "At the beginning of the war President Bush and his generals were worried about Iraq's ability to use weapons of mass destruction against the coalition forces that were to regain control of Kuwait. They had spies everywhere trying to prove the Iraqis actually had WMDs and their location. The Iraqis did have them. But they were well hidden. They quickly buried several caches deep in the desert northwest of the Euphrates River hundreds of miles from Baghdad before the Americans arrived."

"Yes, I do remember that," said Hawk. "The U.S. Secretary of State, that general, was sent to the United Nations to get their support in finding the WMDs."

"Yes sir. The Americans knew the Iraqis had these weapons but were unable to find any trace after they were hidden by Saddam Hussein. It made them look like fools and the American politicos had a field day."

Hawk nodded in agreement and took a long draw on his cigar. He was clearly enthralled in the story.

Doss continued, "In fact, the WMDs would still be buried if it wasn't for a lone Iraqi tribesman who witnessed the building of one cache. Saddam killed all of the workers on the sites. Some believe the Republican Guard officers who oversaw the construction were also killed to protect the location of the weapons. No one alive knew the cache locations until this tribesman told an operative in the area what he had witnessed. We still don't know how many more caches are out there or their location, but the one site has yielded us this great weapon."

"Amazing," said Hawk, placing his cigar in an ashtray, rising to pour himself a drink. He flipped a crystal tumbler over from its top down resting place and reached for the decanter of a one hundred and ten year old Courvoisier L'Esprit. At over nine thousand dollars a bottle, its taste was as fine as it was rare. "So de Terr has the agent?"

"Yes, sir," said Doss. "Captain de Terr is very happy. He can now wreak havoc on the Caribbean and not worry about anyone talking or having to dispose of his victims in a manner that might put his crew in jeopardy."

"Oh, yes. I understand he lost a man in his last attempt against a rather large prize," stated Hawk.

"That is correct. He was one of de Terr's must trusted men as well. I knew him too. In fact, you may have known him. His name was Pappy. He was shot when they tried to overcome a big catamaran off of St. Kitts."

"Damn. Yes, I did know the man. We called him Pappy because he's been around these islands for eons. He was a loyal friend as well as an excellent employee. That's too bad. Have we helped out the man's family?" asked Hawk, truly concerned.

"Not yet. I wanted to speak with you about that," answered Doss, pouring himself a glass of the fine cognac as well.

"A good man deserves a just reward. Pay his family one hundred thousand dollars. But make it very quiet. I do not want to cause the family any more hardship."

"Done! I will take care of it personally," said Doss as he sipped his last swallow and turned to leave.

"Oh, I almost forgot. Did de Terr or his men get the name of this boat that killed our man?"

"It was a very large catamaran, the *Sweet Texas*."

"The *Sweet Texas*," repeated Hawk slowly. His jaw hardened. He was clearly upset. "Tell de Terr to find that boat, kill everyone aboard and sink it. We can't have those types roaming our seas. They have caused us grief already. They will do it again. We cannot afford someone in our way, especially not now. Do you understand?"

"I will speak to de Terr after this meeting," answered Doss.

Hawk paused for a second as Doss wrote a note to himself on a piece of paper off of Hawk's desk. There was a minute of silence as Hawk considered his next actions.

"So de Terr will be testing this new weapon soon?" asked Hawk.

"Yes, sir, I believe he is out at sea as we speak," answered Doss.

"I should think the *Sweet Texas* should be de Terr's first target with his new weapon."

"I would imagine that if it is not, it is very high on his agenda. I understand he did not take the loss of his man well. He will definitely be out for revenge."

"Yes. I would be too."

"Mr. Doss, we need to discuss a course of action that I believe will make us very rich and shock the world at the same time. Please take a seat."

Doss plopped down on a large burgundy leather couch. Hawk took a seat on the opposite end.

"Sounds very interesting," said Doss, sitting up, paying particular attention.

Hawk began his presentation. "As you know, St. Maarten is second only to Grand Cayman in its riches. Money flows in and out of here like water; millions each day on both the French and Dutch sides of the island. Yes, a small bit is ours from our business ventures but it's just a miniscule piece of the entire fortune to be had here. I want it all."

Doss sat still listening intently.

"So I put it to you, my dear Doss... what are we to do?"

Doss sat quietly, gesturing slightly with his hands. "You have a plan?"

"Yes, I do. I want to use this new gas to kill everyone in Philipsburg and Marigot and steal all of the money on the island." Doss sat back stunned. This was big… very big.

CHAPTER TWENTY-EIGHT

May 23, 2013

St. Maarten, Netherland Antilles, 2:10 p.m.

"Shake a leg! We gotta get going!" yelled Hugo to the trio walking to the dingy. "I want to make St. Kitts before too late."

"Hey, I thought we were on vacation."

Hugo grinned widely. "Okay, okay. I give up. You are so very right, Mr. Skoglund. Ya just have to remind me. I keep falling back into that job thing we left behind."

The *Sweet Texas'* Zodiac Yachtline 420 was tied at the end of the dock. The six man inflatable dingy was powered by a forty horsepower gas motor. It was used to ferry people and supplies to and from the catamaran moored in the harbor.

"Not a problem, brother," answered Dane, taking Sherrie's hand to help her aboard the Zodiac. "Your boat, m'lady."

"Why, thank you, fine sir," retorted Sherrie in her best southern belle accent. "Your graciousness is very much appreciated." Dane bowed to show his thanks.

Greg jumped in and stowed the forward line. The sun was shining brightly with just a few high clouds. It was a beautiful day in the Antilles; picture perfect. The clear azure water was calm. All was right in the world. Sailing would be a breeze today.

"This weather is fantastic!" cried Hugo looking up at the sun, letting it bathe his already tanned face. "Sher, if you aren't out on the bow with a bikini within five minutes, you are crazy!"

"Not to worry, Hugo. That's exactly where I am headed while we are underway," answered Sherrie. "I'll bet I can even get Dane to join me!" Dane turned to her and smiled.

"Some of us have to sail this monster," said Dane.

"Ah... even if I do a bit of topless sunning?" countered Sherrie with a wide smile, gently rubbing her small pert breasts through her shirt.

"Damn, Dane," quipped Hugo. "I think she's got ya there. Oh, and Sherrie, I promise not to look!"

Sherrie burst out in laughter. "Like you have never seen a topless woman sunbathing!"

"Well, yeah," said Hugo, looking slightly embarrassed, "but not you." All but Hugo roared in laughter. They were a happy family again.

As they neared their moored catamaran Sherrie opened a small canvas bag.

"Oh, I almost forgot. I got something for you, Hugo." She opened the top for Hugo to see.

"Holy crap, I didn't know they made that many candy bars!" His eyes were as wide as saucers.

"Yeah, I bought out some street vendor. I think there are over ten different kinds of bars in this bag. It'll take you weeks to eat 'em all," giggled Sherrie.

"Oh, hell, are you forgetting who you are talking to?" asked Dane grinning. "This guy can eat a whole steer in one sitting. I'm betting they won't last two days."

"If that happens, someone is going to be very sick," added Greg.

"Not me!" grinned Hugo. "Thank you, Sherrie."

When they reached the catamaran it took no longer than ten minutes and they were leaving the harbor toward the open sea. The two days they spent in St. Maarten gave them time to fix the bullet holes and replenish the stores with fresh fruit, steaks and other provisions. Greg wanted to buy a case of lobsters until his sister reminded him they could catch their own. They sped away on a southerly course. Next stop, St. Kitts. But Dane and Hugo had not forgotten the pirates. They kept a watchful eye about the sea. They wanted a bit of payback.

Meanwhile Captain de Terr and his *May Pop* were cruising northwest of St. Kitts looking for an easy take from the many sailboats traveling from St. Maarten to St. Kitts and beyond. They were unaware the *Sweet Texas* was headed their way.

"Keep a sharp eye out for boats," ordered Captain de Terr.

"Aye, Captain," answered First Officer Brees. They were both on the bridge eager for the chance to test their new toys.

"I want to try out our new weapon as soon as possible. Have you trained the attack crew? Does everyone have the necessary masks and protection?" he asked. "I don't even want to think about losing another man."

Brees stood beside the bridge door. "Yes, sir. We have everything ready." He turned to the helmsman. "Keep watch for anything within our grasp no matter how small."

"Yes, sir," replied the helmsman, checking his course and looking ahead.

Within an hour their next target was on the horizon. The *May Pop* maneuvered to take a position in the sun from the unwitting boat.

"How far out from her?" asked de Terr.

"Not more than a mile," answered Brees, focusing on their target. "I'm sending the skis now." Brees called down to the deck and two jet skis, each carrying a mounted gun with specially crafted tear gas slugs, were dispatched. There was no tear gas in these slugs, only the nerve agent Novichok. The nearly silent jet skis came out of the sun and were on the targeted sailboat before the crew knew what was happening. It only took a single shot of the nerve agent. Within one minute of the bursting of the slug all crew on deck was unconscious and dying.

Without a person steering, the sailboat slowed after turning itself into the wind. The first jet ski came alongside and clipped a lanyard on a side stay. The pirate jumped off of the ski and boarded the sailboat, noted everyone on deck was down and immediately lowered her sail. He checked the crew; all dead, two men and two women. Pity, the women were young and very nice looking. They would have fetched a particularly nice price on the international slave market or would have been kept for 'entertainment' for the crew. He waved an all clear sign. The second ski pirate boarded and the two stripped the boat of all of the valuables, electronics and any weapons. A small block of C-4 explosive was placed under the galley table on the outer hull of the boat. A five-minute timer was attached.

As quickly as they came, the two pirates were gone. A few minutes later an explosion blew out the side and bottom of the sailboat causing it to sink to the bottom.

One thing de Terr and Brees knew now. This nerve agent worked much better than they hoped, even after being quickly dissipated by the normal sea breezes.

"What the hell was that sound?" asked Greg, reacting to the muffled boom.

"I don't know, but it can't be good," answered Hugo, grabbing his binoculars and scanning the area. The location of the sound was hard to place.

"Maybe it was just a sonic boom," said Greg.

All seemed clear until Hugo looked toward the west. On the horizon he could see black smoke.

"Somebody's in trouble," Hugo said, pointing toward the smoke. "Greg, take her over there and see if we can give them a hand." Greg turned the wheel, sending the big cat in a starboard direction headed west. Hugo manned the sails, trimming them to increase their efficiency. The boat shuddered as the sails swung over their heads, fluttering at first and then catching the sea breeze. They popped into trim and the catamaran felt like someone had kicked it into a passing gear. She leapt forward, gaining speed, water and spray flying.

"Hang on all," yelled Greg over the din of the wind in the sails and water. "We are in high gear!"

Hugo stood beside him in case he needed either a hand or relief. Hugo's hand was clamped on the small rail on the port side of the cockpit. When he bought the cat, he wondered why that handle was there. Now he understood.

Dane burst out of the galley with Sherrie just steps behind him. "What's happening?" he cried, looking up at Hugo and Greg in the cockpit. "Trouble?"

"Looks like it," answered Hugo, yelling back down to the salon. "We heard a large boom and now we see black smoke on the horizon. Someone's in trouble all right."

Dane immediately went below and emerged with two H&K MP5 submachine guns. If there was trouble, especially with pirates, they would be ready this time.

"Sherrie, this could get nasty really fast. If trouble starts, I want you down in the hull on the opposite side of the boat. That will give you the best protection if there is gunfire."

Sherrie nodded. She knew this was not a time to argue with Dane. He was going into that SEAL mindset like any other warrior breed. Both Dane and Hugo were extremely dangerous in that mode.

Within minutes the *Sweet Texas* was at the site of the explosion. There was absolutely nothing there except for a few floating remnants of the fiberglass hull and burned Kevlar sails. Hugo scanned the sparse wreckage until he found a bit of a life jacket. Printed on the jacket was the boat's name, *Twilly*. She was out of Sanibel, Florida.

"Damn," muttered Hugo.

"There's nothing left," said Dane, scouring the horizon for any other boat.

"Oh, those poor people," said Sherrie, clutching Dane's arm. "What happened?"

"Don't know," said Dane quietly. "But we need to find out. It could have been an onboard explosion of some type from the look of the wreckage. Hugo, let's circle a bit to see if we see any bodies."

"Already on it!" yelled Hugo from the cockpit. Greg was up on the bow looking for anything important in the water. He had a long mooring pike in his hands. That way he could extend his reach if he saw something.

Within a minute Greg was on to something. "Got something bright pink in the water just ahead," he yelled back. Everyone except Hugo moved forward. Amidst all of the floating bits of fiberglass and wood was a bright pink object two feet under the water.

"What is it?" asked Dane.

"Can't tell, but it looks..." Then Greg saw an arm. "Holy shit, it's a body!" He recoiled at the grisly sight.

Dane immediately turned to Sherrie. "You stay here," he said sternly, laying down his MP5. With that he flew to the forward trampoline where Greg was standing. As Dane got there, Greg was trying to hook the pink clad body floating under the surface. Hugo had dropped the sail, slowing the huge catamaran. Greg's pike caught the object and it slowly rose to the surface.

"Oh, Jesus!" exclaimed Greg as he realized it was the body of a petite young woman; or what was left of it. He quickly noticed that one foot and the lower part of her leg was missing. It was an absolute miracle the sharks had not found her. Smaller fish were nibbling at her wounds.

Dane stood silently as Greg hooked the side of her neon pink bikini bottom and she rolled over. Both men were startled as she turned face up. It was not the obvious fact that she was topless that struck them but the grimace on her face; it was hideous. At first they both thought her face was partially eaten but quickly saw her expression was of absolute terror.

"Let's bring her aboard," Dane said quietly. Greg was struggling to get her close to the boat.

"I think I can reach her," said Dane, lying on the trampoline and across the hull. He reached and caught her hand as she rolled over again. "Got her!"

As they pulled her from the water Sherrie stood in the cockpit beside Hugo with her hands over her mouth. It was not seasickness that overtook her; it was the grisly sight below. She leaned over the side and vomited. Hugo placed his hand on her head.

"That's okay," Hugo assured her. "We've all been there..."

They brought the pink lady aboard. Hugo trimmed the sails and brought the cat into the wind. He jumped down from the cockpit and went below, returning with a blanket to wrap her body and placed her in the salon.

For another hour the *Sweet Texas* trolled through the waters looking for more victims. Finding none, they turned for Philipsburg to report what they found.

CHAPTER TWENTY-NINE

May 23, 2013

St. Maarten, Netherland Antilles, 5:45 p.m.

"Philipsburg Harbor Master... Philipsburg Harbor Master, this is the *Sweet Texas*... come in please...this is an emergency..." Hugo's call lined up a meeting with the Philipsburg police out at the far edge of the harbor. Hugo didn't want to cause a stir by sailing into the harbor with a corpse. Discretion was best.

The police boat pulled beside the cat and boarded. They spent over an hour questioning the group and quickly reviewing the pink lady's mangled body. Dane had deftly hidden the two submachine guns in Hugo's hidden gun safe below in spades. No use in causing a huge stir as to why they had them. It wasn't worth it. The modifications Hugo had made to provide a secure but hidden armory paid off.

It was decided that the woman's body should be taken to the local morgue for a thorough autopsy while the police tried to establish her identity. Dane and his group were asked to stay moored in port until the police said they could go.

So with another night in St. Maarten, the group went ashore to get a bite to eat. Nightfall was over an hour away and the beaches along the waterfront were teeming with sunbathers.

Sherrie looked over the tanning bodies. "Funny how all of these people are having so much fun while others are dying."

"It's like that all over the world, Babe," noted Dane.

"I'll grant you it is a strange world we live in but you can't blame them. They are oblivious to what happened out there today, as we are all oblivious to other people dying all around us. Death happens seven by twenty-four by three-sixty-five. It's just a fact," a somber Hugo lamented.

"Yeah, but still..." Sherrie reached and grabbed Dane's hand. "I feel so sorry for that girl and the others on that boat. I mean, why?"

Dane released her hand and wrapped his arm around her. "We don't know. We may never know. But we will do our best to help the police find out why. In the meantime let's eat and try to put this experience behind us."

"Amen," added Greg. He didn't want to show his sister how much the incident shook him, but it definitely made him think. *That could have been us.* Little did he know that there was much more truth to that statement than he ever knew.

James Doss walked quietly into the back section of a low, nondescript building serving as Hawk's headquarters in St. Maarten. He faced a steel door with a twelve-digit combination lock and a card reader. He swiped his card and punched in a secret code. The door opened. He proceeded to Hawk's office. The door was open. He walked in.

"Looks like de Terr had a successful test of the new weapon," he said, checking a coded radio transmission he held in his hand.

"That sounds like good news," remarked Hawk looking up from the papers on his desk, "very good news!"

"They overtook a large sailboat headed south. They used the jet skis to get close and fired a single gas round. Once it exploded the crew was dead within minutes. They had no chance to send a distress signal. De Terr's men boarded, took their valuables, set a charge and were out of there within five minutes. The explosives took out the boat as de Terr sped away."

"Sweet!" said the boss smiling. "No issues on our side?"

"Not a one," answered Doss. "The gas took 'em out and dissipated before de Terr's men boarded. It was a picture perfect job. No one will ever know how they died."

"Very good," said the boss. "It sounds like we made a good investment after all. How much gas do we have?"

Doss grinned. "We have enough for hundreds of raids like today. With our new plans, we still have plenty but more is in the pipeline."

"I'm even thinking of using the gas to knock off a bank or two on a few of the other close islands as well."

Hawk stood up and walked quietly to the window. "With the added shipment, I don't see any reason we can't move ahead with our new plans. No survivors to talk," said Hawk as he smiled and began to laugh. "Damn, what a setup!"

"Yes, it is if we are careful."

"Where do we eat?" blurted Hugo, trying to lighten the group.

"I hate to say this, but I would love some fresh seafood," said Sherrie.

"After all of the steaks we have had lately, I agree with Sis," added Greg, clapping his hands together, "unless we can find some fried chicken."

"Well, since good fried chicken can't be found here, I guess that's settled. Seafood it is," smiled Dane. "Let's find a place."

"Find a place? What's wrong with Bob Rand's place?" asked Hugo. "He said he has great seafood and he does have the coldest beer."

"Aw, hell, Hugo, why don't you just come out and say it. His place had the best women too," grinned Dane.

"Well, there is that..."

The group burst into laughter as they strolled down the beach headed for Rand's place.

They walked into the bar to find Rand standing at the door waiting on them. "Hey, folks! Where ya been? I've been waiting on you!" he bellowed. "I saw you walking down the beach. If you had gone somewhere else, I would have dragged your asses out and brought you here."

"Damn, Bob, you'll never change," said Hugo, grabbing his hand in a monster handshake. "We are here to eat some fish."

"And I have the best in town. I guarantee it! All caught within the hour."

Sherrie grinned. "Sounds like a winner to me!"

"Me too," came a reply from Greg.

"Here, here, y'all come on over to my private table and have a sit down. Oh, and I have a surprise for you... my daughter is here." Rand looked around searching for her. "Oh, she's probably in the bathroom."

"Well, speaking of the ladies' room, I think I need to make a pit stop," said Sherrie, dismissing herself. "I'll find her and bring her back."

"You do that," Bob said in his regular loud voice. He could probably be heard for a mile.

The group sat down and ordered a round of drinks. Bob told them to forget about the menu; he would get his chef to 'put on the dog' for them. He made sure the drinks were cold and ducked back into the kitchen.

The place was filling up. Most of the clientele were locals. They knew to come here. The food was that good. The cruise ship folks were back aboard. They sailed within minutes. Two minutes later Sherrie returned with a short, gorgeous, blonde-haired beauty.

"Hey, guys, this is Erin, Bob's daughter."

The guys sat there with blank looks on their faces. Erin's beauty was stunning.

"Oh, my God, I have never seen this in all of my life!" cried Sherrie. "All three of you speechless!"

Hugo was the first to speak, of course, as the guys regained their composure and stood up. "Very pleased to meet you, Erin."

"Me too," said Greg, trying to keep it all together.

"Nice to meet you, Erin," said Dane, the most confident of all. "We've heard so much about you from Bob."

"It is an honor to meet you folks too," Erin said sweetly. "Now, which of you is Hugo?"

A beaming Hugo stepped forward and took her hand. He tried to kiss it but Erin jerked it back. "Dad told me I was to specifically avoid you!" she said with a grin. Everyone roared with laughter, except Hugo, who stood there like a child caught with his hand in the cookie jar.

"Wait a minute now..." he interjected.

"Hey, I see you met my little girl! Erin, this is Hugo..."

"Yeah, thanks for the vote of confidence," smiled Hugo. "You warned her, huh?"

"Ha! What did you think, you hound! Do you think I would let you near my daughter after all of our tales of ladies afar?"

"Well…" Hugo said, actually blushing a bit.

"Look at him blush," yelled Dane. "I haven't seen that in ages." The group laughter continued.

"Erin, I do want you to meet this man, Dane Skoglund," said Bob with a serious tone. "If not for him, I definitely would not be walking on this earth today. This man saved my life several times and is one of the best friends a guy could ever have," said Bob, shaking Dane's hand and grabbing him around the neck, giving him a big hug.

"I have heard stories about you for years. Thank you, Mr. Skoglund. Thank you so very much," said a grateful Erin.

Now it was Dane's time to blush but only for a second. "Erin, these are good friends of ours, Sherrie and Greg Knowlton. Brother and sister, I might add."

"Thanks for clearing that up. He's a cutie. I met Sherrie in the ladies' room."

The group sat down and had a dinner that kings would have coveted. The variety of fish was magnificent; huge shrimp, Mahi, Grouper, Snapper, conch and even sea urchin. Broiled, fried and boiled. You name it. They ate it along with copious amounts of potatoes, salad and more than a case and a half of ice cold beer. It was truly a night to remember.

CHAPTER THIRTY

May 25, 2013

St. Maarten, Netherland Antilles, 9:40 a.m.

The group spent a wonderful few days in St. Maarten taking full advantage of the island's offerings. They made time to go over to Maho Beach to watch the planes take off and land.

It was customary for tourists to flock to this beach to brave the blasts of large airliners taking off. With the beach just yards from the runway end, when the planes landed their undercarriages were about six to ten feet above their heads. Either way, it was a rush for everyone. The guys loved it. Sherrie watched as the guys acted like a bunch of teenagers.

The police had also given the group the green light to leave. But Dane wanted to know more. He decided to pay a quick visit to the police while the rest of the crew set about to get the *Sweet Texas* back into sailing mode.

"Hey, bro, did you get all of the gear stowed back into place?"

"Yeah, it's all ready to go, Hugo," answered Greg.

"How's the food and stores, Sherrie? We should be full as a tick," said Hugo.

"Yes, we are good to go. We have enough food for weeks counting the frozen stuff. Did this boat come with a freezer?" Sherrie asked.

"No. I had that added. Dane and I thought it might come in handy on long voyages down here," said Hugo. "You don't see many freezers aboard boats but this one is so big we decided to burn a bit of space and include it."

"Well, it works for me," she said. "It's so much easier to carry all of those steaks you guys crave."

Sherrie turned at the sound of a Zodiac coming closer, hoping it was Dane returning. She walked out on the back deck and saw him slowing to a stop. She waved. "Welcome back!"

"Thanks," said Dane as he tied up the Zodiac.

"Did the meeting go well?" asked Hugo, coming down from the cockpit after checking his instruments.

"Well, yes and no," replied Dane. "We all need to talk."

"Hey, Dane's back," said Greg, popping up from below. "What's up?"

"Everybody take a seat. I have some dangerous news."

"News about the pink lady?" asked Hugo. That question drew an elbow from Sherrie.

"I told you not to call her the pink lady."

"Yes, ma'am," Hugo said quietly.

Dane sat down and looked at all of them. "The crew of the boat we found was killed by nerve gas."

"No way!" said Hugo. "How would someone get access to that stuff?"

Dane explained. "The police are certain that it was nerve gas and they are at a loss to explain it as well. INTERPOL has now been called into the case. I also gave them a few contacts in the U.S. military to get them involved. They are trying to locate someone who can specifically name the nerve agent used. It is vital that they know what it is so they can find out where it came from. Evidently this nerve agent is extremely toxic."

"At least they do know the identity of the woman we found," said Dane looking at Sherrie. "She's Dale Matthews, twenty-six, from our old neck of the woods, Miami. It seems she and three friends were down here on a bareboat cruise aboard the *Twilly*. The group sailed out of Tortola well over a week ago. They were evidently overtaken by someone, pirates if you will, and killed out of spite. At least that's what the St. Maarten authorities say. The boat was reported missing yesterday morning as they did not return to port."

"Damn!" said Hugo.

"That poor girl," said Sherrie quietly. "So pretty and was out having a fun vacation...like us. Now she's dead."

"Exactly," said Dane. "Just like us. Frankly, this has gotten under my craw." He looked at Hugo. "As you know, I don't normally get into other folks' fights, but after talking to the authorities, I believe these are the same bastards that hit us. That pisses me off."

"Oh, hell," moaned Hugo. "One thing I have learned about him is that you do not want to piss this guy off," glancing at Dane. "He's like a coiled rattler, meaner than a snake and ten times as dangerous." Sherrie's eyes widened at hearing what Hugo said. She knew Dane from his years in Miami. She'd briefly heard of his exploits in the Amazon rescuing his sister, Dana, and her husband, Randall. Now she was about to personally witness the warrior Dane that she had never seen. The thought sent a shiver through her body. Fear covered her face.

Dane looked over at Sherrie. "This may get very dangerous before it's over. I would like you to stay with Erin and Bob here in St. Maarten." He looked over at Greg as well. "You too."

Greg thought to himself for about five seconds before he answered. "I totally agree that Sherrie should stay in St. Maarten. But I'm going with you."

"Oh, hell, no," added Hugo. "This ain't no picnic."

Greg looked Hugo in the eyes. "I know. These guys shot me and tried to kill me. This is not a game. I know full well what I'm getting into."

"Okay, you two, calm down," interjected Dane. "I understand where Greg's coming from." Sherrie said nothing. She sat quietly taking all of this in. No one talked for a full minute.

"Well, there goes the vacation," said Hugo. "Gotta go back to work again. Well, at least it's not in some stinking jungle with a bunch of freakin' Nazis."

Greg tried to hold back a smile but couldn't. Sherrie and Dane also cracked a grin.

"Well, that's settled. We drop off Sherrie and then try to flush out these pirates," recapped Dane. "Captain, let's get moving!"

As everyone else began scurrying about the boat, Dane took Sherrie's hand and walked her out on the bow.

"Dane, I'm scared to death. I've never seen or done anything like this before. I do feel that we need to get involved," explained Sherrie. "It kinda feels like when my older brother was killed by those drug lords in Miami. They just drove up, shot him and left him to die in the street. And he did nothing to them. He happened to be standing at the wrong place at the wrong time," she continued. "That trial changed my mind about studying law. All I wanted was to strike at those killers but didn't know who or how to strike. I felt so helpless. They got twenty years. But Martin was still dead. I don't want that to happen in my life again." Dane embraced Sherrie to console her.

"Sherrie, I fully understand how you feel. But this is a real threat to all of us down here. I've got to get involved," he explained.

"I know that. That's not the issue. I am so very scared of losing you." She looked at him with tears in her eyes. "I'm afraid I have fallen so in love with you."

Dane didn't miss a beat. He had figured as much. "Sher, I have never told anyone this outside of my family. I love you too."

Sherrie burst into tears and flung her arms around Dane, giving him a hug like she had never done before. Dane stroked her blonde hair. It smelled so wonderful. And even with a swirling storm coming, he felt on top of the world.

CHAPTER THIRTY-ONE

May 25, 2013

St. Maarten, Netherland Antilles, 10:45 a.m.

It took only ten minutes to call Bob Rand and hook up Sherrie with Erin. Dane walked her over to one of Bob's jewelry shops where Erin was working. Even with the store filled with cash-ladened customers from the cruise ships in port, Erin immediately saw Sherrie and Dane walk in. Both were in awe at the number of shoppers, the number of salespersons and the amounts of money that were being spent.

There was one leathery-skinned tourist clad in a brightly colored sundress that was clearly inappropriate for her age and body type. In her mid-sixties and from New York, she was more boisterous than most other customers. "This is beautiful!" she exclaimed, tugging on her husband's arm. He, on the other hand, seemed completely uninterested in his wife's enthusiasm over jewelry.

"You can't get this design anywhere at home." Again her husband just looked stoically at the jeweler.

"How much?" he finally asked.

"Sir, this diamond necklace and matching broach are the epitome of the finest diamond jewelry available on the island. Its exquisite design and quality of the gemstones are beyond reproach."

"This is so beautiful," the lady said to her husband. "I have to have them. Grace Johnson back home will have a cow when I walk into the club with these."

Her husband looked at the salesman. "Okay. What kind of price can we work? Remember I didn't come off the farm yesterday."

"Of course not, sir." The salesman checked the tiny tag on the two items and pulled a small book from his pocket. After checking a page or two, he replied, "Sir, the recommended price for these two items, the necklace and the matching broach, is $85,000 US. With our discount and your cruise line discount we can make this available for $64,500 US. I assure you one cannot find a finer pair."

The husband did not blink. "How many total carats?"

"Two hundred total. The largest stones are one and a half carats. Please let me prepare it for you."

"Albert, that is a great price," interjected the woman.

"I'll tell you what," said the husband. "I'll give you $62,000 cash. Take or leave it."

Sherrie looked wide-eyed at Dane. "Did you hear that, sixty-two thousand dollars?"

Dane was stunned. He had no idea this business had so much money involved. "Don't get any ideas, Sherrie. I can't afford that."

Sherrie laughed. "Oh, my, I would not want that! I could never wear something as expensive and gaudy as that!"

"Whew! For a minute there I thought I was screwed!"

"Hey, you two!" smiled Erin, walking over to them from across the store. "Dad called and told me what you need. Don't have a second thought, Dane. Sherrie and I will be fine!"

Dane smiled. "Thanks, Erin. I knew we could count on you." He glanced around the store, still listening to some of the prices being quoted. "I had no idea you guys were doing so well."

"Well, Dad set our stores up back when I was young and they have been booming since. Since the tourist trade has blossomed, hundreds of thousands of tourists onto the island are dying to buy, buy, buy!" She looked at Sherrie. "Come with me. I'll get our manager to take over and we will get out of here."

"Sounds great," said Sherrie. For the first time she sounded upbeat.

"Don't worry about Dane and the guys. From what I have heard from Dad, the devil himself would run away if he saw them coming. They'll do fine."

"Thanks for the vote of confidence," grinned Dane. "Sherrie, you stick with Erin. I will be back as soon as I can."

"You be careful. Don't get in so deep that you can't get out. Remember there are police for the really bad stuff."

"The cops are pretty good," added Erin. "I'm sure they can be counted on."

Dane smiled widely and embraced Sherrie. He ended the bear hug with a big kiss. "You be good."

"Sounds like you guys are getting serious," remarked Erin, watching the display of affection.

"Yeah," said Sherrie with a huge grin. "We are very serious."

With that Dane was out the door and headed back to the *Sweet Texas*.

The two girls were happy to see each other; they had bonded after the other night's festivities. Erin offered Sherrie a bedroom at her place out on the beach. Any other time Sherrie would have jumped for joy at such accommodations but this time, under these circumstances, she was subdued. Seeing your greatest love leave on a very dangerous detail was very stressful.

The guys were ready to leave when Dane came back aboard the catamaran. Five minutes later they were bound for St. Kitts again.

"What do you think we are going to find down there?" asked Greg, sitting beside Dane on the upper couch beside Hugo in the cockpit. From the perch atop the catamaran they could clearly observe the entire open sea surrounding the boat. After their earlier run-ins with pirates, they all kept a sharp eye out for other boats. In fact, Dane had deposited two submachine guns in the storage bay under the large seat. If they needed the guns, they would be available in seconds. Even with that worry, all three were happy to be back on the water sailing the huge catamaran. It was exhilarating!

Time was moving into late afternoon. The seas breezes had picked up due to a sizable storm over to the east. As the eastern sky darkened from the clouds, Hugo paid particular attention to the active lightning.

"Getting a bit dicey over there," said Hugo, pointing to the storm. "I think we can outrun the storm and be well past her and in the clear."

"Hope so," said Greg. "I don't want to think about what it would be like to weather a storm like that even on a cat as large as this."

"It's not so bad as long as the lightning doesn't get too severe," remarked Dane. "Hugo and I got into a nasty storm about a week before we picked up you and Sherrie. Now, that storm was a hellish mess. It tossed us all over the place and damn near made both of us sick."

"No... You two guys seasick? I don't believe it!"

"Believe it, Bro," added Hugo. "It kicked our butts. The sea is nothing to be complacent about. If you don't respect her, she'll take you down."

Hugo checked his course and heading. With the sun getting lower and lower and the clouds coming in, the skies looked strange. Rather than the clear blue skies they were accustomed to, these skies were purple to the east and a beautiful red/yellow in the west. The demarcation line between the two skies was very sharp, almost like someone had simply drawn a line across the sky and dared each part to infringe upon the other. Peppering that with active lightning, one had a rather nasty view.

Suddenly a lightning strike hit the water far behind them. Within a few seconds came a mighty boom. One could smell the ozone.

"She's trying to catch up with us," yelled Hugo. "I'm gonna put her in passing gear." Hugo pressed a button and tightened the mainsail. Greg was amazed that it indeed felt like a car hitting passing gear. The *Sweet Texas* lurched forward, causing his head to push back as she increased her speed.

What a boat, thought Greg. He felt very lucky to not only be aboard but to be with these two guys.

CHAPTER THIRTY-TWO

May 25, 2013

At Sea, Northwest of St. Kitts, 6:45 p.m.

"How's that storm looking?" asked First Officer Brees as he entered the bridge.

The helmsman checked his heading and compass before answering.

"The storm is moving fast from east to west about six to ten miles behind us. It should not be an issue for us."

"Good. We need to get to the base as soon as we can to restock," said Brees. "I'll let the captain know." Brees turned slowly to the lookouts. "See anything?"

"No, sir. Caught a glimpse of a few masts about thirty minutes ago and there is a cruise ship on the horizon in front of us. Other than that, nothing," reported the lookout. "Guess the storms have everyone lying up on shore."

"What do you expect for green, fair-weather sailors?" Brees asked rhetorically. The lookout smiled. There were plenty of "go to school one week" sailors in these waters. All it took was money and time. Within one week they earned a captain's license. Armed with little knowledge of how to react to a stormy sea, they usually would rush into port or tie up in a cove for protection.

After about three hours at sea, the coast of St. Kitts twinkled in the darkness. This run from the sea to home base had been uneventful.

Captain de Terr was followed onto the bridge by Brees. They stood over to one side discussing something quietly. The captain reached into his breast pocket and pulled out one half of a cigar. Still listening intently to Brees, he placed the cigar in his mouth and lit it. The light of the match lit up the darkened bridge as a swirl of cigar smoke rose around the captain's head. The quiet conversation ended.

"So we seem to be alone," said Brees. "We'll steer to the cove and stop away from the rocks near the entrance."

"Make sure you aren't too close. I do not want to give away our intentions. How's the moonlight tonight?" asked de Terr.

Brees checked the charts although he already knew the answer. "Waxing crescent tonight, just enough light to maneuver easily."

"Excellent. Come get me in my cabin when we are about to arrive. I want to be on deck as we go into the base," ordered de Terr, taking another draw from his cigar.

Brees checked his watch. "We should be in position by about 11:00 p.m." The captain nodded his acknowledgement and walked through the hatch and back toward his cabin. Brees picked up a pair of binoculars and scanned the horizon on the starboard side. The only ship he could see was the cruise ship reported earlier. She must be making way to Guadeloupe or beyond as she was at least six nautical miles west of the *May Pop* and cruising fast toward the south southeast. Even at that distance Brees could make out the distinctive funnel of a Carnival cruise line ship.

"Stand fast. I'm going below for some coffee. Make way for the base. I'll be back up here in an hour. If anything out of the ordinary is spotted, let me know immediately," said Brees. With that, he was gone.

Greg was now at the helm of the *Sweet Texas*. Dane was below making sandwiches while Hugo took a break in the salon. The storm had passed hours ago, leaving a cool, sweet breeze out of the northwest. The sky was now clear, its brilliant stars spread across the sky. Greg loved it. He was sailing a beautiful catamaran under the crispest and clearest skies he had ever seen. There seemed to be a million more stars than he could remember back in Florida. But that was part of the allure of the sea; especially on nights with little moonlight. The Milky Way seemed to blossom, shedding stars across the heavens.

Greg looked at his watch. It was 10:00 p.m. He realized he was hungry but before he could react, Dane hopped up into the cockpit with a huge pastrami sandwich and a cold Red Stripe.

"Thought you might need this," Dane said, handing Greg the beer and placing the napkin with the sandwich on the cockpit seat. "You're a growing boy that needs his nourishment." Greg smiled but inside wished the guys would treat him as an equal. Sure he was no SEAL and to them he was a kid. But that would change, he promised himself.

As they neared the island, Hugo decided to seek anchorage at a private marina up on the southwestern coast of St. Kitts near Sandy Point. While the large catamaran would be noticed, this was a quiet area. There were nowhere near the numbers of people here as were down in Basseterre. As it approached 10:45 p.m., the *Sweet Texas* was anchored for the night.

The guys sat in the salon with no lights. Although they were not trying to hide, they intentionally did not want to stick out like a sore thumb. Actually, they wanted a quiet evening to just relax a bit. Preparing for bed, Dane noticed something. He sat up and cocked his head to one side.

"There's a boat coming," said Dane looking out toward the north, "fairly decent size." Hugo ducked inside and emerged with the largest pair of binoculars Greg had ever seen.

"Where the hell did you get those?" he asked.

"Picked them up back in Tortola," explained Hugo. "They are long-range binoculars used by commercial sailors to scan the horizon while at sea."

"Well, I guess so," remarked Greg. The Zeiss 20x60mm Image Stabilized binoculars were some of the best one could buy.

"We should be able to see them with these," smiled Hugo.

"If we can't, it won't be for the lack of equipment," Greg said smiling quietly. "Those are the largest binoculars I have ever seen."

Dane stepped over beside them. Normally he would not be concerned but with their latest experiences, he did not want to take any chances. "They are certainly not in a hurry. They must be fishermen coming back from a long day of fishing." Hugo cranked the binoculars trying to get a clear picture in the darkness.

"Whoa, Hoss," whispered Hugo. "That's the boat that shot at us."

"Are you sure?" asked Dane. "I never got a good look at her. We were a bit busy firing back."

"And I didn't see a thing!" said Greg. "I was flat on my back."

"While I was trying to evade them, I did get a good look. One thing that was strange... their anchor was painted red. This boat looks like our man and it has a red anchor on deck."

"Hugo, are you sure?" asked Dane.

"Have you ever seen me not be when it comes to someone shooting at me?"

Dane tilted his head to one side. "No, I can't say that I have. Where are they headed?"

"Looks like they are headed north. I don't think they have seen us but their present course will bring them within several hundred yards of us. They must feel damn safe. They must feel they are in home waters," added Hugo.

"Okay, let's keep an eye on her and see where she goes. I don't want to lose her in the darkness," whispered Dane as the boat passed within two hundred yards of them and proceeded on a northern course.

CHAPTER THIRTY-THREE

May 25, 2013

Along the Northwest Coast of St. Kitts, 10:50 p.m.

The *May Pop* slowed to a near idle. Her forward speed was about seven knots. Everyone aboard was below or sleeping except for the single helmsman on the bridge. He was exhausted and on the verge of sleep. His eyes were bleary and his head kept nodding over. If the captain saw him in this condition, he would have been put off of the boat permanently. He was totally unaware of the large catamaran in the shadows on his starboard side, moored in the darkness.

He had the boat on a northwesterly course heading for a specified location on the chart. The GPS readout said the *May Pop* was almost home. There were only a few more miles until they entered the small cove and the underground entrance to their lair. Finally… they were home after nearly a week at sea gorging themselves on unknowing prey, unarmed sailboats. Their take was very good; however, they had lost Pappy and the one other crewman.

The helmsman heard footsteps through his catatonic state. He instantly recovered. First Officer Brees opened the hatch to the bridge and stepped in.

"What is our status?" he asked. The helmsman checked the GPS and compass.

"Sir, we are coming up on the house. We should be in the cove within ten minutes."

"Very good," barked Brees, not particularly interested in the helmsman. He checked the forward scanning radar and found nothing out of the ordinary.

The helmsman checked the clock above his head.

"Sir, I have had no visual contact with any other boats within the last hour and a half; just a few skiffs, nothing larger."

"Very well, contact the house and have them open the bridge. Then proceed into the cove. As soon as the curtain opens we can enter the cave."

Brees picked up a pair of binoculars and personally scanned the shoreline. He was looking for any sign of someone watching from a beach. In this area there was nothing but a very small rocky beach with brush out to the water's edge. Two houses were the only structures near the water. One on each side of the small cove, they were connected by a footbridge crossing the width of the cove entrance.

The house to the south was the main. It sported a long, wide open veranda spanning the length of the beach side. The cottage on the north side was the guest quarters. The only access to the guest house was the small footbridge hanging down within a few feet of the water's surface. The bridge served another purpose other than access. It shielded the narrow channel and the larger cove beyond. During the day a casual passer-by would see the two houses and believe it to be someone's luxury beach house. That was exactly what de Terr and Brees wanted. No-trespassing signs covered the area warning away the locals and tourists alike.

The entire area was private property owned on paper by several non-descript owners from Europe and America. Shielded by all of this was the real owner, Hawk.

Seconds later Captain de Terr stepped onto the bridge.

Brees beat him to the punch. "Captain, all is in order. We are beginning our final entrance to the cove."

"Bridge open?" asked the captain, removing his cap and running his hand across his closely trimmed hair.

"It is opening now."

"Good. We can use a few days down time. It also does us good to be free from the sea awhile. Too many folks may be looking for us. Make this a quick docking."

"Aye, Captain," said Brees. "Helm, come to six zero degrees. Slow to two knots." Brees grabbed his night vision binoculars and scanned the coast off their bow. "I see the cove. The bridge is swinging open. Maneuver into it and make ready your anchor. I will be on deck." With that, Brees placed the binoculars in the cabinet behind him and stepped out onto the bridge catwalk, starboard-side.

It was a very dark night. A stiff sea breeze blew at about ten knots. The crew would have to be on their toes as they entered. Brees looked at his watch. It was exactly 11:20 p.m. Very good, he thought. He had told the captain they would be anchored by midnight. He had plenty of time to spare.

The *May Pop* slowly crept into the small, shallow cove past the open foot bridge. She seemed to disappear as she pushed aside encroaching vegetation on each side. This was a perfect spot to hide a boat. The cove itself was protected but also the entrance to the underground cave was disguised – their base. Once the boat got in there, it could hide indefinitely.

The *May Pop* pushed past the bushes and came to a stop as the brush acted like a door closing behind them. The helmsman turned off the engine and stood to, waiting for the permission to enter the cave. He glanced down on deck and saw Brees gesturing to two crewmen.

Off to both sides of the cove were two hidden guardhouses protecting the cove and the cave entrance. They looked like old World War II bunkers. The guard positions were built back into the surrounding rock with rear access passages leading back inside the main cave. Heavy vegetation concealed the two guardhouses, rendering them nearly invisible. Brees looked at the bunker on the starboard side and gave a wave. He got a short flash from a green signal light. All was okay. Brees returned his attention to the crew and the matter at hand.

"Get the push poles ready and get the men up here. I want her docked as soon as possible," ordered Brees.

"Aye, sir," responded the crew leader, scurrying about making ready for the cave entrance. Brees stood on the bow, his eyes squinting, trying to see the entrance. In the dark it was very hard to see. The entrance to the cave was hidden behind a series of dark, heavy nets backed by a heavy black tarpaulin that hung from the top of the cave to just beneath the surface of the water below. The combination of nets and the tarp concealed the cave entrance even during the day. The guards in the two bunkers controlled the chain hoists that moved the heavy nets aside so the *May Pop* could slip inside.

The deck crew brought out long push poles, one for each man. The eight men stood four to a side along the length of the boat. They drove their long poles into the water, hitting the bottom a mere six feet below. Holding the ends of the poles, the crew pushed the boat forward through the water. When the last man reached the stern, the men picked up their poles and returned to the bow and began the pushing process again until the *May Pop* passed through the gates and was inside the cave.

"We are clear!" Brees informed the crewmen, his voice echoing from the walls of the cave. "Stow the poles and make ready for the tow boat." While the men put the poles away, they could hear the humming sound of a tow boat coming to meet them from deep within the cave. The twenty foot tow craft was very much like a small tug boat but was powered electrically. Sound carried very well in the cave so the quiet electric boat fit the needs of boats making clandestine stops at the base. Its relatively silent and powerful electric motors could pull any type boat that could fit in the cave.

The crew leader watched the tow boat stop and turn. Even within the cave its maneuverability was excellent.

"Cast the tow rope," he ordered while another crewman made fast the rope to the *May Pop*. As they tied off the ropes, the gates to the cave began to close. The men on the tow boat tied off their end and motioned their readiness. As the rope stiffened under the pressure, there was a slight lurch as they began to pull the much bigger boat deeper into the cave.

Once the gate was closed and the *May Pop* was about forty feet into the cave, several sets of soft red lights automatically turned on to give the sailors a way to see what was transpiring. The only sound was the low hum of the tow boat and the soft lapping of the water against the hull of the larger boat. They were safely home. Brees let out a sigh of relief.

CHAPTER THIRTY-FOUR

May 25, 2013

Moored Along the Northwest Coast of St. Kitts, 11:30 p.m.

"Where the hell did they go?" asked Greg. The large boat they were watching had vanished into the night. "Do you think they saw us and took off?"

"No, I don't think so. They couldn't have run. We would have heard the engines," answered Dane. He too was perplexed.

"Oh, they are there," said Hugo coolly. "I watched them all the way. They slowed to a crawl and steered into a cove just beyond those rocks," he added, pointing up the coast.

"I don't remember seeing a cove on the charts," said Dane. "You think it is man-made?"

"Could be," answered Hugo. "They definitely entered some type of inlet or cove."

"Guess there's only one way to find out where they are," grinned Dane.

"I knew you were going to say that," smiled Hugo. "Hey, Greg, how's your swimming skills these days? Want to go on a moonlight swim?"

"Hell yeah, I'm game!"

"Wait a second, you guys," interjected Dane. "Let's think about this a bit. First, we need someone to stay with the boat." Dane looked at Greg. "And I don't want to belittle your swimming skills but we may be in the water for quite a while. Hugo and I are trained to do that."

Greg grimaced. "Yeah, Sherrie told me you guys were SEALS and professional lifeguards. I do see where you are going. It makes sense. I'll stay with the boat."

"Hey, this boat is important to me. She needs protection while we are gone," added Hugo. "And it's the only way we have to get out of here."

Greg and Dane laughed.

"I'm serious," pleaded Hugo. "We can't just flap our wings and fly away."

It took only forty-five minutes for Dane and Hugo to prepare for their incursion. They decided to take the Zodiac and paddle their way up to the cove. They didn't want to use the motor as they went in; it would make too much noise. But they may have to use it to make a fast getaway if things went wrong.

The two dressed below deck in black wetsuits, deciding to forgo the hood, boots and gloves. They blackened their faces and hands to conceal them. They would be much harder to be seen in the dark. After a brief collaboration they decided on armament. Hugo opened the hidden armory in a room behind a secret panel that replaced the port side fore crew cabin and brought out two Glock G21 Gen4 .45 Auto pistols. Both were equipped with tactical lights and laser sights. Each carried two extra thirteen round magazines in addition to the one in the pistol.

"You ready?" asked Dane standing in the dark salon.

"Is a pig's butt pork?" answered Hugo in one of his patented Texas answers.

"Guess that means yes," smiled Greg.

"Okay, Greg, I plan to go up the coast only a few yards from the shore. We'll judge the water depth as we go. I want to stay in water deep enough to drop the motor and make an escape but I don't want to get too far out and stick out like a sore thumb," explained Dane. "You should be able to see us all the way up until we enter the cove." Greg nodded and gave Dane a thumbs-up gesture.

"If anything happens, Greg, you must stay with the boat. We are counting on you to be here." Dane turned to Hugo. "We'll tie off the Zodiac and enter the cove. It's probably safer for us to swim in, especially since we have no idea what we will come up against."

Hugo adjusted his wetsuit. "I have a feeling we may be face to face with these guys once we are in the cove. We need to stay together in case things get nasty. Agreed?"

"Absolutely," answered Dane. "Ready?"

"Go time, baby," grinned Hugo. Dane turned back to Greg.

"If anything happens to us, stay here. At dawn, sail this puppy back to Basseterre, dock her and wait there. We will meet you if we don't get back earlier. Do you understand?" said Dane.

"Yes, sir," replied Greg fully, feeling the gravity of the situation.

"You feel comfortable handling her by yourself?" asked Hugo. He had a professional and personal reason for asking.

"Yes, I do," answered Greg quickly. "I've learned a lot from you, Hugo. I guess all that time at the helm will pay off. Don't worry about me. I can handle the boat, no problem." Hugo gave Greg a slap on the arm followed by a big grin. Dane smiled to himself. The kid had learned to be comfortable with the *Sweet Texas*. Thank goodness.

With that, Dane and Hugo climbed down into the Zodiac and cast off their lines. Within seconds they disappeared from view. Greg scrambled up to the cockpit and grabbed Hugo's binoculars. It took a few seconds but he finally saw them in the darkness heading up the beach.

CHAPTER THIRTY-FIVE

May 26, 2013

Inside the Cave, 12:50 a.m.

"It's good to be home," remarked Brees as Captain de Terr joined him on the foredeck.

"Yes. We are lucky to have such a fine place to hide. Most people in our business don't have that luxury," sighed de Terr. "By the way, I got a message from the Hawk. We have an appointment via Skype in a couple of hours. Looks like we are to get some new orders."

"Hmmm, sounds interesting," replied Brees. The *May Pop* was well on her way to the dock deep within the mountain above. Twenty minutes later deTerr spotted Levi Smith standing on the dock.

"Damn. Smith is here. I hate that pig. If I were Hawk I would take him out to sea and send him to the bottom with a necktie of concrete blocks. The guy is as stupid as a bag of hammers," ranted de Terr. Brees could not help but to laugh.

"Frankly, I think a bag of hammers is ten times smarter than Smith!" cracked Brees. The two laughed heartily. It felt good to shed the pressure of piracy on the high seas.

"Well, let's go see what the idiot has to say," said de Terr, slapping Brees on the back. "At least the bastard has cigars."

The *May Pop* was only a few feet away from the dock.

Smith was dressed in what looked like jungle garb, khaki shorts and shirt, and wore a John Deere cap. He was scurrying about the dock guiding his men as the large boat approached.

"Get those ropes ready," he screamed. "Get off your asses and get this boat tied off. Move it!"

The dock crew was working as fast and as efficiently as possible. They didn't appreciate this fat man screaming at them. Just as Brees and de Terr hated Smith, so did the men in the cave. The boat nudged the dock as the *May Pop* crew and dock crew exchanged mooring lines and began to make fast the boat to the dock.

Smith was all smiles as he approached the two men stepping off the boat.

"Welcome home, Captain de Terr, and you as well, Mr. Brees. We are very happy you have returned safely to our lair."

"Yeah, yeah, save it for someone who cares, Smith," barked Brees. Captain de Terr didn't even look at him. Smith leapt forward to catch up with de Terr.

"I have your rooms ready for you. Do you want something to eat? Remember we hired a great cook. He can throw a couple of steaks on and have you ready to eat in fifteen minutes," said Smith, waddling beside de Terr, trying hard to keep up.

"Yeah," said Brees. "Two steaks would be great. Make them rare with a salad, potatoes, onions and ice cold beer."

"Absolutely!" said Smith, motioning to one of his men to get the cook started.

"We'll be in the lounge," said Brees. "Are there any women about?"

"Ah, yes," replied Smith. "I'll have some company join you in a few minutes. Meanwhile please relax and enjoy yourself."

The two men stepped into the wooden front structure facing the wide dock. The pirate cartel had spent thousands of dollars to enlarge and improve this lair. The structure was originally several small storage rooms. They excavated and enlarged the cave area around the dock to house not only storage but crews' quarters, guest rooms, full kitchen and dining facilities along with lounges and recreation areas. To most that lived there permanently it was a far cry from the squalor and poverty of living in the real world.

The men were fiercely loyal to the Hawk. He took care of them, housed and fed them. Best of all, he paid extraordinarily well. They had all that they wanted and were happy with their surroundings, except having Smith around. They all hated Levi Smith.

CHAPTER THIRTY-SIX

May 26, 2013

In the Water at the Cove, 1:10 a.m.

"I don't see a thing," whispered Hugo as they approached the rocky area where the large boat had disappeared. "It's got to be here somewhere." Both Hugo and Dane were scouring the coastline for a clue, any clue.

They were approaching a large area of underbrush that flowed down the mountainside right down to the water's edge. The small cove had to appear natural. They knew the boat went somewhere and this secluded area looked perfect.

"There it is," he said quietly, motioning to Hugo. "See that opening?"

"Yes, sir, that seems to be what we are looking for," said Hugo. Dane looked to the shore and saw a good place to stash the Zodiac.

"Over there. We can put the boat over in those bushes and swim in." The two men paddled quietly over to the shore and nudged the Zodiac up under part of the underbrush that was overhanging the water.

"Perfect place!" said Hugo. "No one can see it from land or sea."

"Let's tie her up and see what we have found," answered Dane.

Minutes later the men began to swim away from the boat and into the small cove. It was 1:35 a.m. What little moon was expected raised high in the sky but did little to cast any light on the two. They swam quietly, listening intently for any foreign sound. By not wearing the neoprene hoods with their wetsuits, they could hear much better.

They moved stealthily into the opening, staying glued to the right side of the cove. They were both amazed by the size of the open area. They had been right. This was once a natural cove but had been cultivated carefully to hide something.

As they moved deeper into the cove, Hugo suddenly froze and tapped Dane on the shoulder. They both silently disappeared back into the brush.

"What's up?" whispered Dane. There was no response from Hugo other than him pointing to an area on the opposite side of the cove about twenty feet above the water. Suddenly in the blackness there was a tiny red glow.

"Cigarette," said Hugo. "There's someone up there. It looks like a watchtower or something."

"That makes sense," added Dane, "a lookout perhaps."

"Definitely. Stay here. I'm going to get a bit closer." With that Hugo ducked so only his head from the eyes up was above water. With his blackened face and jet black hair, he was nearly invisible. Dane watched as Hugo floated out into the middle of the pool without making any ripples in the water that would give him away. He watched Hugo turn slowly in a circle so he could get a good view of the entire cove. After a couple of minutes, Hugo floated back to the underbrush hiding place.

"We've definitely got lookouts," whispered Hugo. He turned to face the cove. "Over there is a lookout post. That's where we saw the cigarette," he explained. "But there is another post literally over our heads, about twenty feet above us. I heard talking from up there. We have to assume they are the guardians of the cove."

"So we have lookouts protecting what... an empty cove?" queried Dane. "And more importantly, where is that ship?"

"I did notice that the far end of the cove looks very sheer, almost like a door or gate. There's the same heavy growth cascading down the face of the cove end. It could be an entrance."

Dane thought about what Hugo saw. "It has to be an access point of some kind. That would account for the guards," Dane speculated. "Did it look big enough for the ship we saw to enter?"

"It's pretty damn big," Hugo explained. "That must be the answer."

"Well, there's only one way to find out," Dane said, peering out from under the bushes. "Let's go check it out."

"10-4! Let's go see what we can find."

Both men floated out from their cover and lowered themselves in the water to eye level. They moved slowly, stealthily, like snakes stalking their prey.

They moved to their right, staying as close to the edge of the undergrowth as possible. Their slow movement eliminated ripples in the water. They only hoped the men in the lookout posts above did not have night vision capabilities. If they did, the two men in the water would stand out easily.

Slowly they moved, inching forward. Finally they reached the right side of the sheer wall. Hugo reached out and touched the vines hanging down to the water. They were live plants. He moved some aside and reached farther into the growth. That's when he felt it. He felt canvas. Dane was right! This is an entrance.

"It's a portal of some sort," he whispered to Dane. "I felt something like canvas with some kind of support behind it.

"How far down does it go?"

"I'll check." With that, Hugo slid under the surface and moved toward the gate. He was about eight feet deep and swam under the gate and into the cave on the other side. He moved over to his right until he touched the rock wall of the cave and unhurriedly, very slowly rose to the surface.

What he saw was astounding. In front of him was a huge cave he estimated to be thirty to forty feet wide and sixty feet tall. It was dark with little or no light coming through the huge tarps. In the distance he saw a soft glow of red night lights similar to those on submarines. Hugo scanned the walls of the cave looking for signs of lookouts. He found none. The cave walls were sheer right down to the water. There was a slight flicker of red light along the walls as ripples rode in and out from the sea currents. After gaining as much information as he thought possible, he returned to Dane outside.

"Holy crap, Dane!" he whispered while gasping for air. "There is a huge cave on the other side of this wall big enough for the ship to pass. This has to be their hideout."

"See any guards?" asked Dane.

"Not a single one. It's very dark down here. I can see red interior lights farther down the cave. There's definitely someone home."

"Let's see… it's 2:10 a.m.," said Dane. "We should be able to get in and see what's going on and back to the boat within a few hours. That should give us plenty of time to get back to Greg before dawn. I say we take a look."

"Follow me," grinned Hugo. The two men submerged to about eight feet and swam under the gate, emerging on the other side.

"Good God! I've never seen anything like this," said Dane quietly as he looked around the cave.

CHAPTER THIRTY-SEVEN

May 26, 2013

At the Pirate Base, 2:20 a.m.

Brees and deTerr sat at a family-sized dining table. It was nothing fancy, just large and rustic. Another man brought out two large platters of food. Each had steaks, fried plantains, pigeon peas and fry bread. There was another platter of jerk chicken and other root vegetables. A second man brought in a basket of fresh fruit and salad.

"A feast fit for a king," said Smith, walking into the room and sitting across from the two sailors. Neither Brees nor de Terr looked up. "I hear that you have been very successful in your raids on this voyage," Smith said in an upbeat manner. Then he stopped. "I also hear you lost Pappy. I was sorry to hear that. He was a very nice person."

De Terr continued to eat like a man who was starving. Manners be damned, he ate with his hands, leaving the utensils untouched. He took the jerk chicken, wrapped it with fry bread and ate it. The captain used his own knife to cut sizable chunks of steak to eat as well.

Brees, on the other hand, did use his fork but his table manners would have made most cringe. The two men ate in silence except for the slurping and smacking sounds they made while eating.

Smith seemed uneasy. His first cordial attempts to talk with de Terr and Brees were totally ignored. He decided to try again.

"Captain de Terr, the Hawk has arranged a conference call for 4:00 a.m. to discuss a new project. After you eat, you can get some sleep. I will charge one of my men to wake you for the call."

Brees looked at Smith with disgust. De Terr never interrupted his meal.

"We know about the call. That's why we are here, you idiot!" hissed Brees. "Who asked you to join us here anyway?"

"Well, I..." stuttered Smith.

"Listen, fat man, we don't need you. We are quite able to handle this by ourselves," sneered de Terr, finally looking up from his food. "For some reason Hawk keeps you around. That's his business. As for me, you could die right now and I wouldn't give a damn."

"Well, Hawk sees my abilities to manage this place and handle his affairs with this cargo and other shipments," Smith said pompously. "I have his full confidence."

Brees and de Terr laughed out loud. "You pig! Hawk keeps you here because no one else would live his entire life in a cave like some troll," said Brees.

Smith was getting mad. He slung off his cap and stood up. "I've had about enough of you..."

In one quick motion Brees pulled his gun and placed the barrel end mere inches from Smith's sweating forehead.

"Don't kill him," de Terr said calmly. "He will bleed all over our food and I'm not finished eating yet. And you will have to tell Hawk that Smith is dead and he needs a new troll."

Smith stood motionless. He didn't utter a word. Brees smiled.

"Did you crap in your pants, Smith? I smell something funny," asked Brees with a wide grin.

Smith stepped back and walked oddly out of the room. Had he soiled his pants? No, but he did feel a warmth running down his leg. Damn, he hated those two.

It took only twenty minutes to slowly move deeper into the cave. The soft red light shed an eerie look over the wet walls and the dark water. Hugo estimated the water to be at least fifteen to twenty feet deep after executing two dives to find the bottom.

Both Dane and Hugo kept an eye on anything that moved. As they left the mouth of the cave they noticed a small dock on each side of the cave wall and a man-made opening the size of a submarine hatch just above each. They surmised that this was the entrance to the lookout bunkers they saw outside.

Dane checked his watch. It was 2:45 a.m. "We only have three hours or so to get back to the cat," he whispered to Hugo. Sound carried extremely well in the cave. "We'll keep going until 4:00 a.m. and then make a decision on what to do." Hugo nodded his agreement.

As they rounded another slight bend they saw regular lighting ahead. They both froze more by force of habit than actually needing to freeze. No one ahead had a chance of seeing them this far out into the darkness, red light or not.

"Looks like we found their home," whispered Hugo. In the distance they could see a large boat with the name *May Pop* tied to the dock. Hugo also saw several other smaller boats as well. All were tied to the same dock.

"Seems to be a crowd," added Dane. "Come on..." They continued swimming at a snail's pace as to not create a wake, staying close to the cave wall. They were prepared to submerge under the water at a moment's notice.

Hugo led while Dane followed checking their six from time to time. Both men's heads acted as if they were on swivels. They reacted to every miniscule noise. Even with the regular lighting the men were aware of plenty of dark shadows concealing a missed guard or crewman who just happened to be in the right place at the right time to discover them.

"This is amazing," whispered Hugo, turning back to Dane. Only their heads pierced the water's glistening surface. "Surely they didn't build this."

"No. It looks like it has been here for quite a while," answered Dane. "You sure there was nothing on the maps about this?"

"Not a thing."

"It's almost impossible that a natural cave or grotto has been here forever and undiscovered," said Dane quietly.

Hugo stopped suddenly. He caught movement across the water. Slight ripples were coming from the opposite side of the cave. Hugo motioned to Dane and they both silently slid under the water. After a full two minutes, both rose, exposing only their eyes and taking in air through their nose. The ripples had slowed. Across the cave, Dane saw a small boat at another dock with two men sitting astride two boxes in the boat. Both were smoking. He wondered if these two were guards returning from the lookout post.

Dane tapped Hugo on the head and pointed across the way. Hugo nodded his head. He saw them too. They continued silently.

The voices of the dock workers grew louder as they moved closer. Dane and Hugo reached the end of the dock and deftly continued under the decking hidden from sight from all sides. Hearing the heavy footsteps above, they slid quietly through the water until they were directly under the main building attached to the dock. They rested briefly but continued to listen, moving from one place to another to follow the more interesting conversations they could hear from under the floorboards.

The buildings built in the cave were basic. They included several levels built up the side of the cave walls, all resting on the grand pilings that anchored the dock. The walls and floors of the structures were simple pine boards. The results were cracks, some one-half inch wide. The men liked it because it was easy to wash down, the wash water simply draining through the flooring and into the water below.

But the cracks enabled anyone under the floor to clearly hear and sometimes see what was happening in the rooms above. Dane and Hugo used this as an advantage. They listened intently to the conversation above.

CHAPTER THIRTY-EIGHT

May 26, 2013

At the Pirate Base, 3:50 a.m.

Dane checked his watch. It was now 3:50 a.m. He knew the sun would rise soon. He also remembered they needed to return to the catamaran by sunrise or Greg would sail without them. After a quick check, the guys decided to stay another thirty minutes. With that, they would have plenty of time to leave the cave, retrieve the Zodiac and get back to the *Sweet Texas* with time to spare. The conversations above were getting very interesting.

Smith strode into the dining room to join Captain de Terr and Brees. It was time for the call. Within seconds the phone rang. Smith answered.

"Yes, sir, they are both here. I will put you on speaker phone."

"Gentlemen," squawked an electronically altered voice from the speaker phone unit at the center of the table. "I hope you are doing well, Captain de Terr and Mr. Brees. I have heard you encountered a few issues, but all of that is behind us now, correct?"

Yes. I'm..." interjected Smith.

"Yes, Hawk," interrupted de Terr, giving a stern look at Smith to keep his mouth shut. "All issues have been addressed and we are fully capable of acting on your behalf."

Brees stared at Smith as if to tell him in no uncertain terms that his life depended on his silence.

"That's wonderful, Captain. It is very comforting to have such great men as you and your crew working with Mr. Doss and myself. We have quite a lucrative plan for you," explained Hawk. "I'll let Mr. Doss explain."

"Good morning, gentlemen," started Doss. "You are aware of the new weapon made available to you on your last run."

"Yes, Mr. Doss," answered Brees. "It was very effective."

"As it should have been," continued Doss. "As you were told, we were able to weaponize a small supply of nerve gas. We obtained the gas a few weeks ago from one of our cohorts in the Mideast and you were the first to use it successfully. We now believe it is time to put our new weaponry to the ultimate test."

The captain looked at Brees and smiled. Smith smiled as well until a glance from Brees wiped the smile away.

"What type of plan do you have for us?" asked de Terr.

"We plan to rob all of the banks in Philipsburg, St. Maarten," Doss stated bluntly.

There was stunned amazement. The silence in the room was eerie.

"I…" started Brees.

"No, that's quite all right. I do imagine my statement took everyone by surprise," explained Doss. "We have the capability using the nerve gas weapon to either kill or incapacitate the entire population of Philipsburg. With the entire population incapacitated, our people, wearing the proper insulated gear, sweep through the banks and collect the contents of all of the vaults. Also our teams will move in on the major jewelry stores and collect the gold and gems as well. The actual value of the haul will stagger the minds of the authorities once they are able to respond. In the meantime, we will ferry the gold, gems, currency and bearer bonds back to the safety of the cave in St. Kitts. We will be able to store the product and then ever so slowly release it to our accounts in Geneva."

De Terr, Brees and Smith sat speechless. Deliberately they began to process the scope of the plan and, more importantly, the value.

Hawk waited for a few seconds and then addressed the question on everyone's mind.

"As you digest this plan, let me say this will make us all multimillionaires. You three, Captain de Terr and First Officer Brees as well as Mr. Smith, will never want for anything else on this earth," boasted Hawk. "We will all have enough money to make our own heaven on earth anywhere on the globe. In fact, you may even want several heavens."

"That sounds wonderful, Hawk," said de Terr with a huge smile. He turned to Brees, who had the largest grin on his face he had ever seen.

"This plan is perfect!" announced Smith, slapping his hand down on the table.

"Whoa. Fellows, let's not get overcome with joy yet," said Hawk. "Besides, that speaker phone microphone is damned sensitive. You nearly blew my eardrums out with that banging. We have an enormous amount of work to complete before we execute this plan. Mr. Doss and I will be working on arrangements beginning this morning. Captain de Terr, Mr. Brees, your job is to begin the selection of your most trustworthy men to participate and become rich. These men must keep secrets. If they do not, they die. It is as simple as that. No questions or degrees of guilt. Just dead! Do you fully understand?"

Yes sir," answered de Terr, Brees and Smith in unison. Hawk let his short speech sink in for a few seconds.

"So gentlemen, now that you have heard the plan, I command your unconditional support. Do I have it?" Hawk asked.

"You have my full support," said de Terr decisively.

"Hawk, you have mine as well," added Brees.

"Of course you have mine," said Smith with a sleazy grin. "I will support it until I die."

"I can arrange that," whispered Brees in Smith's ear. Smith merely smiled nervously and stepped away from the table.

"If we are finished, I believe we all have things to do," said Smith, acting as if he was the center of the planning and actions at the cave.

"Have a good morning, gentlemen," croaked Hawk. Then there was only a dial tone.

"Come; let's get some sleep. We have additional work to do later today." De Terr slapped Brees on the shoulder. "Smith, are our normal quarters ready?" de Terr asked.

"Yes, they are ready. Please call one of my on-call guards if you have any further needs," said Smith. The captain and his first mate left the room.

As they walked down the hall, Smith looked at his watch. It was now 4:35 a.m. He needed to get some sleep as well but wanted to think about how he might pull this heist off and get rid of de Terr and Brees.

Under the floor, Dane looked at Hugo. Their eyes were like saucers.

"You caught all of that, didn't you?" asked Dane.

"Yeah, but I don't believe it! I'm still in shock," answered Hugo. "They are going to kill hundreds if not thousands of people, not to mention stealing millions."

"We have to get back to the boat. It's only a little more than an hour until daylight. We don't want to miss our ride," said Dane. "You ready to roll?"

"Lead on Mr. Skoglund. It's time to go home." The two men slowly moved from under the building to the outer edge of the dock. There they took a long, deep breath and ducked ten feet below the water before swimming toward the cave opening.

They took turns rising to the top to take bearings. Soon they were at the cave gate. Hugo was again the first to dive below and into the open cove. Dane followed. They purposely arose outside the corner of the cave by the gate edge. This was the darkest area of the cove. Hugo spotted the lookouts and kept a sharp eye as he and Dane very slowly made their way to the underbrush at the mouth of the cave.

A few minutes more and the two retrieved the Zodiac and were on their way back to the *Sweet Texas*.

CHAPTER THIRTY-NINE

May 26, 2013

Philipsburg, St. Maarten, 6:25 a.m.

The two ladies had been up for an hour. Erin warned Sherrie of the early rising, explaining the things to be done before their stores opened to another day of tourists from the cruise ships. Erin maneuvered her red Jeep through the narrow streets of Philipsburg. There were errands to be run. There were locals scurrying through the streets headed for their jobs. Sherrie was in awe of the hustle and bustle going on so early in the morning. What she thought was a sleepy island paradise had a very active vibe.

"I had no idea you needed to be up at this unholy hour to get ready for the day," said Sherrie, struggling to get moving. Her last week or so on the catamaran included sleeping late and from time to time a few other more amorous activities before bailing out of bed to greet the day, usually about 10:00 a.m.

"We get to work early but we usually wind down early," explained Erin. "Before we can open the stores, we have to replenish our stock. Each night our stores report their sales. We have folks who work each night to pull stock and reorder anything we are low on. You also will notice that the banks here are open at 6:00 a.m. Many actually run two shifts."

"Why two shifts?" asked Sherrie.

Erin explained that the banks preferred two short shifts to one long one. Experience had shown it made for a more alert and dedicated employee. As a consequence, fewer errors were made. It was a win-win for both sides.

"Getting ready each day includes going to the bank to manage our cash. You would be amazed how many "tourists" come down here with American cash. We don't ask any questions," continued Erin. "Remember this is actually part of the Netherlands. We are not required to adhere to U.S. cash laws," grinned Erin, "and we don't."

Sherrie nodded. She'd heard of off-shore banking but never realized it occurred in St. Maarten.

Erin smiled. "Here I have known you for only a few days and I'm telling all my secrets."

"Erin, I have no one to tell so your business management principles are safe with me," laughed Sherrie. Erin looked at her oddly. "Oh, did I not tell you I graduated from law school back in the States?"

"No, you didn't," answered Erin, clearly shocked. "Maybe I should not have talked so much."

"Ah, hell, no! I gave up the lawyer gig several years ago," Sherrie said, suddenly looking stoic.

Erin glanced at Sherrie's face. "Sounds like a very interesting story behind that."

"Sadly, yes, there is. I gave up law after my older brother, Martin, was murdered by drug lords in Miami."

"Oh, my God..."

"Yeah, multiply that feeling by ten thousand and that's how I felt." Sherrie continued. "The cops caught the guys who did it and I thought they would pay dearly for it. What I didn't know was their lawyers were much better than the Dade County prosecutors. They got all of the charges thrown out of court. There was absolutely nothing we could do short of an armed vendetta. And believe me, I thought about it."

Erin slowed and made a quick right-hand turn. She stopped the jeep in front of a nondescript three-story building painted in a drab tan color. There were no windows on the first floor, just a heavy steel door.

"First we need to check on yesterday's cash flow and inventory. Those reports should be on my desk. Then we will go to the bank and end up at our main store on the waterfront. All of this by 8:00 a.m. when the cruise ships begin to arrive."

"Sounds like a plan," said Sherrie, looking over to see the sun begin to rise over the hills to the east. A slight fog hung in the air but it seemed to be cleansing the air rather than causing any visibility issues.

Once parked, they went inside, the door closing securely behind them. It looked more like a closet rather than an office building. Sherrie looked puzzled. They were in a small twelve by twelve foot vestibule, cameras at all corners of the room. Suddenly there was a voice.

"Good morning, Miss Erin."

"Good morning, Betty."

A buzzer sounded and the two girls walked through a heavy steel door. An elderly island lady smiled and called them over as they entered another anteroom.

"A fine good morning to you, Betty," said Erin with a big smile. "Family doing well?"

"Oh, yes, ma'am. My son was accepted to the college in America. We are oh so proud!"

"Betty, that's wonderful. Where will he go to college?" Erin asked, genuinely happy.

"Miss Erin, he will go to the University of Miami," she said, nearly in tears. "God bless him."

"Yes, Betty, God bless him and you and your family," said Erin, leaning down and giving the older woman a kiss on the cheek. "You tell him I expect good grades," she added. "Betty, this is a friend of mine, Sherrie. She will be helping me out for the next several days. Her father is a good friend of Dad's."

Betty broke into another wide smile. "Hello, Sherrie. Welcome. I am so glad to meet you."

"Thank you so much, Betty. I am happy to be here!"

"Betty, we will be in my office if Dad or anyone needs me. I'll let you know when we head off to the bank and to the stores," said Erin.

"Yes, Miss Erin. Thank you."

The girls moved on to Erin's office just down the hall.

"That lady is so proud of her son," said Sherrie quietly as she sat down on the large leather sofa across from Erin's desk.

"Betty has been with this company for forty-two years. She was here when Dad bought into the business. The former owner had one stipulation in the contract... we had to keep Betty. She was once thought to be a contractual quirk, but now Betty is the heart and soul of this company. I can't think of anyone else in the world that deserves more happiness."

"That's quite a story," said Sherrie, looking around the office while Erin reviewed the overnight reports. The art on the walls of the office was beautiful. Intrigued, Sherrie looked closer at a few of the pieces. Rembrandt... surely not an original... was it? There were also paintings by Andrew Wyeth. Sherrie knew of Wyeth and those certainly looked like originals. If all of this was true, the walls of this office were worth millions.

"Ah, Erin, I have ask... are these originals?"

"Why, yes, they are," she replied calmly. "That is one of the best ways Dad and I invest for our future. Original art is one of the easiest ways to invest enormous amounts of money and no one seems to flinch. And if the artist is dead or dies, the price continues to grow year after year. Not a bad investment at all. Since this building is our headquarters, the security is such that we can feel at ease displaying them here."

Finally Sherrie was starting to grasp the degree of wealth Erin and her Dad had amassed. Erin returned to her review of the nightly reports.

After about ten minutes Erin stood up.

"Well, there is an issue that I must take care of. Come with me. It should only take a minute."

"Problem?"

"No, not really, just a normal occurrence," replied Erin.

The two ladies walked down the hall and entered the elevator. Erin produced an access card and swiped it. A small pad came out of the wall where she placed her right forefinger on the red flashing light. After a second the light turned green and the elevator rose to the third floor. As different as night and day, the third floor was vast and for the most part empty. No one was running about. Only a few boxes littered the floor.

They walked over to another door and used the access card to enter again. This room was sparkling white with nothing in it. It was clear it was an anteroom of some sort. Once the door behind them closed and locked, the lights grew dim. One wall became perfectly transparent. Sherrie was impressed as the guards opened a hidden door to let them into the high security area of the Rand headquarters.

CHAPTER FORTY

May 26, 2013

Aboard the Sweet Texas, off St. Kitts, 7:45 a.m.

The cat was screaming across the azure blue waters on a northwestern course toward St. Maarten. The hulls hissed as the spray flew from their edge knifing through the calm seas. In Texas laymen's terms, they were hauling ass.

Hugo was at the helm. Dane was below briefing Greg on what they found and the sinister plan they learned.

"Oh, crap," cried Greg, "Sherrie's back there!"

"That's why we are going back to get her out now. This Hawk guy sounds ruthless. His number one man, Doss, is even worse. But we may have time on our side. They said they needed to finish their plan of attack. The only problem is that I don't know whether that is today or next week."

"Damn," said Greg, clearly concerned. "What are we going to do?"

"First I'm going to find Sherrie and get her aboard here with us. Then Hugo and I will get to the authorities and tell them what we heard and show them the cave." Dane looked at Greg and smiled. "Don't worry. I won't let anything happen to Sherrie or us. Those guys talked like they needed a few more days to get everything in order and recruit their small army. Meanwhile, we will be ready for them," assured Dane. "Come on, let's go enjoy some sunshine."

Dane arose and led Greg back on deck and up to the cockpit. Hugo was in his own world. He was using his bare feet to steer the cat, his feet on the wheel and a cold beer in his hand. Mountain's *Mississippi Queen* was blaring over the cockpit speakers.

"Mississippi Queen... She taught me everything... Way down around Vicksburg... Around Louisiana way lived a Cajun lady, aboard the Mississippi Queen... You know she was a dancer..."

Hugo glanced over and saw Dane and Greg. He stopped singing and welcomed the two up top.

"It's a beautiful day in Miami," he screamed, "and not too bad down here." Hugo grinned from ear to ear. The sun was already bright and the heat was rising. The small amount of cold spray that reached the cockpit was refreshing.

"Looks like we are making good time," Dane said over the sounds of water rushing past the large catamaran hulls.

"Yes, sir, we are screaming," declared Hugo with a nod to Greg and Dane. "Come on up and enjoy this glorious morning. Greg, are you awake enough to take the helm?" Hugo stood and stepped back from the helm.

Greg smiled widely. "I'm always ready to guide the *Sweet Texas* to paradise," he said, stepping around Hugo and taking the wheel. "When all of this is over, I'm going to have a very hard time giving all of this up."

Hugo patted him on the back. "Greggie, who says we gotta give this up?"

All three laughed. It looked like Greg had '*earned his spurs*' in the Texan vernacular. He was fast becoming one of the guys. And he was damned proud of it as well.

"We should be in port by a little past ten if this wind holds out," explained Hugo. "You want to radio ahead to get Bob to meet us?"

"Not a bad idea," answered Dane, enjoying a fine wall of sea spray. "I can get him to contact the cops and we'll have everyone there when we moor. That would save some time. And since we don't know Hawk's timeline, any time we save could make a difference. You guys enjoy the ride. I'm going below to make the call."

As Dane turned to go below, another large spray engulfed the threesome, drenching them.

"Man! That is sweet!" cried Hugo, wiping the seawater from his face. "This is what sailing is all about." Greg was beaming. He felt he had died and gone to heaven. He loved sailing this boat.

CHAPTER FORTY- ONE

May 26, 2013

Philipsburg, St. Maarten, 7:48 a.m.

The issue turned out to be a larger problem than Erin had thought. She met with the accounting and cash managers, putting them almost an hour behind schedule. Finally they were alone again.

"One final item and we are out of here," she said. Sherrie had managed to get a cup of coffee and was finishing it off. As she put the cup down she accidentally pressed a button on the phone. Suddenly a voice could be clearly heard on line 3.

"...I don't care what he says," said a voice. "If he won't cooperate, kill him. This operation is too big to be slowed by his interference." There was silence. Sherrie looked at Erin. Now she was listening. Both were spellbound.

"But he says he needs more money, Mr. Doss," another voice said nervously. "If I tell him no, he may talk."

"Dammit, you tell him that if he speaks one word of this operation to anyone, one of Hawk's men will personally come over and cut the guts from his body and feed them to the fish. Then they will turn on his family. Believe me, they will do *exactly* that! Take whatever actions are necessary to get him in line. I'm sure he will not like Hawk's remedy to the situation. Let me know the verdict immediately."

"My God, who is it?" asked Sherrie. "I wonder what operation they are speaking about."

"If he is on our phone system, it's someone in our building. There is a Mr. Doss working here but he is in distribution," answered Erin. "I don't..." She stopped in midsentence as the men began talking again.

"If we are to use this nerve gas to rob the banks in Philipsburg, we will have his cooperation. Tell him to cooperate or we will find someone else to deal with. That means he, his family, even his dog will die," said the menacing voice.

Again silence for a second or two. "Yes, Mr. Doss."

"For both of your sakes, I hope he comes to his senses. You know you and your family could also suffer from this decision."

The ladies continued to listen.

"Sounds like someone is planning to rob several banks and kill a lot of people," said Erin.

"Nerve gas. Did you hear that? We found a body from a sunken sailboat a few days ago. The lady was killed with nerve gas! That stuff kills anything and everything it touches. That's nothing to play with," added Sherrie. "These guys have to be the ones that killed her." Erin reached down and pressed the line key and the phone went silent.

"We have to go tell Dad what we heard," said Erin, gathering a few papers quickly. "He should be down at the bar by now."

A second later the door to the room burst open. Three burly men dressed in suits, wielding automatic weapons entered.

"Do not say a word or you will be shot," one of the men said, all three pointing their guns at the two women.

"Who the hell are you?" yelled Erin, rising and coming around the table. She did not recognize any of them. "How did you get in here?"

Without hesitation, a second man stepped forward. Using his huge hand, he grabbed Erin by the face, literally lifted her off the floor and slung her over against the wall like a rag doll. She did not move. She looked dead.

Sherrie was stunned. Her eyes were like saucers. What was happening? Who were these guys? She opened her mouth to talk. She was greeted by a huge fist crashing into her face. All she saw was stars and a brilliant flash, then nothing. Sherrie crumpled in place on the floor like a sack of potatoes.

Mr. Doss walked into the room and closed the door. He stood there silently for a full minute. Then he reacted.

"Take these two away from here..."   He stopped and considered a location. "Take them to the cave in St. Kitts. But keep them alive until you hear directly from me. We can't afford to have these two in our way knowing what they heard. Arrange their transfer now. Tell no one about this. Find their car and get it out of here. Ditch it in the ocean. As far as anyone is concerned, these two ladies just vanished. You will answer to me if you fail," hissed Doss, glaring at the three goons.

Mr. Doss was pissed. Major big time pissed. Now he had a significant problem.

Within twenty minutes, the two ladies were drugged, packed up and secretly loaded aboard a private plane headed to St. Kitts. Arrangements were made with Mr. Smith in St. Kitts to expect two high security prisoners.

CHAPTER FORTY-TWO

May 26, 2013

Aboard the Sweet Texas, off Philipsburg, St. Maarten, 9:05 a.m.

Hugo heard the Philipsburg harbor master clearing Royal Caribbean's *Jewel of the Seas* to enter the port. Although not a huge ship, the Radiance Class ship of 90,000 tons carried 2,500 cruisers ready to spend money.

"We have a cruise ship in front of us but she should be docked by the time we get there," said Hugo, stepping back into the salon fresh off of the radio in the upper cockpit.

"Good. We can get ashore, meet Bob and the police and find Sherrie. He said he would meet us on the dock beside the bar."

Greg popped up from below.

"Breakfast is ready if anyone's hungry."

"Now, that's the nicest thing I have heard all day," smiled Hugo. "Whatcha got?"

Dane shook his head with a grin. He knew Hugo so well. He was always hungry and always ready for a beautiful girl. That's why he liked him so much. Hugo was the brother Dane never had. And it showed through their devotion and support of each other.

"I made some grits, eggs, sausage and hot coffee!" cried Greg.

"Grits?" yelled Hugo back. "You said grits?"

"That's what he said," answered Dane, smiling. He knew Hugo loved grits.

"Hey, who's sailing this boat?" asked Dane with a grin.

"Woo wee! Grits! Just like back home in Texas," grinned Hugo. "Hey, Greg, watch the boat while I eat, please. Just let her lie here and we will go in just after that cruise ship clears." With that Hugo bounded down into the salon and began filling his plate.

"Yes, sir," cried Greg, smiling, climbing up into the cockpit. He loved sailing this vessel. How he wished it was his own. Dane joined Hugo in the salon for breakfast.

"Okay, Boss, what's your plan?" asked Hugo between bites.

"When we moor, I want to head over to see Bob and go get Sherrie. I figure his contacts in Philipsburg will help us try to unravel what we saw and heard. When I radioed him earlier, he was as surprised as we were. Guess he knows his jewelry stores are most likely on this maniac Hawk's list."

"Sounds reasonable," said Hugo, dipping into the pot for a second helping of grits. "I still can't believe they want to knock over the banks with nerve gas. That's sick!"

"Yeah, and it is very deadly. They could end up killing hundreds of people here on the island."

Hugo nodded in agreement as he took a sip of coffee.

"How we gonna stop them?"

Dane put his coffee cup down. "Hugo, *we* are not going to do anything other than report what we saw and heard. No more Amazon heroics for me. Once we inform the authorities, they can do what they need to stop those folks."

Hugo finished his meal, took a drink of coffee and looked at Dane.

"You are thinking about Sherrie, aren't you?" he said softly. "Frankly, I can't blame you."

"Yes, I am. For once in my life I have to start thinking about someone other than me," answered Dane seriously. "We have something good going and I don't want to mess it up by getting killed."

"Yeah, that would put a hitch in your get-a-long," smiled Hugo, patting Dane on the back. "Let me see how Greg is doing."

It took about thirty minutes for the *Jewel of the Seas* to make the dock, clearing the harbor for traffic. Ever since 9/11 the security around cruise ships was heightened. No one wanted to imagine what some crazed terrorist might do to unleash bombs or gunfire on an unarmed cruise ship and its passengers. And no one wanted to find out. Therefore, all comings and goings of cruise ships in ports all over the world were carefully controlled with discreetly armed security boats patrolling the harbor waters, keeping all boats away from the giant ships.

Hugo informed the harbor master of their arrival and was assigned a mooring buoy. Ten minutes later the trio headed to the shore.

"Let's head to the bar's dock," said Dane, driving the Zodiac. "It's almost 10:30. He said he would meet us with the police there."

"To the bar dock," shouted Hugo as the Zodiac cruised through the harbor at the speed limit. En route, they passed parallel with beachfront. The area was already filled with beautiful ladies sunning themselves and svelte guys vying for their attention.

"Lordy, look at this scenery!" cried Greg. Dane stopped his thoughts.

"What did you say?" asked Dane surprised.

"I said look at the scenery," answered Greg, spreading his arms toward the beach.

"Ha ha!" laughed Hugo, bending over as if in pain, "a man after my own heart."

"Hugo, you are leading this young lad astray," laughed Dane. Greg sat there with a huge grin. The trio resumed their short voyage down the beach. Dane felt like a father of teenage boys.

CHAPTER FORTY-THREE

May 26, 2013

Philipsburg, St. Maarten, 10:00 a.m.

James Doss walked down the hall into his office. He decided to let Hawk know of the possible security breach. But he did not want to tell him everything; at least not yet. He sat heavily in his desk chair and folded his hands before him in a tent. His thoughts were raging. How was he going to handle this situation? There was too much at stake for any one of them to not slam down any dissent or get rid of any obstacle. After a full five minutes of thought, he reached for the phone.

"Yes, Mr. Doss," answered a deep voice. "What can I do for you?"

"Hawk, we have a slight issue." Doss decided not to cause an overreaction. He would handle the two ladies personally. "There may have been a leak in security. However, we have taken care of the issue. The persons involved have been eradicated. Our plans are still secure."

"Very good, Mr. Doss," replied Hawk. "That is the way I like to handle problems. I love to find out after the problems are successfully handled. Thank you for passing that information on to me."

"Yes, sir," answered Doss, inwardly relieved that Hawk trusted him to do a good job. He put down the telephone and sighed in relief. But it was not over. There were some very hard decisions to be made.

Smith and one of his cronies were awaiting the Cessna Caravan as it landed at the R. L. Bradshaw International Airport on St. Kitts, on the north side of Basseterre. The short flight took less than an hour.

As the plane taxied over, Smith turned, said a few words to his cohort, who motioned for a vehicle to meet them on the tarmac. Immediately a black Chevrolet Express van emerged from the hangar behind Smith and approached the still moving Cessna. The windows, including the windshield were heavily tinted. It looked like a funeral van.

When the plane stopped, the left rear cargo door popped open. Even before the engine exhaust fumes subsided, Smith was the first one aboard. His man followed, standing in the door. Within a minute, Smith reemerged, jumped down from the plane and motioned for two large men to come get the cargo. One of Smith's men helped slide a bundle out of the cargo door and into the hands of the two awaiting men. They turned and carried it to the back of the van.

Smith opened the van doors and the bundle was heaved in. The pair stepped back over to the plane to get a second bundle and also placed it into the rear of the van. They jumped in as well. Smith's man exited the plane quickly and ran over and got into the rear of the van. Smith closed the door, checked and walked to the passenger side and got into the front passenger seat. The van drove off slowly.

The van travelled up the Caribbean Sea side of the island toward Sandy Point Town. Between the Brimstone Hill Fortress and Half Way Tree, the van slowed to a stop on the right side of the road. Smith's man stepped out of the back of the vehicle. He lingered at the edge of the road waiting for the single car following them to pass. Once out of sight, the man walked into the underbrush and reached into the side of a tree. He pulled a hidden switch. A six foot wide section of the underbrush moved aside on rollers, revealing a covert entrance. The van quickly turned into the entrance and cleared the "gate". Smith's man closed the entrance and jumped back into the truck. As the underbrush moved back into place, the opening simply disappeared.

The van continued inland down the overgrown dirt road for about a mile as it approached a large drain culvert painted in the same green hues as the surrounding vegetation. It was uniquely camouflaged as to blend in with the undergrowth. From above it was virtually invisible. Off to each side two guards stood by watching the entryway.

The van slowed and Smith waved to one of the guards. Then they drove directly into the culvert with only inches to spare on each side.

Smith turned around to check the two bundles in the rear.

"Are they awake yet?" he asked.

"I don't think so. Neither has moved a muscle," replied Smith's man riding in the rear.

"Good. I want to get them in a cell before they awake. It would make everything easier." Smith strained his eyes, looking through the windshield as the vehicle moved from the culvert into a much larger tunnel.

The total length of the tunnel was nearly two miles. It ended in a man-made cavern hewn out of solid rock far beneath the Brimstone Hill fortress. It was connected by smaller tunnels to the underground docks where the *May Pop* was moored.

Ostensibly a garage, the cavern was twenty feet high and sixty yards square. A number of fluorescent lighting fixtures hung from a metal grid anchored eighteen feet from the floor. The van slowly entered the cave and headed toward a set of double doors on the far side.

"Park over there," ordered Smith, pointing to the doors. Two armed guards flanked the opening. The van parked and its rear double doors opened. Several men rolled a flatbed cart to the van's rear. The two bundles were off-loaded and quickly rolled through the cave's doors.

The cart was rolled down the long hall and into a complex of several rooms carved out of granite. The walls were finished and painted an off-white color. The air was cool, about sixty degrees, but dry. They moved to the far side and stopped in front of a large, heavy steel door. The two bundles were lifted off the cart and carried into a room approximately twelve feet square, a holding cell.

One man reached into his pocket and pulled out a six-inch folding knife. He flicked his finger and a super sharp blade snapped to the ready. He proceeded to slice the sides of the canvas bag, paying particular attention to not cutting the contents.

"That's enough," Smith said. "Leave 'em there. Now everyone get out!" Smith stood over the bags and waited until everyone left. He stepped over to the doorway and looked to make certain the others had moved on down the hall. He pulled the door closed making certain he had a key. Quickly he stepped over to one of the bags and pulled it open. Erin's arm fell out. She was still out cold. Smith smiled and opened the second bag. This one held Sherrie. She too was unconscious.

Smith felt a warming sensation between his legs. Here he was alone with two beautiful girls and they were unconscious. He knelt beside Erin and reached into the bag and pulled her upper torso out onto the cold floor. The pig smiled as he slowly ran his hands through her hair and down her neck. He turned to see that the door was still closed. He let his hands move down to Erin's breasts. They felt so very soft even through her shirt. Smiling like a Cheshire cat, he unbuttoned the buttons of her shirt and pulled it back, exposing her dainty white bra. He giggled as he caught sight of the tiny pink bow of ribbon at the center of her bra between the cups. He grasped the center of her bra from her chest and pulled it up. Both of her small breasts popped out, fully exposed to Smith's prying eyes. He reached down and squeezed them both. He was excited to feel the softness and warmth of her naked breasts. His hands ran over her breasts multiple times, exciting him even more. He wondered how much longer these two ladies would be out. Squeezing Erin's breasts once again, he decided he wanted more. He was becoming aroused.

His thoughts raced. He could do whatever he wanted to these girls and no one would ever know. His mind grew darker and darker. He removed his hands from her chest and stood up. He had to adjust his crotch due to his increased size. He reached down and dragged Erin from the bag onto the floor. He pulled off his shirt and began to unbuckle his pants. He was going to take her right here and now. While Smith was unzipping, Sherrie moved and began to moan. Damn! The other one was waking up! He decided to continue. In his condition he figured taking Erin would only take a minute and he would be finished long before the other girl was awake.

Suddenly there was a hard knock on the door.

"Hey Smith, you in there?" boomed a loud voice outside the door.

Bam! Bam! Someone was beating on the door. Smith panicked. His pants were now down around his knees. Suddenly the door lock turned and Dante Brees stepped in.

Brees stopped dead in his tracks. He could not believe what he was seeing.

"You damned pig!" screamed Brees. "What the hell do you think you are doing?" Brees stepped closer and, using his foot, kicked Smith over onto his back. "You stupid son-of-a-bitch." Brees looked at Erin and then Sherrie. "Damn, you are a dead man!"

"Pull your pants up," snarled Brees. "Wait 'til Hawk hears about this. He will slice your balls off and feed them to you on a plate." Brees turned and stepped outside.

Smith was scrambling to hide himself and try to get his pants back up.

"I was... it's not what you think... I was only..." He knew he was screwed. Nothing he could say would save him. Hawk would simply kill him. He stood up and pulled up his pants and recovered his shirt. This was bad, he thought, really bad.

CHAPTER FORTY-FOUR

May 26, 2013

Philipsburg, St. Maarten, 11:00 a.m.

The trio walked into the bar and immediately saw Bob Rand sitting at a corner table surrounded by paperwork. He was talking to someone on the phone while continuing to review and sign the many documents and bills in front of him. The sea breeze was blowing in through the open air windows and several tourists were already three sheets to the wind. One of the bartenders saw them and headed over their way. Hugo waved him off, pointing to Bob. The bartender smiled, waved and returned to his work at the bar.

Bob looked up at the guys.

"Hey there, pilgrims. Kinda early for you guys, huh?" he asked with a big grin. His grin subsided when he saw Dane's face, dark and foreboding.

"Bob, we have a major problem," he began. "We have stumbled upon a plan to target your businesses and the banks here on the island."

Bob's face went stoic as he stared at Dane.

"What do you mean my businesses?" he said quietly, now fully engrossed.

Hugo began. "Bob, we ran across some pirates a few days ago, a pretty foul bunch. We happened upon them again and this time followed them to their hideout over on St. Kitts." Bob was all ears. "Last night Dane and I decided to visit their little underground lair and learned of a plan to rob your businesses, your jewelry stores and several major banks here in Philipsburg."

Bob sat up straight. He was wearing a slight smile. "Well, I personally would pity the poor fool that tried to rob any of my stores. We have armed guards hidden both inside and outside of each of them. They would not stand a chance of getting away with it."

"Well, that's all well and good, but what if everyone, your employees, guards, and even your customers were totally incapacitated by nerve gas?" added Dane.

"Nerve gas?" gasped Bob. "Where in the hell is someone going to get nerve gas? That's pretty nasty stuff."

"Damn right it is," said Hugo, sitting down at the table. "But we heard it all, right from the horse's mouth, as we would say in Texas. This is no joke, Bob."

"Good God. Have you told the police about this?"

"No. We just returned from St. Kitts and we wanted to talk to you first. We figure with you the police would be more apt to listen to our story." Dane continued, "And I wanted to get Sherrie and, if you want, Erin aboard our boat for safekeeping. Just in case."

"Yeah, I agree, especially with the girls. When is this supposed to go down?" asked Bob, rubbing his chin.

"That's just it," said Hugo. "We heard their plans but we don't have any timeline."

Bob sat for a moment. Then with a huge grin he said, "Aww, damn, boys. You think I'm going to believe you? You are pulling my leg, right? Just pulling old Bob's leg."

Dane looked at Hugo and then Greg. "Bob, I wish we were. This is as real as it gets."

Bob's face turned ashen. "You aren't joking, are you, Dane? This is real?"

"Damn. I wish I were only joking."

Dane and Greg sat down beside Hugo. After a moment of thought, Dane broke the silence.

"I figure we get the girls and have Greg take them back to the cat. If things get really messy, he can take the *Sweet Texas* out to sea for safety."

"Sounds like a plan," said Bob. "Let me call Erin. Sherrie's been with her all day long. Knowing Erin, they are over at Orient Beach. You know that topless beach where all the young folks go?"

"Interesting," said Hugo.

"Not now…" cautioned Dane.

Bob reached for his cell phone and dialed Erin. He was perplexed at the result.

"The cell company said that her phone was unavailable at this time. She always has her iPhone with her. Even if she is busy, it should go to voice mail. That's very odd."

"Could they be at your main store?" asked Greg.

"Sure. Or maybe over at our headquarters/warehouse," said Bob, looking a bit worried. "This is not like Erin at all."

"I say we run by the main store to see if they are there and then by the warehouse if we need to," said Dane, standing.

"Want Greg and me to shoot over to Orient Beach? We could check it out and be back in a few hours," asked Hugo. "We could kill two birds with one stone by spreading out our resources."

"As enticing as that sounds, no," answered Dane. "I don't want us to split up, at least so far away. If we do find the girls, I want Greg to get them to the boat as soon as possible."

"I have to agree with that," said Bob, standing and reaching for his keys. "Come on. My truck's out back."

The guys exited the bar through the rear door and piled into Bob's Ford F150 crew cab.

"Nice truck!" smiled Hugo. "I grew up with pickups."

"I have to say that it comes in pretty handy around here, although the gas mileage could be better," said Bob.

They drove over to the main store. "You guys stay here. I'll talk to the manager in charge." Three minutes later he emerged with a worried look on his face. "They haven't seen Erin all day. She was supposed to stop by to attend to a problem but never showed up."

"Let's go to the warehouse," said Dane. Before he got his statement out of his mouth, Bob started the truck and was driving toward the headquarters of the Rand Corporation about six blocks away.

Bob parked the truck in front of the nondescript building. The guys got out and followed Bob to the front door.

"Kinda plain, ain't it?" asked Hugo in his Texas drawl.

"Yeah, it is," replied Bob. "Sometimes less is better when you have a lot of jewelry and cash about. These are our offices and our vault."

The men came through the door and immediately were faced with Betty at the reception desk.

"Hello, Mr. Bob! How are you this very fine morning?"

"Good morning, Betty," smiled Bob warmly. "Betty, these are my friends from back in the States, Dane, Hugo and Greg."

"A very good morning to you too gentlemen. How can I help you, Mr. Bob?"

"Betty, has Erin been by this morning?"

"Why, yes! Missy Erin and her friend Sherrie were here earlier. I think they still may be here. I did not see them leave."

"So both of them were here?" asked Dane.

"Yes, Mr. Dane. That Miss Sherrie is a very pretty girl, you know. She is a hard one to forget."

Dane smiled at Betty. "Yes, ma'am, she is very pretty and very hard to forget."

"Aww, you her man?"

"Yes, ma'am, I am," Dane admitted, slightly embarrassed.

Bob turned and looked outside. "Betty, I don't see Erin's Jeep."

Betty looked past the men. "It was right there in the same parking space you are in. They must have left."

"Would you please page her to see if she is in the building?" asked Bob.

"Yes, Mr. Bob. Of course I can."

They waited a full two minutes for Erin to call back to Betty's desk. There was no call.

"Sounds like they are not here," said Greg.

"Yeah," added Bob. "Let's drop by the police station next." With that, the men thanked Betty for her help with Hugo finishing it off with a gallant kiss on her cheek. Betty loved it.

CHAPTER FORTY-FIVE

May 26, 2013

Beneath Brimstone Hill, St. Kitts, 1:00 p.m.

Erin stirred. Her thoughts were still clouded. She opened her eyes and tried to focus. Sherrie was moaning, still in the bag with only her face showing where Smith had previously opened it. Erin could not move. All she could remember was someone hitting her…nothing else. She felt cold. She looked down and saw her naked breasts. What the hell had happened? Her mind raced. Had she been raped? She concentrated for a moment. No, she did not feel any discomfort down between her legs and her pants were still on. She was relieved.

But how did her shirt and bra get this way? Sherrie moved. Her hand came out of the bag and her head slowly rose.

"What the hell happened," slurred Sherrie, trying to get up on her elbows to see. Then she saw Erin. "Damn, what did they do to you?"

"Apparently someone felt me up pretty good. I don't think they did anything else, though," Erin answered quietly. "I woke up with my boobs hanging out."

"I can see that," said Sherrie. "Are you all right?"

"Yes, I think so." Erin slowly rolled to one side and slowly pulled her bra back down and tried to sit up. "Whoa, that is a problem."

"What do you mean?" asked Sherrie, who also attempted to sit up but was overcome with dizziness.

"My head is swimming," said Erin. "How are you?"

"Just dizzy. I think someone drugged us. Where are we?"

The two girls looked around at their surroundings. Nothing looked familiar.

"Think we are still at your warehouse?" asked Sherrie.

"I don't know. I don't recognize anything. It's cold as hell in here. We can't be in our warehouse."

They continued to recover as they sat there for another hour awaiting the unknown.

At 2:30 p.m. Mr. Brees decided to check on the two women. He did not trust Smith to even be near them after that stupid stunt he pulled. If he had not intervened, Smith would have probably raped them both and killed them to hide his work. He would have said they tried to escape. Smith was a pig but Brees also knew he was a dead man. Hawk would surely kill Smith for his actions.

He placed the key in the lock and opened the door. The two girls sat against the opposite wall.

"Hello, my sweets! Looks like you are doing much better now."

"Who are you and where are we?" demanded Erin. "You can't do this to us. My father and his friends will kill you for this!"

"Now, now, missy, calm down a bit," soothed Brees. "My name is Mr. Brees. You are all right now and safe."

"Safe my ass!" cried Sherrie. "You tried to rape her."

Brees stepped back. "Oh, no. I did not do that. I don't need to treat a woman that way. That pig Smith did that. I stopped him from raping you both. He will pay dearly for his actions, believe me. You may be able to cut off his balls yourself!" The girls stared at Brees, stunned. "Believe me, I am very sorry."

"Where are we?" asked Sherrie, now slightly quieter.

"You are at our base."

"How the hell did we get here?" cried Erin.

"Well, it seems you overheard something that you should not have," explained Brees in an uncharacteristically soothing voice. "We had to get you out of the way until our plans are complete."

"What plans are you talking about? We don't know anything about any plans."

"Oh, well, we cannot take that chance. See, we know you heard part of a conversation, an important conversation. So you were drugged and brought here by plane this morning," explained Brees.

"This morning… is it still Sunday, the 26th of May?" asked Erin.

"It most certainly is, pretty lady. Now, you girls just relax and I will get you some food and items so you can clean up."

"Screw that!" said Sherrie. "Let us out of here and we will be out of your hair."

Brees smiled widely. "No, that cannot be, at least not yet." He turned and left the girls in the holding room.

"Well, that was interesting," said Erin. "Evidently they think we know something that somehow messes up their plans, whatever they are."

"Well, I say screw their plans. I want out of here." Sherrie stood up and walked around the room, patting her hand on the wall as she walked. "These walls are solid. They are rock or concrete that seems painted. We aren't going to be able to get through them. The door's our only chance."

"Agreed," said Erin. "Think we could create a diversion like they do in the movies and jump the guy who comes to see what's going on?"

"Don't think so. That Brees guy is pretty big. And I do remember those huge guys back in Philipsburg. We can't fight them."

"Yeah, you are probably right," said Erin, growing more concerned at their plight. "We might have a better chance if we play along as demure, helpless little girls and strike when we have a chance, maybe when or if they move us."

"Agreed. But this is one little girl that will have no problem kicking any of those guys in the balls as hard as I can. That would slow them down significantly."

"Whew. I'm sure glad I'm your friend," said Erin. "I would hate to get on your wrong side."

"Yeah, when you grow up with brothers, you learn how to hit 'em where it hurts the most." With that Sherrie sat down beside Erin to await their fate, whatever it was going to be.

CHAPTER FORTY-SIX

May 26, 2013

Philipsburg Police Station, St. Maarten, 2:30 p.m.

Bob led the group into the police station. It was an older building. Even in the Caribbean tax dollars were tight and the police and fire brigades were tightly run with little funds to spare. Coming in the door they encountered a long bar-like half wall staffed with several nicely dressed female and male police officers. The walls were painted an aquamarine blue. It seemed the paint was simply laid over the top of several previous layers. The station was clean but nothing to write home about. A cooling sea breeze blew in through the open windows. The old wooden floor creaked as the group walked to the first officer.

"Good afternoon," Bob greeted the young lady officer. "I would like to see Inspector Stamper, please. He knows me. I am Bob Rand."

"Yes, Mr. Rand. I know you. My brother Randolph works for you in one of your stores. Let me see if Inspector Stamper is in."

"Thank you very much," smiled Bob. The guys looked about the police station.

"Reminds me of the police station in Austin, Texas," said Hugo. "Saw the inside of that place too many times in my younger days."

"I'll bet," said Bob with a grin. "I'll venture you were holy hell as a youngster."

"Yeah, I was wild sometimes, but my dad would always jerk a knot in my ass when I needed it. Too bad I needed it a lot. He decided to put me to work in the family garage so he could keep an eye on me. He worked my butt off but, frankly, he made me the man I am today."

"That he did," added Dane. "Ol' Hugo here can field strip a car as fast as you or I can field strip an M16. And that's fast!"

Greg laughed. "He can also sail a boat like a bat out of you know where too!"

"That I taught myself with the help of my bud Dane here." He slapped Dane on the back just as a fiftyish-year-old short, thin man walked over to them.

"Raymond! How are you, my friend?" smiled Bob. "Guys, this here is Ray... ah, Inspector Raymond Stamper. He's been a friend of mine ever since I came to this island. And a good friend he is too!"

"Glad to meet you, Inspector," said Dane, shaking the Inspector's hand. "I'm Dane Skoglund. This is Hugo Winsor and Greg Knowlton. We are from Miami."

"A pleasure to meet you gentlemen," smiled the Inspector. "What can I do for you?"

"We need to talk to you, Ray. These guys came across something big today. Really big. Something you need to know about," explained Bob.

"Come on back here where we can talk in private," said the Inspector, leading them back behind several desks and into a small conference room. "Can I get you something to drink? Coffee...soda...water?"

"An ice-cold Coke would be great," said Greg.

"Me too," added Hugo.

"Debbie, bring us five cold Cokes. Make sure they are cold, please! Around here that means take them from the bottom of the ice cooler. Now, gentlemen, what do you need to see me about?"

"I guess it would be best to start at the beginning," started Dane. "Hugo, you and Greg jump in as we go."

The inspector brought out a pad of paper and pulled a small tape recorder from his pocket. "Do you mind if we record this?" he asked.

"Not at all," answered Dane. "In fact, I think you may need to in order to get everything that we are going to tell you. It all started several weeks ago when Hugo and I brought his catamaran, the *Sweet Texas,* over to St. Maarten from Tortola where he took possession of his new boat."

"The *Sweet Texas*?" asked the Inspector. "I have seen her mentioned in several inter-island reports lately. This is your boat?" he asked.

"Yes, it's my boat," answered Hugo.

"Go on," said the Inspector.

Over the next two hours, the guys recounted their experiences with the pirates, the lady in pink, Greg getting shot and their nighttime visit to the pirates' lair. All in crystal clear detail. Each word recorded and a multitude of the Inspector's questions answered to the best of their ability. After it was all over, the Inspector looked at Bob Rand.

"That is quite a story, Bob. What do you think of all this?"

"Ray, I have known Dane and Hugo for a very long time. We came through the Navy together and served as SEALS in several Mideast conflicts doing things that I still cannot tell you without having the full force of the United States Government come raining down on me. These guys are professionals in every way. If these guys told me the world was ending in ten minutes, I would believe them. Or let's put it this way; if they say it's so, I say it's so. They are the only persons on earth I would say that about."

"That's a pretty strong way to put it," said the Inspector. "So you still can't find Erin?"

"Yes, and that concerns me greatly. It's not like her to disappear like this," said Bob. "Something's not right."

"And my sister is with her too," added Greg. "Something is wrong. I can feel it."

The door to the conference room opened. Raymond's assistant, Debbie, was there.

"I have something you may want to see," she said, handing the Inspector a well-worn manila folder. "I'll be outside if you need me."

"Thank you, Debbie," said Raymond, opening the folder and beginning to read. He read for a minute or so and then placed the folder on the table in front of him. "We just found your daughter's Jeep in the water in the Lowlands area near Little Key. A pilot reported seeing a red vehicle of some sort in the water about a half mile offshore. It had to be dumped there."

"Damn!" said Bob sternly. "Those sons-of-bitches have my daughter!"

"Wait a minute," said Dane in a calming voice. "We don't know that. Besides, how would these guys know about Erin and Sherrie and us?"

"He's right," added the Inspector. "It doesn't make sense. It has to be a coincidence. Maybe someone stole it and got cold feet and decided to dump it fast. A smart person would have ditched the Jeep far offshore."

Dane and Hugo nodded in agreement.

"Maybe, but where are the girls?" asked Bob.

"I don't know but we will find them," said the Inspector, standing. "Debbie!"

Again the door opened and Debbie stepped in.

"I want two detectives in here right away. We have a lot of work to do." He stopped the recorder and handed it to Debbie. "Please have that transcribed now. I need it as soon as humanly possible. If someone needs to stay after their shift to get it done, do it."

"Yes, sir," snapped Debbie and off she went.

"Let's see…it's almost five. I say we get a quick bite to eat and then we will get the authorities in St. Kitts on the phone. Maybe we can work out a plan to visit this 'Pirates' Lair' tomorrow night and see what is going on there."

"Agreed," said Dane.

"In the meantime, I will put out a full alert for any strange doings about the island and have my full force out to see if we can find the girls here in St. Maarten. I'm going to tell you not to worry, but I'm a father as well. So I know my plea will fall on deaf ears. Please try to relax as much as possible. We are going to need our expertise tomorrow if we visit the lair."

Hugo rubbed his chin. "Ah, if we are going to visit the cave, we are going to need some, let's say, unique equipment, you know, firepower."

"He's right," agreed Dane, looking at Bob, who nodded his agreement.

"Well," started the Inspector, "let me see what we can do about that. Frankly, I don't like arming civilians. It causes issues."

"Inspector, these guys are not civilians, as you know. As I explained before, they can handle weapons and authority to the highest degree. There will be no issues," said Bob bluntly. Inspector Stamper looked at each of them, returning his stare to Bob.

"I am inclined to agree with you, Mr. Rand."

All of the men shook hands and the Inspector returned to his duties. The four guys left the police station and returned to Bob's bar.

CHAPTER FORTY-SEVEN

May 26, 2013

Beneath Brimstone Hill, St. Kitts, 8:45 p.m.

Both Erin and Sherrie tried to get some sleep. Neither had succeeded. Each time they heard footsteps outside their locked door they froze, thinking someone was coming to get them.

For one thing, they were very hungry. They had not eaten since early in the morning. They also did not have water. They found an old wash pail over in one corner. They both agreed to use that as their toilet; they had no other.

Eight hours had passed since they talked to Brees. All they knew was they were at a base of some kind. Where, they had no idea.

"I think they may have forgotten about us," said Erin quietly.

"Sure looks that way," agreed Sherrie. "I would hope they would at least feed us and give us something to drink."

"I wonder where we are. It almost looks and feels like a cave. Painted stone walls and it's so cold. I don't know anyone in Philipsburg who can afford to run their air conditioning this low," said Erin.

"Hmm, a cave might be right. The walls, floor and ceiling are all rock. The cold could definitely be from being underground," added Sherrie.

Without warning, there was a knock on the cell door.

A voice came from the other side of the door. "Are you decent?" It sounded like an older man.

The two girls looked at each other in fear.

"Ah, yeah, we're decent," blurted Sherrie.

There was a heavy snap as the lock disengaged. The door swung open revealing a small, slightly built man of about seventy years old.

"Well, hello there, ladies," he announced. "My name's Orrin and I brought you some food and drink. Now, if you two will stay calm and keep your seat, I will leave you this cart. I cooked all of this myself. There's chicken, peas, bread, a jug of cold water and a few cans of soda. I'll come back and get the cart when I bring you breakfast tomorrow morning. Is there anything else you need?"

"Yeah, we don't have a toilet," said Erin. "We could really use one."

"And some blankets," said Sherrie. "We are freezing."

"Heh, heh, I think I can gather up those for you. But I can't get no toilet. I can get you a thunder bucket," answered the old man.

"A what?" Erin asked.

"I didn't think you would know what that was. Maybe you know it as a pee pot," said Orrin smiling nervously.

"Oh, okay. I know what you are talking about now," said Erin slightly embarrassed.

"Okay, you girls eat and I will be back in a few minutes with the blankets. It does get a bit cold in the caves."

Both girls picked up on that statement. So they were in a cave!

"Yeah, I'm surprised the cell is so dry, it being on St. Maarten. Most caves are full of water since it's an island," said Sherrie, fishing for more clues.

"Oh, this is a nice place. I've lived and worked here for almost 25 years. Hawk is good to us and we are good to him," said the old man. "And besides, we aren't on St. Maarten."

With that comment, Orrin turned and left the cell, locking the door behind him.

"Not on St. Maarten!" cried Erin. "Then where the hell are we?"

Sherrie sat there compiling the clues in her head. "I don't know, Erin. I don't know. When he comes back with the blankets, let's try to get him to talk to us. Maybe we can get some more information."

The girls attacked the food cart, eating their fill within minutes. They both decided to save some food and drinks for later in case they got hungry during the night. With their stomachs full, they both lay down to rest. That's when they heard footsteps outside their door. The lock snapped again and Orrin peered in.

"You thought I forgot you? I brought you two pillows and some blankets," he said, placing them inside the door. "Oh, and I almost forgot, here's a pee pot for you. You two sleep tight."

"Wait," cried Sherrie, getting up on her knees. "What does this Hawk guy want with us? What did we do to him?"

"I don't rightly know, ma'am," replied Orrin. "Leastwise, they don't tell me. I'm only one of the cooks and not even the head cook. I do my job good and they pay me well."

"You sound like a very important fellow here in the cave," Erin interjected. "They wouldn't eat if it weren't for you."

Orrin smiled widely. "You can say that again. I may not be the head cook but I can cook better than he can."

"What kind of things do you cook?" asked Sherrie, trying to get him to talk.

"I can make anything. I make cakes, cookies, pies and cook all kinds of fish, meat and vegetables. My mammy taught me how to grow vegetables and raise chickens, pigs and goats. I learned from her how to cook all of it. I make the best goat stew in the islands."

Sherrie continued to prod. "Goat stew is one of my favorites. I love the way they cook it in Jamaica."

"Ha ha!" laughed Orrin. "They can't hold a candle to mine. I ain't seen anyone from Jamaica that can out cook me!"

"I don't know, Orrin. Jamaican goat stew is pretty damn good," said Sherrie.

"You let them come here to Kitts and I'll show them how it's done," cried Orrin. "I've lived here for nigh on to seventy years and mine's the best."

"Okay. When do we get to try some?" asked Erin.

Orrin stopped, looked behind him and then looked at the girls. "I tell you what. We will probably make some tomorrow since the men from the *May Pop* are here. That's about a dozen more mouths to feed. I can get you some then. How's that?"

"That sounds great," said Sherrie. She had what she wanted…information.

"I best go now," said Orrin softly. "Don't want no one to accuse me of botherin' anybody."

"You aren't bothering us, Orrin. We enjoy talking with you," said Erin.

"Yeah, you are our friend," added Sherrie. "Thanks for the blankets and the pee pot!"

"Sleep well. I'll bring you breakfast in the morning." With that the door closed and Orrin was gone.

"Well. So we are on St. Kitts. At least we know where we are," said Erin with a slight grin. She liked the way Sherrie had of getting information out of men.

Sherrie nodded but was frowning.

"What's wrong, Sherrie?" asked Erin.

"The *May Pop*. That's the pirate boat that shot my brother and tried to kill us. Erin, we are in really bad trouble. Until now I had no idea how bad it was," Sherrie said calmly but clearly disturbed.

Erin stared at Sherrie. "Damn!"

CHAPTER FORTY-EIGHT

May 27, 2013

Philipsburg, St. Maarten, 8:10 a.m.

"Morning, guys!" yelled Hugo to Bob and the Inspector as they met on the dock in front of Bobby's Marina. "What's the news, Inspector?" asked Dane.

"Gentlemen, you have really opened a Pandora's Box. I spoke with the St. Kitts authorities last night. They are very interested in your story. It seems they have had several reports of outright piracy in their waters, including several murders. They believe you may have stumbled across the people responsible for all of these crimes."

"So they are going to help us out?" asked Hugo.

"Most definitely," answered the Inspector smiling. "They want these folks as bad as we do. They have asked that we come to St. Kitts immediately."

"We can take our cat," offered Hugo.

"Hell, we can take my jet!" cried Bob.

"Jet?" exclaimed Hugo. "You got a jet?"

"Hell, yeah, Hugo. How do you think we get from island to island and back to the United States whenever we want? I bought my first one two years ago and recently upgraded."

Greg was dying to ask. "What kind is it?"

"It's a new HondaJet. And baby, let me tell you it is one sweet ride!"

"A jet made by a motorcycle and car company? I don't know about that one," Hugo said curiously.

"How many does it seat?" asked Greg, who was getting more excited at the idea of flying in a small jet.

"It seats five and, of course, a pilot and co-pilot. And it has a nice cargo section too. I got my jet rating a few years back so I usually co-pilot. It has plenty of room for us."

"Bob, I swear you are full of surprises," grinned Dane. "You never cease to amaze me."

"So that means we are going on his jet?" asked Greg, about to pop with excitement.

"Hell, yeah, son," bellowed Bob. "We are flying in style! Let me call my pilot and have him ready the plane and send someone over to pick us up."

"Sounds like a plan!" said Hugo, shaking Bob's hand.

"Bob, we really do appreciate this," said Dane, putting his hand on Bob's shoulder.

"Hey, it's my little girl and your girlfriend. We can't afford to hold back. Ray, you ready?"

"I need to stop by the office and pick up a bag but other than that, sure," added Ray.

An hour later the group was on the jet leaving the skies of St. Maarten and stretching out over the azure waters of the Caribbean Sea on their way to Basseterre, St. Kitts.

Greg spent most of the flight sitting in the co-pilot seat. Bob yielded it as soon as they took off so the guys in the back could talk. Greg was in heaven. Already a techno junky, he was totally enthralled with the futuristic cockpit of the HondaJet. The all glass avionics systems were straight out of Star Trek. It had touchscreen controllers and three large high-resolution displays that flooded the pilot with every piece of flight information one might imagine. Greg wanted one of these.

The pilot keyed his microphone for an announcement. "Gentlemen, we will be arriving in St. Kitts in twenty minutes. It almost takes longer for us to get into the airport's flight control path than it takes to fly there. Relax and we will be there very soon."

Greg watched the clouds stream by as they flew on a southerly heading. This was so cool! Sailing was a thrill but this was literally out of this world. He was like a kid in an ice cream parlor. He wanted more and more and more.

"So you like flying," asked the pilot.

"I love it," replied Greg with a huge smile. "It's like sailing without water and a hundred times faster."

"You want to take her for a minute or two?"

"Are you kidding? Absolutely!"

"Okay. Take the controls softly in your hands and hold the jet stable. Just watch this screen and keep the wings level," said the pilot. "It's that simple. The jet will almost fly itself. In fact, it's so simple that I can't tell anyone... I don't want to lose my job."

Greg grinned and then immediately turned serious. He placed his hands on the yoke and felt the slight movement of the controls.

"Just keep everything steady and you will be fine," assured the pilot.

"This is so freakin' cool," said Greg.

Bob turned away from the conversation in the cabin to see Greg flying the jet. "You better be careful, son," he joked.

"Yes, sir, I will."

"No; I don't think you understand. I have no qualms with you flying; it's just that now that you have, you won't want to stop. That's how I got into this flying stuff," said Bob with a smile. Bob liked Greg. He was a good kid that wore his heart on his sleeve and was as eager to please as anyone he had ever met. He inwardly wondered if Erin might have an interest in Greg.

Twenty minutes later the small jet popped through a puffy white cloud and Greg relinquished the controls back to the pilot. They began their final approach after contacting approach control at 119.6 MHz. They were directed to runway 07. The jet twitched a bit in the hot humid air but she rode through it like a champion. The wheels touched down at 9:40 a.m. The weather was beautiful.

The ground control tower asked that they taxi to the police hangar at one end of the main terminal.

Waddle Nelson, the Commissioner of the Royal St. Christopher and Nevis Police Force, stepped out of his vehicle parked inside the hangar. He thought, no use waiting on the plane out in the hot sun. He surveyed the two police planes and helicopter the force owned to be able to move quickly between St. Kitts and Nevis, the two islands of which he was responsible. He turned toward the hangar door as the whine of a small jet became louder. He watched the sleek mini jet easily navigate from the outer tarmac and stop directly in front of the hangar with the nose of the jet, including the cabin door, just a foot or so inside the shade of the building.

As the engines whined down, the door popped open and slowly lowered itself, creating a stable stairway to disembark from the jet.

Inspector Stamper led the small team down the steps.

"Waddle, my friend, how are you?"

"Commissioner Nelson, it is great to see you again. It has been too long."

"Yes, it has. Too long indeed," answered the Inspector, giving him a hearty handshake.

"Your mode of transportation has improved greatly since we last talked," said Nelson, admiring the new jet.

"Oh, a friend was generous enough to let us borrow it for the trip," the Inspector shot back.

Nelson smiled widely. Each group of authorities on these islands had 'friends'. Most of these 'friends' sported very, very deep pockets. Waddle Nelson liked to flaunt his personal friendship with Mick Jagger of The Rolling Stones, who owned a home on Nevis.

"Sounds like you have a rather strange issue to speak with us about?" asked Nelson.

"Yes, quite. But first let me introduce my colleagues, Mr. Dane Skoglund, Mr. Hugo Winsor, Mr. Greg Knowlton, and you may have met Mr. Bob Rand of St. Maarten.

The Commissioner shook each man's hand and stopped at Bob. "Yes, I do recall meeting Mr. Rand here. It seems my wife has made some beautiful purchases from some of your stores."

"And we do appreciate your business," said Rand very courteously. "I hope she still finds the items to her liking."

"Yes, she does. She wears them at all of the parties," explained the Commissioner.

"That's wonderful," said Rand. "When this is over, I want you and your wife to come over and I will personally make sure you get the finest discount known to man."

"Why, thank you, Mr. Rand," acknowledged the Commissioner. The Commissioner was used to getting good discounts throughout the islands.

"Well, gentlemen, I suggest we go to the station headquarters and discuss this issue you and Mr. Stamper have found."

The men piled into the black Ford Excursion and drove away.

CHAPTER FORTY-NINE

May 27, 2013

Beneath Brimstone Hill, St. Kitts, 9:00 a.m.

The girls did not hear the cell door open. Both were sound asleep. Orrin peeked in quietly. In the darkness he could see the two cuddled in the far corner of the cell.

Brees was rounding the corner with a cup of coffee when he heard Orrin. "Hey! What are you doing there?" he yelled, surprising Orrin and waking the girls.

"I was told to feed them," said Orrin, clearly scared of Mr. Brees. "I meant no harm to them. I'm also here to change their bucket."

"Bucket? What kind of bucket are you talking about?" asked Brees. Then he realized Orrin was talking about their toilet bucket. "Oh, okay, that's all right. You go ahead and attend to the girls." He was relieved. After what he found Smith doing, he was on the alert. If they were harmed in any way, Hawk would hold everyone responsible. Brees only wanted Smith to get what was due. These girls were extremely important trade value if anything went awry.

Brees stood at the open door sipping his coffee while Orrin picked up the pot and shuffled it outside of the cell, replacing it with a new one.

"Hey!" yelled Brees, "That's nasty. Watch out and don't spill it or I'll have you down here cleaning this place on your hands and knees!"

"Oh sorry sir, I won't be making a mess." Orrin hated Brees. He treated Orrin like a dog.

Brees stepped into the cell and held the door open while Orrin attended to the captives. The girls, now awake, sat there without saying anything. Having Orrin clean their cell was normal. For Brees to be there watching was not. They hoped this was not something sinister.

"You ladies have a nice night? Do you need anything else," asked Brees nicely? The two looked at each other in general disbelief. Sherrie chose to answer.

"We could use a shower and two toothbrushes," said Sherrie.

"And more blankets. The floor is cold and hard," added Erin.

Brees smiled and nodded his head in agreement. He took another sip. He relished seeing two beautiful women under his control. His mind raced thinking of the things he could do with them both.

"Oh, and one more thing," started Erin. "When are we going to be freed? We have no idea who you are, where we are or, for that matter, what the hell you think we know. My father is Robert Rand of the Rand Corporation in St. Maarten. When he finds out we are missing, he will have the police looking for us everywhere. He will not rest until we are found."

Brees' smile soured. He took a last sip of coffee and slung the remainder of the cup at the ladies.

"You stinky little bitches do not seem to understand that with one word your throats could be cut, concrete blocks shackled to your feet. Your next stop is twenty thousand feet below the water... forever. See if your fair daddy can find you then." Brees laughed and left Orrin with the ladies.

"That Mr. Brees is a nasty one," said Orrin. "I served under him for a few months when the *May Pop* had no cook. He is a bad man."

Sherrie sat up and leaned forward. "He's the captain of the *May Pop*?" she asked.

"Oh no missy, that be Captain de Terr. He captains the *May Pop*. Mr. Brees is de Terr's First Mate. Second only to the Captain but he is worse than de Terr." Orrin placed the new bucket in the corner and walked into the hallway.

"What is the *May Pop*?" asked Erin, totally lost. "Sounds like some flower."

Sherrie leaned over to speak with Erin. She didn't want Orrin to hear.

"It's the pirate boat I was telling you about yesterday. Girl, we are in a world of hurt here," said Sherrie in a whisper. "These people kill without regard. They have slaughtered people merely to steal their belongings. Erin, we have to find a way to get out of here. There is no limit to what they will do to us."

Orrin brought in a small cart of food. "I couldn't get any goat stew for you. They ate all of it. But I did get you some pork and potatoes and some bread."

"Thanks, Orrin," said Sherrie, giving him a purposeful smile. Orrin seemed to be a kind-hearted person.

"Don't worry. Old Orrin will take care of you. I'll bring you food, water and a new pot each day. You just tell me if you need anything and I will get it for you," said Orrin, backing toward the door.

"Remember the toothbrushes and a shower," noted Erin. Orrin smiled and tipped his cap to acknowledge her request.

Erin looked closely at Sherrie's face. "You are scared aren't you?"

"You would be too if you had seen what these animals do to people," Sherrie said quietly. "When we sailed off of St. Maarten, we were attacked by the *May Pop*. My brother Greg was shot by those devils. Then a few days later when Greg was better we sailed for St. Kitts. On the way we came across another sailboat that was attacked by pirates, probably the *May Pop* as well. They used some kind of gas to kill the entire crew, a man and his wife. Erin, it was horrible."

Erin sat back against the damp wall. She stretched out her legs. Now she was worried. She didn't know Sherrie really well, but anything that would rattle her like this must be disturbing. She looked around the room. It still smelled like urine and everything seemed wet all of the time. The nastiness was starting to get to her.

"What do you think they will do to us?" asked Erin.

"I really don't know. They may kill us or use us as their whores or sell us into slavery in the Mideast. All of those are not good," explained Sherrie. "Not good at all."

"Well, by now someone knows we are missing," said Erin, trying to lighten the mood a bit. "Dad and your friends will be out looking for us."

"Yeah," snapped Sherrie. "And how the hell will they know to come to St. Kitts and find us in a cave?"
Erin nodded her understanding. It didn't sound good any way they looked at it. Sherrie was right. Her father and the guys may know they are missing but they have no clue as to where to start to look for them. Erin sighed as she realized there was not much hope. This did not bode well for either of them.

CHAPTER FIFTY

May 27, 2013

Police Force Headquarters, Basseterre, St. Kitts, 10:50 a.m.

The small motorcade from the airport danced through local customs by virtue of the Commissioner's wave. The short motorcade trip to the Police Force Headquarters took less than fifteen minutes with a police escort.

The group arrived to a small welcoming committee consisting of the entire St. Kitts police day watch; all ten of them standing on the steps of the headquarters building. They all went straight into a large conference room on the second floor.

One thing was very clear on this island. Commissioner Waddle Nelson was in full charge. His word was law for all practical purposes. Even if it was not, the courts would take months to render any opposing rulings, if they dared.

The Police Force Headquarters building was first class in many ways. It had to cater to the royals and superstars that regularly visited the islands, especially Nevis. The elite stay in regal personal homes or the ultra-private and personal Nisbit Plantation Beach Club, recognized regularly as one of the best hotels in the world.

The conference room was well appointed with richly paneled walls and several large portraits of prior commissioners and old sea captains. A rich smell of wood polish permeated the room. The chairs were large and comfortable, finely upholstered with a linen cloth. This was clearly a nod to the heat and humidity in the tropics. Fine leather seats would have been beautiful but very uncomfortable. They also would not have lasted very long in this environment.

"Very nice," whispered Hugo to Dane as they walked around the table to take a seat. "Reminds me of the funeral home back in Austin."

"It is, isn't it?" answered Commissioner Nelson. "We try to make everyone who visits very comfortable." Hugo looked at Dane, embarrassed that he was overheard.

"Commissioner Nelson is always a gracious host," said Inspector Stamper. "We have had the occasion to work together on many projects over the past several years and he always takes very good care of us."

"Well, we certainly do appreciate the hospitality," said Bob matter-of-factly. "But we have a job to do, getting my little girl back." Dane, Hugo and Greg nodded in agreement.

"There are some technicalities that I must adhere to before we move forward. As you must know, as a Police Commissioner, I cannot merely bring in new men, arm them and send them in this type of situation."

"Okay. I'll buy that," said Bob. "What are these technicalities?"

Inspector Stamper opened a folder in front of him and said, "Gentlemen, please do not be offended by what I am about to say. This is from Commissioner Nelson and me." Stamper looked over at Bob Rand.

"Mr. Rand, I have always held you in very high regard. Frankly, that is why we are sitting here now. But even so, we must adhere to our duty as the duly elected police authorities. We do not know these men that you have brought along. We have been briefed by you as to their tactical prowess and their military experience. However, we need some sort of proof that we can base our decision upon," explained Inspector Stamper. Nelson sat quietly, paying particular attention to the faces and reactions to Stamper's words.

There was a collective deep breath taken. Greg had a small smirk on his face. Just wait until Dane tells you guys off, he thought. After five seconds of complete silence, Dane spoke softly.

"Gentlemen, I completely understand. Beyond Bob here, you do not know us at all. If I were in your place, I would be acting exactly as you are. That said, this is a problem that we can remedy relatively quickly with a few phone calls and faxes. However, let's keep our eye on the ball in this situation. We have real pirates who have openly and willingly killed people and shot Greg here," turning to Greg. "That is a fact. We now have two ladies missing, one Bob's daughter and the other a very close friend of mine. Do what you must, but do it quickly or the blood of those two women will be on your hands."

Inspector Stamper fidgeted in his chair. Commissioner Nelson tried to show a calm front but his eyes and his sweaty brow gave him away.

"How do you know this cave and your missing friends are connected?" asked Nelson.

"At this time we don't," answered Dane. "But I find their disappearance and this whole situation to be very coincidental. I personally believe they are linked."

"I do too," added Rand. "We all think they are in that cave." Rand paused for a second. "Well, at least we hope they are. They have to be there."

Nelson cracked a slight smile. "Mr. Rand, I appreciate your concern but you have no proof."

Dane leaded forward, placing his hands flat on the table in front of him. "Okay. We have no proof. But we have a gut feeling. That's good enough for me. Besides, if the girls are not there don't you believe it is important to stop this plan?"

"A gut feeling?" mocked Nelson leaning back in his chair. "I'm sorry. We cannot act on gut feelings."

"Guys, when this man gets a gut feeling, you better act on it. He is very seldom wrong," sneered Hugo staring at Nelson. Hugo was not happy.

"So what do you need to certify our identity?" asked Dane trying to defuse Hugo's growing anger. Hugo sat back in his chair.

"Some of our history remains classified. The U.S. government will not respond to an information request in that arena," explained Hugo. "Would a normal background type check suffice? Anything beyond that may be a problem."

Commissioner Nelson regained his composure and decided to play a bit of hardball. "It may be a problem for you but not for us. You are asking to come along on official police business. And I am still not convinced your ladies are in there."

"Look," stated Bob. "You do what you feel is adequate to vet these guys but you better do it fast. I don't have to remind both of you I can bring significant pressure on this situation from far above your heads, pressure that could result in changes in management. Do you understand? We want to work with you. We will cooperate as much as humanly possible, but there is a limit to our patience and understanding, especially when it comes to my daughter."

Commissioner Nelson, not used to being talked to this way, sat up in his seat. "I don't think you understand..."

Inspector Stamper placed his hand on Nelson's arm, interrupting his statement. He whispered something into Nelson's ear. After a few seconds, Commissioner Nelson sat back in his chair and wiped the sweat from his brow.

"After further thought, I think we can get this cleared up to everyone's understanding and move on." Nelson reached for the telephone in front of his position at the table. "Captain Jones, can you step in here a moment?" They all sat in silence.

Captain Desu Jones opened the door to the conference room and stepped in. He closed the door and stood at attention. "You asked for me, sir?"

"Yes," said Nelson in a calm voice. "Please take down these men's names and run a standard background check on them." Nelson nodded toward Dane, Hugo and Greg. Dane nodded back his agreement. "Use the priority status. I want this information back as soon as possible."

"Yes, sir," acknowledged Captain Jones. He stepped out of the room for a moment and returned with a notepad. He began with Dane and circled around the room until he had all of the three men's information. Then he excused himself and left the room.

"Captain Jones will get the information we need and then we can move along with our plans," said Nelson. He was trying to be accommodating but also wanted to show that he was in charge.

"How long will it take?" asked Bob. He was clearly ready to move as fast as possible.

"Two, maybe three hours," answered Nelson. "We are a long way from our background clearing house and are usually not priority one when it comes to such checks. That is why I asked Captain Jones to use a priority status. Hopefully we can get this done as quickly as possible."

Dane looked at his watch... it was almost 12:30 p.m. Damn, he thought. If we have to wait all afternoon for this information, it could be tomorrow before we get our gear together and plan our way in. His frustration was growing.

"I suggest you all go get some lunch and let's hope we can have some information by then," suggested Commissioner Nelson.

"A very good idea," added Inspector Stamper. "We could talk over some of the particulars we discussed back in St. Maarten. Bring Commissioner Nelson up to date. That should save us some time so when we get the okay we can move immediately." Stamper looked at Nelson and nodded his head as if asking Nelson to agree.

"Yes. That sounds like an excellent idea," said Nelson, rising to his feet. "I will treat. We have some very good restaurants in Basseterre."

Hugo looked at Dane with a frown. He did not like it but it looked as though they had to play along to get all of the niceties done.

With that, the five men left the room, led by the Commissioner. It was time for lunch. And Hugo was hungry.

CHAPTER FIFTY-ONE

May 27, 2013

El Fredo's Restaurant, Basseterre, St. Kitts, 1:00 p.m.

The men walked into the crowded restaurant lead by the Commissioner. One of the servers saw Nelson and quickly retrieved the manager from the back room.

"Commissioner Nelson. It's so very nice to have you here. Will you and your party be lunching with us today?" asked the manager.

"Yes," answered Nelson. He was trying to show his importance to the other four men with him. "We will have the private room, please. This is a business lunch."

"Most certainly, sir," answered the manager. "I will go attend to the arrangements myself." He motioned to the bar. "Please have a seat at the bar. This should only take a minute or two." He waved his hand at the bartender, who came running across the room. "Please take care of Commissioner Nelson and his party. Of course, their drinks are on me."

"Thank you," said Nelson graciously as they moved to the bar. "I do like this place. They are most cooperative."

Hugo stepped close to Dane.

He spoke softly, almost a whisper, "Looks like a shakedown to me. This guy must rule the roost and everyone kowtows to him."

Dane nodded his agreement. "Yeah, we have seen this type plenty of times, haven't we?"

After each ordered a drink, the manager scurried out and announced the private room was ready. The men took their drinks and retired to a small dining room with a large picture window overlooking the beach. It was nothing special, simply an adjunct dining area that was away from all of the hustle and bustle of the main restaurant. They all sat down with Nelson ordering a feast for the men. The manager quickly took the order and left the room.

"So tell me about this situation that we must handle," said Nelson, sitting as if he owned the place.

Stamper began. He told Nelson of how the men had come to him with their story about pirates and their missing friends. They discussed at length Dane and Hugo's visit to the cave and the plans they had overheard. Commissioner Nelson was at first just listening, not paying particular attention to the story. Once they got to the hidden cave, pirates and nerve gas, his eyes were focused on Dane and Hugo as they responded to multiple questions from Nelson and Stamper.

The conversation quieted when the manager and three servers began bringing in several platters of food all creatively displayed. Hugo's eyes widened. This was going to be a feast!

The men ate and continued to discuss Hugo and Dane's visit to the cave.

"So," said Nelson, "There is a cave under Brimstone Hill? While I find everything else you said plausible, I am having a very hard time believing this cave and underground docks. How did this cave get there?"

"If I had to guess, it's probably an old vent from millions of years ago when the mountain was a volcano. There's some evidence of more work being done over the years to enlarge or enhance the cave but the original cave is intact. Like I said, that's just a guess. I'm almost certain it is not man-made. To create a cave of that size would take years and hundreds of men. There's no evidence anywhere of that type and size of construction project taking place. Would you agree?" asked Dane, turning to Hugo.

"Absolutely. After seeing the size of this cave or cavern, it has to be natural," added Hugo. Nelson crinkled his brow. He was actually interested. The Commissioner thought for a second.

"How many men did you say were there?"

"It's hard to say," started Dane. "We saw more than a dozen men directly but we also heard maybe a dozen more. You agree, Hugo?"

"Yes. I figure there are several dozen men down there given the fact that we saw guards, dock workers, a reasonably sized boat that might have a crew of twenty men or more. Then there were the cooks and servers we heard serving the meals. In my opinion, I would say there could be as many as seventy-five people in that cave right now."

Nelson was still not convinced.

"Mister Winsor, are you serious? How can there be a cave that we do not know anything about with a complement of seventy-five people?" queried Nelson.

Bob Rand slammed his hand down on the table. Both Nelson and Stamper were startled. Dane and Hugo did not skip a beat.

Hugo whispered, leaning slightly toward Dane, "Uh oh..."

"Look, dammit. I am not going to sit here and listen to you call us liars. I know Dane and Hugo. They would never lie about something like this. We know for a fact these so-called pirates have nerve gas and we also know what they plan to do with the stuff. Let's get off our asses and move here!"

Dane smiled but covered his mouth with his napkin. The two policemen were not used to being spoken to in such a manner.

"Now look here, Mr. Rand," said Nelson leaning forward.

"No, you look here," said Bob loudly. "We have set this situation on a silver platter for you. Go ahead and ignore it if you want. But if you do and people die, you will be shoveling shit on some God-forsaken island for the rest of your life. And if my daughter is hurt due to your ineptitude, well, you will pray that you get to that island in one piece."

Nelson was furious. "How dare you threaten me!"

Dane looked at Nelson. "Sir, he is not threatening you. He is promising you. And I will tell you the same. If my friends are hurt in any way by your ineptitude, I will personally see that you are imprisoned for gross misconduct. But if this does go down like we think it could and you do nothing, I would say your superiors will have your ass in a sling long before we can get to you. Do you understand me?" Dane's voice was low and calm, almost serene.

Inspector Stamper immediately understood and jumped into the fray, taking control of the conversation. "Please gentlemen, I do not think the Commissioner is saying he will do nothing." Stamper glanced at Nelson as if to tell him to keep his mouth shut. "I believe we can all work together and solve this mystery, foil the pirates' plan and get the ladies back to us safely. Don't you agree, Commissioner?"

Nelson was still red in the face. But he was also a man that knew when he had met his match and needed to back off. He certainly did not want this to escalate to his superiors.

"Most certainly," said Nelson quietly. "I'm sure we can work this out. What do you suggest?"

Dane sat back and took a breath. Bob was still fuming but at least he was keeping his mouth shut.

"I want to go into the cave after dark, find the girls if they are there and do as much as we can to thwart these pirates' plans. We do not have to stop them. All we have to do is screw their plan up and cause them a delay while you, Mr. Commissioner, call in the cavalry and shut the place down completely. I'm certain that foiling this deadly plan would go a long way to further your career." Dane played right into the hands of Nelson.

"Alright, I agree," said Nelson, wiping his mouth and daubing his head with his napkin. "Let me call my office and see if we have had any issues lately in and around the Brimstone area that might bear out some of what you said." He reached for his cell phone and talked with Captain Jones for just a few minutes. After he ended the call, he seemed in a much better mood.

"Very well then," said Nelson smiling. "I think we can move ahead with a plan to go into the cave as soon as we get your credentials approved. I have asked Captain Jones to have everything ready when we return from lunch. If all is well, we could be looking at going in there tonight. Is that too fast?"

"No sir, that sounds good to us," said Dane. "We are ready to go now if need be."

"Very well," interjected Stamper, truly glad the combative nature of the conversation was put behind them.

The men continued with their meal. Now each had their own reasons to move ahead without delay.

After about twenty minutes, Stamper asked, "So gentlemen, have we finished our meal?"

"I'm done," said Hugo.

"Me too," said both Greg and Bob together.

"Well, if we are ready, let's get back to my office and get this mission started," said Nelson, now fully supporting Dane and Hugo's plan. Now he realized there might be glory for him.

CHAPTER FIFTY-TWO

May 27, 2013

Police Force Headquarters, Basseterre, St. Kitts, 3:00 p.m.

The group returned to Police Headquarters and regrouped in the conference room. As they entered, Captain Jones handed Nelson a folded piece of paper. The men sat down to resume their conversation.

"Gentlemen, Captain Jones has informed me that your backgrounds check out. Now we can legally get down to business. I will be creating a temporary deputy job for each of you to make it perfectly legal for you to bear arms and accompany the police to the cave," announced Commissioner Nelson.

"Very good," said Inspector Stamper, nodding with approval to Dane, Greg, Hugo and Bob.

For the next hour the group discussed several plans, all centering on a stealthy entrance to the cave from the ocean side. Then there was a knock on the door.

"Come in," said Nelson.

The door opened and Captain Jones walked in and closed the door.

"Excuse me, gentlemen, but I have some very interesting information that we have uncovered within the last several minutes."

"Go ahead, Captain," said Nelson. "We all need to hear what you found."

"On a whim, I asked my staff to review any issues that were reported in the general Brimstone Hill area. I had them go back about ten years to see if anything out of the ordinary came up. Well, we did get a few items but most were explained away, except one. Sir, as you know, we ask the island's security companies to file a report on any security systems installed, upgraded or repaired. It gives us an idea of the systems on the island and their capabilities and use. About three and a half years ago there was an upgrade/repair item for a security gate south of the Brimstone Hill Fortress entrance."

"And how does that come into play here?" asked Nelson, beginning to get impatient.

"Well, sir," explained Jones, "That area has no buildings of any kind. Why does one install a security system in the middle of nowhere?"

"Captain Jones, is that all you have?" asked Nelson, now clearly upset. Before he could answer, Hugo broke in.

"Wait a second." He looked at Jones. "Has anyone been out to check this out?"

"Yes, sir," answered Jones. "I had one of our patrols take a look."

"And what did they find?" asked Nelson.

"Nothing sir, absolutely nothing," said Jones.

"What do you mean nothing?" asked Nelson.

"The patrol went past the described location several times and saw nothing but overgrown bushes and the like," answered Jones.

"Wait a minute," interjected Dane, looking over at Hugo. "The cave entrance from the water was camouflaged by overgrown bushes so that even if one found the small cove you still could not see the entrance to the cave. I wonder if we have that same tactic being used here."

"What do you mean?" asked Greg.

"I wonder if there isn't a secondary land entrance to the underground lair that is camouflaged as well," queried Dane. "I would find it hard to believe that the only entrance to the pirate's lair was by sea. There would have to be some way to get into the complex by land. Captain Jones, you said this was an upgrade or repair. Do you have any record of the original installation?"

"No, sir. None," answered Jones.

"That would not surprise me," added Hugo. "A place this secret probably had off-islanders do the original installation. They were unaware of the requirement to report the system to the police or openly told not to report the system. They simply came in from wherever, installed the security system, got paid well and left. Now, several years later, when changes were made, someone slipped up and filed a report. That would be the only answer."

Commissioner Nelson looked at Captain Jones. Jones nodded in agreement.

"So we have a somewhat sophisticated security system installed in place where there is nothing. It does sound fishy to me," added Bob.

"I have to agree," said Dane. "I think we may have stumbled across a second entrance. That does change our plans. We will have to split up our group, sending one in by water and the other in by land."

Nelson sat there for a second. "Stamper, what do you think?"

"It sounds plausible to me, Commissioner. I agree with Dane this time. I believe we are looking at two distinct entrances. When we move in we must cover both entrances or everyone will simply vanish out the back door."

"Agreed," said Nelson.

"Yes, I do too," said Bob. All of the others nodded their heads in agreement.

"All right. We must plan a two-pronged attack," said Dane. "Now, how do we do it?"

"A better question is when we do it," said Nelson. "It's after 4:00 p.m. now. Can we plan the assault, get the men together, sufficiently arm them and do this by about 11:00 p.m. tonight?"

"That would be pushing it," added Dane. "We have to get this right the first time. These pirates are merciless. We have seen them kill and they will kill again. On top of that, they may have two very important hostages, Sherrie and Erin. We cannot make a mistake."

Bob sat up straight. "But we can't wait. The longer those girls stay in there, the more danger they are in; if they are still there."

"What do you mean still there?" asked Greg. "Where would they go?"

Hugo looked at Greg. "It's not that. These guys could decide to sell the girls as slaves or do whatever else they would do to make money off of them. They are not interested in ransom. It has been several days and no one has contacted us. So I agree we should move as fast as we can but not so fast as to jeopardize the mission."

"Well put, Mr. Winsor," said Nelson. "Now we are faced with the million dollar question... can we go tonight or should we wait until tomorrow?"

The group got silent. Hugo was scribbling notes on a piece of paper. He passed it over to Dane and Greg. Dane read the note and sat back in his chair. "I vote for tonight, but very late, like 2:00 a.m. Everyone will be asleep and only a small guard staff will be on site. And, most importantly, they will be sleepy as well; perfect for our entrance."

"Can we get the necessary armament by tonight?" asked Hugo.

Nelson replied, "We have a full complement of the necessary firearms here in our armory. We can go take a look when we leave here."

Bob stood up. "I'm headed to the restroom and then we can put this plan together."

Now, that's a plan I can follow," said Hugo. "I need to visit the boy's room too."

"Let's all take fifteen and return ready to get to work," said Dane. "We have a lot to go over before 2:00 a.m."

"Very well," said Nelson.

CHAPTER FIFTY-THREE

May 27, 2013

Beneath Brimstone Hill, St. Kitts, 4:30 p.m.

Erin and Sherrie sat against the wall. Even with the blankets they were cold. The cave was cold. The cell was always wet. They were dirty and their clothes reeked of urine and a rotten smell. At least they were being fed.

"Sherrie, what are we going to do?" Erin had never experienced this type of filth.

"What do you mean?" answered Sherrie.

Erin turned and looked Sherrie in the eye. "What I mean is we have been here for two days, I think, and I haven't seen a way to escape. Even if we could get out of this cell, I have no idea where we are or how to get back outside."

"Yeah, I know what you mean, but we can't give up," said Sherrie. "They seem to want us for something or they would have gotten rid of us by now."

"I wonder if we were kidnapped for ransom," stated Erin.

"Could be. Our guys would pay it and get us back, but I would bet on a rescue.

Of course, that assumes they know where we are," said Sherrie. "And we don't know that. But if anyone can find us, it's going to be Dane and Hugo."

"You have a lot of confidence in those two."

"Well, let's just say they are pros at this type of thing. They have a background that would scare the devil himself," grinned Sherrie. "And the devil should be scared."

"Military guys, huh?" asked Erin.

"Elite military, Erin. They tracked down and eliminated a whole bunch of Nazis in the Amazon last year when Dane's sister was kidnapped."

"Hey, I heard something about a Nazi new order discovered and destroyed in the Amazon."

"Well, that was Dane and Hugo," said Sherrie with a smile. "These guys are super nice but can go super bad-ass in an instant. If anyone can find us, Dane will."

"Well, in that case we better pack and be ready to go when they get here," smiled Erin.

There was a noise outside the door. It was being unlocked.

"Hell, are they here before we are ready?" asked Erin.

The heavy door opened and Mr. Brees stepped in.

"How are you ladies?" he asked. "Orrin been keeping you fed?"

"Yes, he has. But we still do not know why we are here," said Sherrie.

"All in good time, ladies, all in good time," said Brees. "But I do have a treat for you. Hot showers. Get up and come with me. I warn you not to try to escape. You are many meters below the ground with very few ways outside. You would be captured again within minutes. And the captain would not be amused. The last person who tried to escape was given a hundred lashes. Somewhere during the punishment they died." Brees hid his slight smile. He wanted to scare the girls. No one had ever tried to escape. But he wanted the girls to know he was serious.

The two girls slowly stood up against the wall opposite Brees. Now they were scared. They wanted a shower but both were worried about the circumstances. Brees motioned for them to follow him. As they left the cell, they turned right and walked several feet down a corridor. This was definitely a cave. The walls were hewn out of solid rock and the floor was uneven although much smoother than the walls or ceiling. Every sound echoed, even the sounds of their shoes on the rock floor. And there was that incessant cold wet air.

The girls noticed several other rooms or cells on both the right and left as they walked down the corridor. Some had heavy doors like theirs while some had no doors at all. Sherrie noticed the lighting was fluorescent, powered by an electrical conduit running the length of the cave on the ceiling. Someone did a great deal of work in here to make this a livable area.

Finally they turned another corner to the right and were faced with a huge steel door. Although it was painted, evidence of rust around the edges of the door bore proof of the dampness in the cave. Brees stopped and opened the door with his set of keys.

"We are going down to our living quarters where the showers are. Do not talk to anyone. Some of these men would move heaven and earth to get to you," warned Brees.

The girls said nothing. They merely nodded and followed Brees.

Once through the door the environment changed greatly. The walls and ceiling were now wood, much like a normal house. The humidity seemed much lower as well probably due to a breeze running through the building. Now they began to see others. They passed several men working on building repairs. They received long stares. Brees was right; many of these men would love to get hold of two women.

They walked past a dining room, several bunk rooms and a large common area. As they walked by, the men in the common area stopped everything to look at them. The building was large. It housed nearly a hundred men and a few older women who served as cooks or housekeepers.

The girls were paying very close attention to their surroundings and the path they were taking. They mentally mapped the route just in case they may have an opportunity to flee.

"Here we are," announced Brees. An older woman was standing beside the door with some clean clothes. "You can take a shower here without anyone bothering you. She will get you anything you need. There are also clean clothes for you."

Sherrie stepped up to the door and looked in. It was a large common shower room. On the wall to the right were six shower heads. The floor of the shower room was bare wood with wide cracks in the planks, presumably to drain the water from the shower. There was a single ten foot long bench on the far side of the room. On the wall opposite the showers were six single lavatories. She and Erin stepped into the shower room.

"This lady will guard the door. The door will stay open. If you give her any trouble, she can call us to come help her. I will be waiting across the hall to take you back to your cell," explained Brees. "Go ahead. Get your showers and get dressed."

With that, Brees turned and walked away to the room across the hall. The old woman followed the girls inside the room and placed the clean clothes on the bench. Sherrie and Erin watched as the woman walked back to the door and stood there. The girls removed their nasty clothes and placed them in a pile by the bench. As they stepped up to the shower, the old woman said something and tossed a tube of shampoo over to the shower area.

"Thank you," said Sherrie, picking up the shampoo. Meanwhile Erin had turned on the water expecting a cold dribble. She was very surprised to find a strong stream of hot water. The girls enjoyed the warmth of the water. After two days in the cold, dank cell, this was heaven. For a few minutes they felt almost normal again. That is until Erin turned around and saw Brees standing at the door smiling while watching them shower. Erin tried to cover herself and motioned for Sherrie to do so also. Sherrie glanced back and faced the wall, showing Brees as little as possible.

"Can't we have a little privacy?" yelled Sherrie. "Or is this how you get your kicks, watching women shower?"

"Looks very, very nice from here," said Brees with a wide grin. "I merely wanted to ensure the old woman was all right, but you two do look very tasty." With that comment, Brees laughed loudly and returned to the room across the hall. But this time he pulled a chair over by the door so that he could still see the girls.

Not aware of Brees' view, Erin and Sherrie continued their shower and washed their hair. Once they finished, they dried themselves and put on the clothes they were given, a pair of cotton trousers that they both had to roll up to be able to walk and a white t-shirt.

"Seems like they conveniently forgot the underwear," said Erin.

"Let's hope that is not a harbinger of things to come," added Sherrie.

The two girls looked at the old woman.

"Do you have any shoes for us?" asked Erin. She mumbled something in what sounded like a foreign language and shook her head no.

"Barefoot it is then," said Sherrie. "It's going to be a cold night with only this."

"Well, I see you are cleaned up," grinned Brees. "You look and smell much better. In fact, you look so good that I think I will let you eat in my private dining room. Follow me, please."

The trio again walked down the hall past two doors and into a small dining room with a beautiful mahogany table. There was seating for eight. This room was carpeted and had a single window. It was hard to see out due to the bright lighting in the room. But even so, Sherrie was able to see water outside. What confused her, however, was the darkness outside the window.

Erin's eyes were drawn to the art in the room. No great art critic, she did recognize several pictures she had seen before. There were two Andy Warhol pictures, what looked like a Monet and two Picassos. She wondered if these were real or merely cheap imitations.

"Please sit down, ladies," Brees said graciously. "Captain de Terr sends his regrets. He was unavoidably called away on business."

"How are you called away on pirate business?" asked Sherrie without breaking her stare on Brees.

"Pirates? My dear, there are no pirates here. We are independent businessmen who work hard to make a meager living," protested Brees.

"Yeah, tell that to the boats that you have plundered and the people you have killed," snarled Sherrie. She decided not to pull any punches.

Brees' smile disappeared from his face. "My good woman, I believe you are mistaken. We do none of that."

"Funny, you shot my brother when you tried to take our boat and you killed that poor lady on the other sailboat," said Sherrie. Erin's eyes were as big as saucers. What the hell was she doing?

"So you were on that large catamaran," said Brees quietly. "One of my closest friends was killed by one of you."

"Yeah, well, sorry…" smiled Sherrie. "He died trying to kill us. We got him first." Brees glared at Sherrie.

"Why don't you and your friend eat," said Brees. He threw down his napkin. "My appetite has suddenly turned by your foul mouth. Remember you are at my mercy here. I could turn you over to my crew and let them use you two like whores. In fact, that may be the best thing for your humility." Brees stood and stepped toward the door. "Yes, I think my crew could use some entertainment, but only after I screw your brains out." With that Brees was gone.

"Sherrie, what the hell do you think you are doing? We are going to be raped by his entire crew!"

"No, we are not," explained Sherrie. "I just wanted him to admit he was the one that shot Greg and killed the family we found. He won't hurt us. Like I said, we are being held for ransom and they need to protect their asset, us."

"I hope to God you are right, sister. He didn't look like he was kidding."

"No, but he did look a bit concerned," said Sherrie. "He knows now he has kidnapped someone who has friends that will stand up to him. He's not used to that. Now he's wondering what's going to happen. It's time for him to worry a bit instead of us now that the shoe is on the other foot."

CHAPTER FIFTY-FOUR

May 27, 2013

Police Force Headquarters, Basseterre, St. Kitts, 7:35 p.m.

The group had worked through dinner. But they devised a plan of action. There would be a two-pronged attack; one by the sea route and the other by land. Dane and Hugo with Inspector Stamper would lead the sea assault. Bob and Commissioner Nelson would lead the land incursion.

"Okay, what are we missing?" asked Hugo, playing devil's advocate.

"We just touched on weaponry," said Dane, looking over at Nelson. "What do you have in the way of assault weapons?"

Nelson picked up the phone and spoke a few words quietly. Within seconds, Captain Jones bolted through the door and joined them at the table.

"Captain Jones can update us on the arms we have available. Captain?"

"Thank you, gentlemen," he started. "We have in our armory several weapons that may interest you in this endeavor. First, in the way of pistols, we have Glock 40 caliber and 9mm pistols and Beretta M9s. As I am sure you know, these are the best hand-held weapons for combat. For assault weapons, we have the fully automatic Colt 9mm SMG and the M27 IAR (Infantry Automatic Rifle). For shotguns, we have the Remington 870 combat shotgun and the new U.S. Marines' Benelli Super 90. We also have sniper rifles, the older M40 and new M110."

The guys looked at each other in amazement. They could not believe what they were hearing. These folks had a veritable war-ready arsenal. Where in the hell did they get this stuff?

"The M110 is just being issued to the U.S. military," said Hugo, scratching his head. "These guys are hooked up."

"I see you are a bit taken back by our armament," smiled Commissioner Nelson. "We have been well armed due to some let's say U.S. involvement down in this area. While they don't advertise their actions, they are nevertheless very gracious when it comes to arming us for self-defense."

Bob looked at Nelson. "You mean to tell me you have clandestine U.S. support here in St. Kitts? I don't believe it!"

Hugo chuckled. "Well, Bob, they are pretty damned up to date to be on their own. Some of this has to come from a well-armed army."

"United States Marines, to be exact," smiled Nelson, tapping his fingers on the table in front of him.

"We in this region have been the benefactor of the United States due to our location and the drug running that occurs from time to time," added Stamper. "We help out. We look the other way and we get rewarded with supplies."

Without cracking a smile, Dane asked, "How about explosives?" Nelson waved his hand toward Jones.

"We have all types of non-lethal and lethal grenades, grenade launchers and a few dozen LAW rockets. We, of course, have dynamite, C4 and other items, including Claymores."

"Well, one thing's for certain," grinned Hugo. "We can go in there as hot as we would like!" There was a low chuckle throughout the room as the men began listing in their heads the arms they would need.

Twenty minutes later they had their arms list finalized.

The Commissioner nodded to Captain Jones. "Go ahead and gather the needed arms but don't let anyone else know. The sergeant in the armory, of course, will know but no one else." Jones looked a bit puzzled as he looked at the list and back at Nelson.

Hugo saw this and chimed in. "Ah, I think the captain may need a bit of help. That's a hefty list there. I'll give him a hand."

"I can help too," said Greg standing.

"Sure, come on along," said Hugo. "A nice strapping young guy like you makes a great pack horse." Dane laughed at the sight of Greg's face, a mixture of excitement and horror.

The trio left the room. It was 8:45 and beginning to get dark outside. Dane and Bob stepped outside for a bit of fresh air. The sea breezes were kicking up. But the breeze was refreshing after the hours they had spent in the headquarters. The humidity was high, the air being heavy rather than fresh. A faint rumble in the distance announced an approaching evening storm.

"Well, Dane, what do you think we will run into?" asked Bob quietly. He reached into his shirt pocket and pulled out two Cuban Cohiba cigars. "Smoke" Dane took the cigar, bit off the end and accepted the light from Bob? It was a medium sweet smoke. Bob lit his and they both stood on the sidewalk in front of the Police Force Headquarters enjoying the calm.

"I'm not sure but we had better be ready. I can't believe these so-called pirates have operated this long without being detected. That tells me we are up against a very sophisticated enemy, one that has discipline, courage and firepower. They also have money! And that, Bob, is what worries me. Bad guys with money can buy very bad things to kill people. We know they have nerve gas in their hands. Whether the gas is in their lair, we don't know. But I would not assume anything. I plan on it being there. We have to surprise them and kill them before they know what hit them."

Bob stroked his beard, now sporting a two-day growth. "I have to agree with you," said Bob. "We have to go in like there is no tomorrow. Like that time in Fallujah. Kill 'em all and let God sort 'em out."

CHAPTER FIFTY-FIVE

May 27, 2013

Beneath Brimstone Hill, St. Kitts, 8:20 p.m.

Erin and Sherrie were returned to their cell after having a very good meal of fish, various vegetables, rice and plantains. There was even chocolate cake for dessert.

While they were gone someone had cleaned their cell and placed two cots with pillows and blankets to replace the hay on the floor. Over in one corner was a small chemical toilet and toilet paper.

"Well, it seems we are important to someone," said Erin, surveying their new digs.

"I told you we were safe. We are worth too much to someone. Probably that Captain de Terr Brees told us about earlier," said Sherrie.

"I can't figure it out. Why are we so important to the captain?"

"That I don't know," sighed Sherrie. "I simply wish they would let us go."

"Well, since I don't think we are going to come up with an answer any time soon, I would suggest we get some sleep," said Erin, taking a closer look at the cots. "Hey, these aren't bad. They're much better than the hard floor."

The two girls were almost ready for bed when there was a knock on the door. A few seconds later the door lock turned and the door slowly swung open.

"Missies, can I come in?" said the raspy voice. It was Orrin. "I hope you found the new things the captain left you. He wanted me to check on you one last time to make sure you are comfortable."

Sherrie turned to Orrin and smiled. She could not help but like the poor man. It was his kindness in this hell-hole that made it tolerable. "Thank you, Orrin. We do appreciate you helping us."

"Yes, you have been a Godsend," added Erin.

"Aww, I only wanted you to be comfortable. It gets very cold down here."

"I bet it does," said Sherrie, trying to make conversation. "We are used to being out in the sun and ocean breezes. When we don't have that it is really hard to survive."

"I know what you mean," said Orrin, loosening his grip on the door. "I can only spend a few days down here in the cave until I have to go outside and get fresh air and sunshine. "

"I wish we could do that," Sherrie said. "Is there any chance we might get to go outside?"

"I can't say," said Orrin, glancing behind him to see if anyone was watching.

"We would be so thankful to anyone that would let us just go outside for a few minutes. We would come right back in, I promise," begged Sherrie. Erin sat on her cot. She knew what Sherrie was doing and decided to let her go for it.

"Well, you know, I might be able to do something, but we should wait until everyone else is asleep. With only the guards on duty, I may be able to take you out for a minute or two."

Without warning Brees was standing behind Orrin. "You little whelp!" he screamed. He stepped forward and punched Orrin hard in the abdomen. Orrin doubled up and hit the floor like a sack of potatoes. "You let these two out and I will kill you. Do you understand me?" As Orrin rolled on the floor trying mightily to catch his breath, Brees kicked him in the face. Brees' boot smashed Orrin's nose and blood flew all over the floor.

"You damned brute!" screamed Sherrie. She rushed over to Orrin and knelt beside him. Not only was Orrin's nose broken but he had lost a tooth, maybe two. Erin rushed Brees. He simply brushed her off like a gnat, spun her around and slapped her so hard she slammed against the wall, falling to the floor.

"Stop it, dammit, stop it!" screamed Sherrie. Brees stepped back, relishing his work. Orrin was a bloody mess and the other girl was out like a light. He looked at his hand and laughed.

"She sure can't take a punch," he grinned. "And it was only a slap."

"You are such a big man," said Sherrie angrily. "You do a great job of beating up old men and girls. You are such an ass."

"Watch your mouth, girlie, or I will knock your butt out too. I don't want to hear any more of your mouth. Is that clear?" he snarled.

Sherrie stared at him. It was a stare that would have caused many men to shrink away. Sure Sherrie was pretty, but she could be as mean as hell if she needed to be. But now was not the time. She noticed all of the yelling and commotion had yielded several more of Brees' men, now peering in the open door.

"Need any help, sir?" asked one of the crew.

"No," answered Brees. He looked at the man but spoke to Sherrie. "But if this happens again, I'll let the boys here have you."

Sherrie's stare continued. Finally she spoke, "In time, I will see you dead." Brees threw back his head and laughed. He turned to his men.

"Oh, I am so scared," laughed Brees as his men joined in the laughter. "Drag the old man out and clean him up. Then lock the door and post a guard here. No one but the captain or I is allowed in here." With that he grinned at Sherrie and stepped toward the door. "Oh, by the way, no food for a few days. Sorry, we have a shortage." Brees was still laughing as he left the cell, his men dragging Orrin behind.

The door slammed shut and all was quiet again. Sherrie moved over to Erin, who was beginning to stir.

"Erin, are you all right?"

"What happened?" she answered, still groggy from the slap and collision with the wall.

"That ass Brees slapped the crap out of you. Don't you remember?" asked Sherrie.

Erin sat up and placed her palm on the side of her face. It was blood red. "Now I remember. He must have hit me when I tried to get him to stop hurting Orrin." She regained her composure and immediately began whipping her head around looking for Orrin. "Where is he?" she cried. "Oh, God, don't tell me they killed the poor man."

"Shhh…" said Sherrie quietly. "Orrin's okay. They beat him up good but he seemed to be all right when they took him away. But after that, I don't think we will see him again, at least not for a while."

"For a while?" Erin blurted out. "How long do you think we will be down here?" For the first time Erin began to sob. "I guess the real answer is we are never going to get out."

Sherrie hugged her and gave her a big squeeze. "Hey, girlfriend, we will get out of here. I know it. Dane and Hugo will track us to the end of the world. They will get us out."

Sherrie laid her head against Erin's. She certainly hoped what she said was true. But in reality she had no clue as to what was or was not happening in the outside world.

CHAPTER FIFTY-SIX

May 28, 2013

On the road to Brimstone Hill, St. Kitts, 2:10 a.m.

The group rode in two simple panel vans so as to not be noticed. The teams were ready; fully armed, camoed, and slightly nervous. About two miles from the hill the trucks pulled over to the beach side of the road.

What there was of a moon was fully obscured behind clouds from the storm earlier that night. The constant sea breeze blew through the group, adding to their nervousness. The fresh smell of the sea clashed with the job that must be done.

The local policemen were not accustomed to an all-out assault on a fortified position. Several of the men were veterans of various militaries but none had seen any action.

Team One included Dane, Hugo, Greg, and Captain Jones along with two of his men. Team Two consisted of Inspector Stamper, Bob, and four more policemen. Commissioner Nelson and several of his men would stay behind and coordinate as needed.

Team One would make the water assault. They were to enter the water south of the cove and get into the pirates' lair via the waterway Dane and Hugo had used a few days ago.

Team Two's route was much more dangerous. They would breach the fences out by the roadway and gain entry to what they believed was a cave entrance from the wooded area southeast of the cave. Their route was more perilous since the group had very little information as to what they might find. They knew the entrance existed, but beyond that fact, they knew nothing of how many guards they might encounter or any other defensive conditions. But they had the advantage of an easy retreat if the assault went wrong.

The water assault was much more dangerous in retreat; there was only one way out.

The group stood silently pondering their operation. Each man reviewed his responsibilities in his head. They also considered the lives of the two women thought to be inside.

"You all have your maps. Take a last look if you need to. You have your rendezvous points. You know your escape routes. Any questions?" asked Dane quietly.

"Looks like the moon and clouds are cooperating with us," said Hugo, reaching in his pocket for chewing gum. "At least we will have the cover of darkness and not be lit up by moonlight." Several men scanned the sky above and nodded in agreement. Very few words were spoken.

Greg was clearly nervous. He had no idea what he was getting into but knew that they must rescue the girls; that is if they were in there.

Dane scanned the area with his well-trained eyes looking for any abnormality that might foretell trouble. There were no boats at sea. He gazed up and down the road. He saw nothing again. Finally he listened. He heard wind rustling leaves on the trees but nothing else. He turned to the group.

"Okay, men. This is it," he began. "Rule one... go slow but steady. We cannot afford to go on a hell bent charge into these compounds since we don't fully know what we are up against. That's especially true for you guys, Bob. We do strongly feel there is a cave down that hidden road. One that leads into the mountain and is somehow connected to the sea cave Hugo and I found. But we have no idea of their strength."

"Yeah, but at two in the morning I'll bet three-quarters of them will be asleep. The ones awake and on guard will be sleepy and not expecting an armed incursion," grinned Bob.

"You are probably right but don't count on it. If you assume an elite fighting force, we have one up on them already. Inspector, are you ready?" asked Dane.

Stamper looked at his men, all who gave a "strong thumbs up".

"We are ready!" exclaimed Inspector Stamper.

"Okay, gentlemen, time to lock and load," said Dane quietly.

With that, he cocked his assault rifle and pressed the safety to the on position. The others checked their magazines and side arms and readied their weapons. In the quiet, the snapping and clicking of the safeties and ammo magazines sounded deafening.

"Move out" came Dane's command and the operation began.

The two teams began their assault. Team One raced down to the beach close to the shore and proceeded north toward the cove entrance to the cave.

Team Two did the same racing down the side of the road to just south of the hidden road to the back entrance of the cave. It was on.

CHAPTER FIFTY-SEVEN

May 28, 2013

Beneath Brimstone Hill, St. Kitts, 2:20 a.m.

First Officer Dante Brees sat at the table with his drink. He looked at his watch. It was very late but he knew there was nothing scheduled for the morning. He smiled to himself as he recalled beating Orrin.

"That piece of crap was going to let those two girls out to get a breath of fresh air," he said quietly. Captain deTerr sat across the table with his cigar, a Perdomo 20th Anniversary Maduro. He seldom smoked anything other than Cubans but this was one of his favorite Nicaraguan cigars. Besides, it was from a box he stole from the sailboat they scuttled. You can't beat the price, he thought.

He looked Brees squarely in the eyes. He took a slow draw on his cigar and meticulously exhaled the smoke in little rings. He tapped the ash into the ashtray on the table in front of him.

"You know that if those two girls had gotten away I would have sliced your gut open and fed your intestines to the fish," he said in a very matter-of-fact voice.

Brees knew he was not kidding. De Terr was a monster. He had seen de Terr personally kill several of his crew as well as many, many others. The man was a psychopath.

He loved to inflict severe pain before allowing his victim to die. Just a few weeks ago Brees had witnessed de Terr interrogate a man found in the woods just outside the compound. When the man could not answer questions put to him, de Terr stripped him of his clothes and tied him to a chair. If front of several of the crew de Terr simply took a knife and began slicing large cuts into the man's legs and arms. His screams were hideous. He was careful not to cut any large arteries or veins as that would cause the man to bleed to death quickly. De Terr wanted him to die slowly and painfully.

As some of the crew grimaced at the sight, de Terr simply laughed as he continued to question the man. Finally, after slicing the man about his entire body, de Terr bent down and whispered something to the man, whose eyes widened wildly. Almost instantly, de Terr's knife was buried in the man's gut and ripped him crosswise, spilling his entrails in a pile on the floor. The man's face turned from horror and pain to a blank stare as he died looking at his insides on the floor.

De Terr coughed, bringing Bree's mind back to the present.

"Any more news on the big job?" asked Brees.

"Yeah. Since we are alone I can tell you exactly what is happening. As you know, we have received the shipment of nerve gas.

"Yes, I know," answered Brees. "I took personal charge of getting stored and secured."

"Very good."

"So when are we going to get the details?" asked Brees.

De Terr smiled. "Tonight we will find out more."

Brees grinned widely. He knew this job was going to make him a multi-millionaire. He was ready to spend his share. "Hell, yes!" he cried.

"Calm down, my friend," assured deTerr. "You must show restraint. This has been a long time in the making and we must do it well."

"Yes, sir!" said Brees loudly, leaning back in his chair. "My God, we will all be rich!"

"Now, now, Mr. Brees, take it easy. Not all of us will be rich but only a select few; Hawk, his confidants and you and me. We will never have to want again. That I guarantee you. But first, I have been told we will have visitors tonight."

"Here? Who would want to come here to see us?" asked Brees. He thought for a moment. Who in his right mind would want to come here? "Is Hawk coming?"

De Terr smiled and stood. "There is a very good chance of that, Mr. Brees. But right now I need to go get ready for our visitors. Stay here. I will return in a few minutes and fill you in."

As deTerr left the room Brees sat back and took a large gulp from his drink. He loved rum. He was raised on rum by his parents and even spent time with his uncle distilling the golden elixir. But that was long ago. He and his family were poor. They had little to eat except what they could glean from some farmer's fields or gather in the jungle. He swore to himself that when he was older he would never be poor again. That was the rationale for his becoming a pirate.

CHAPTER FIFTY-EIGHT

May 28, 2013

Outside Brimstone Hill, St. Kitts, 2:40 a.m.

Team One reached the water entrance to the cave. They were ahead of schedule. Hugo led them into the water. It took only twenty minutes to jog down the beach and enter the water about one hundred yards south of the cove. They silently slipped into the dark water and began to slowly swim to the cove entrance. At the cove, Hugo turned and waited until the entire group was around him.

"As you enter the opening, be aware that there are two lookout posts up above the entrance to the cave, one on each side. We have to hug the right shore and move very slowly as to not create any large wave action. It's probably too dark for them to see but we still need to be careful. As planned, I will take point and Dane will trail all of us. We go in and rendezvous under the dock. Everyone understand?"

There were nods from everyone.

"Okay, let's get to it," said Hugo as he turned and stealthily moved around the bend and into the cove. The group moved slowly just as Hugo asked. All eyes were on the opposite shore, trying intently to spot the lookout nest.

They moved slowly. Only their heads protruded from the water. By not creating any waves, the group moved silently, unseen by the guards they knew were above. Upon reaching the far right outer edge of the cave opening, the group gathered again. Hugo scanned the far side of the cove watching the guard station intently. This time there was no tell-tale glow of a burning cigarette or cigar; just total darkness.

Hugo slid down the line and reached the edge of the cave gate. He pulled it back slightly and peered into the darkness inside. He saw nothing. He turned and looked back at the men and motioned for them to swim in one by one. The only sound was the waves outside the cove and the strong breeze blowing onto shore.

When the last man entered, Hugo waited until Dane brought up the rear.

"Okay, here's where the real work starts," said Dane in a whisper. "Stay in line and hug the right side here. As you can see, there are some ripples and a few waves so our movement can be slightly faster than out in the cove. Hugo will lead. As we told you back in town, our objective is the docks that you will see about a half mile into the cave. Stay sharp. Stay alert. These folks are not looking for visitors and once they see us, they will not like it at all. Everyone ready?"

Again a series of blank face nods betrayed their anxiousness. But they were willing to move on.

Dane looked at Greg. His eyes were wide, showing fear as to what was to come. "You okay?" Dane whispered.

"Ready and willing," answered Greg. "Let's get the girls."

Dane nodded and smiled. The kid was scared but he was brave enough to keep going. He respected him for that even though it was his sister in there.

The group continued their swim down the side of the cave in the dark with Hugo taking point and Dane trailing. After a few minutes they could see a dim light coming from deep in the cave. The group simply lowered their heads deeper into the water and kept swimming and sliding down the side of the cave.

Now they could see a bend ahead. Then they could see the dim, almost muted lights over the water at the dock. Hugo raised his fist to stop everyone. One last check before they began the last several hundred yard swim to the dock and safety. Hugo turned to each man and gave a thumbs-up signal. All returned the same. They were ready to go.

Before Hugo could turn around, a huge bright spotlight lit up the cave and bathed the group in light. The entire group was illuminated but just as quickly the group sank low in the water. Two or three bursts of an automatic weapon rang out in the cave. The water around them foamed with hot lead. Instantly the entire team was under fire and in the worst place, a few hundred yards from cover. Hugo slapped his hand on the water and the group dropped below the surface, each grabbing for the snorkels strapped to their chests. Thank God Hugo had decided to add the snorkels at the last planning meeting.

One of Jones' men twitched violently. He had been hit. Jones grabbed him and pulled him up against the rocks and into a tight niche. Both came to the surface just inches from the search light now scanning the area.

"You all right?" asked Jones.

"Just a nick on the arm," answered the man. "It stings like hell, but it's not a problem. I can go on."

Jones felt a tug on his leg as Dane surfaced as the light scanned out into the middle of the cave. The man held up a thumbs-up sign and all three sank below the surface again.

Hugo had moved ahead. He was determined to put out the light. Even with his gear he swam through the water like a torpedo. Once he had a bearing on the dock, he dove to a depth of about eight feet and took off.

Dane gathered the others and pointed down. The light was returning to the side of the cave they were on. They too dropped below the surface with only their snorkels breaking the surface.

As the pirates continued to scan for the team, Hugo approached the dock. Looking up he could see the figures of two men standing beside the light. He slowly rose to the surface under the dock at the men's feet. He looked back in the cave. No sign of Dane and the others. That was good news! He waited until the searchlight scanned over to the opposite side of the cave again and pounced.

Hugo took two knives from their scabbards on each side of his chest, reached up and placed one hand on the deck of the dock. Taking one quick move, he lurched out of the water until his shoulders were level with the deck. Before he fell back, he used both blades to sever the Achilles tendon on one leg of each of the pirates. The pirates felt the sharp sting of Hugo's blade and collapsed together on the deck. Before each could scream, Hugo pulled himself up onto the dock and dispatched both men quickly with his knives.

There was immediate silence. Hugo's eyes raced from side to side trying to detect any movement, any threat. There was none. But he knew others would be there quickly after the burst of gunfire. Actually, he was shocked no one else had come running out.

Hugo turned back toward the water to see the snorkels of the rest of the team approaching the dock. He replaced his knives and broke out his automatic weapon. He was ready to lay down covering fire if needed. He scanned the area again and turned his attention to the team. Jones was climbing out of the water via a short ladder over near the cave side. One of Jones' men was floating about three feet from the dock, his weapon ready in case it was needed. Dane followed Jones onto the dock. They squatted in a group until all of the team was feet dry. Dane looked over Jones' shoulder. His eyes were drawn to an inscription in the rock...1699. Dane pointed at the date.

"This has been here a while."

They had made it in.

CHAPTER FIFTY-NINE

May 28, 2013

Beneath Brimstone Hill, St. Kitts, 2:40 a.m.

Team Two found the hidden road although it was more like a trail than what one would call a road. It really was a narrow set of two dusty bare areas packed between a myriad of trees, bushes and assorted undergrowth. It was clear this entrance was not to be advertised. In fact, if someone stood directly in front of it, most folks would think it a long abandoned road, nothing else.

A moderate sea breeze blew through the leaves serving to cover the footsteps of the group. The only problem was that the wind noise and the rustling of the leaves made it hard to hear anyone stalking them. Bob was in the lead on the right side of the trail with Inspector Stamper and two more men. They quickly made their way up the road, stopping only when they encountered a gate and checkpoint. They could see a single red glow in the five foot by five foot guardhouse. One of the guards was smoking. Inspector Stamper turned to Bob.

"Looks like only one guard," he said quietly.

"Don't know... maybe more but only one smoking," answered Bob, keeping his eye focused squarely on the guardhouse.

Stamper stared at the guardhouse, trying hard to determine if there was someone else inside. "I can't tell. There could be another guard but it looks as though there is very little room in that guardhouse."

Bob nodded and motioned for one of the men on the team to move up and take a look. The man he picked was an ex French Foreign Legion sapper whose job it once was to sneak into enemy territory and silently kill as many of the enemy as possible. And he was very good at his previous job.

The man quickly and silently made his way up to the guardhouse and knelt beside the door. He peered in to find a single guard staring out the window, a cigar in his hand. Seconds later the guard was dead and the cigar was lying on the floor. The sapper motioned for the team to move up. One down.

The small group scurried in single file up to the protection of the guardhouse. Beyond the guardhouse the road narrowed even more. The group silently moved up the left side of the road until they came to a sudden open area. There it was, the cave entrance! It was apparent that the trees around the small clearing had been purposely grown to provide a canopy overhang. This entrance was nearly invisible from above.

The group formed up with Bob as he peered at the cave entrance. There were two men working on a truck over to the far right of the opening under a bright hand-held work light. Both of their heads were under the hood. There were no signs of weapons.

"That looks like the only folks out here," Bob said, turning to Stamper. "If we move along this side behind those crates and barrels, we can get inside without them seeing us," he said, pointing to the left

Stamper looked over the area quickly. "Yes, I think we can. With that bright light those guys will not be able to see us over on this dark side. It looks good to me."

But something was wrong. Stamper felt it. It didn't make sense that such a high security operation would only have one guard and have two bozos working on a truck outside with a bright work light, and at 3:00 a.m. But maybe they were just too confident in their security. He tried to brush away the thoughts forming in his mind as just his thinking too much.

Bob broke his crouch and motioned for the group to follow him. He moved to his far left, nearly in the underbrush, behind a few crates and fuel drums. Once there, they took another look at their position.

"We have good cover here," said Bob, glancing back at Stamper and his men. "Leave one of your men here to cover our escape. He will have the perfect position for cover fire as we come out."

"I agree," answered Stamper. He turned to one of his men. "Stay here and cover us. If all hell breaks loose and we don't come back, work your way back to the road and go report to Commissioner Nelson. He can get us help fast. We will hold out until you return. If all goes as planned, we should be back out in thirty or so minutes. Hopefully we will have the girls. If not, well, we will cover that later."

Stamper looked at Bob. "Ready?"

"Is a pig's butt pork?" answered Bob with a smile.

Stamper looked at him as if he were crazy. What the hell did that mean?

The group, now down to Bob, Stamper and three of Stamper's men headed toward the cave entrance.

Again working around from the left side, they reached the cave entrance and stopped to check for a guard. There was none. Stamper still wondered why there was only the one guard. The one they killed was not sufficient for maximum security. This time he could not hold back his thoughts.

He tapped Bob on the shoulder. "Bob, there should be more guards."

Bob turned to Stamper. "Why's that?"

"It just does not seem right that merely one guard is on duty for this entrance. Unless those two grease monkeys are supposed to be guards as well," reasoned Stamper.

"You see anyone else out here?" he asked Stamper.

"No. It's more like a feeling than anything else. I just can't put my finger on it. If this was my lair, I would have ten or more guards and security patrols," explained Stamper.

"Yeah, I see your point, but at the same time I don't see anyone else out here. Maybe they are merely lax about their security."

"I can't see that, Bob. These guys are good, really good. And they have money, funds enough to have tip-top security. I sense a trap."

"We can sit here and speculate all night," said Bob. "But," looking at his watch, "we only have a few hours before sunrise and we damn well better be out of here by then. So we can sit around and look for more guards or take advantage of what looks like their screwup and get this job done."

Stamper looked at Bob. It was against his gut feeling but finally the words came out, "Do it."

With that, the group scooted around the corner and into the cave. To say it was dark was an understatement. It was as dark as pitch once the weak light from the work lamp the workers were using faded from their view.

The team moved down the side of the cave with Bob feeling their way along. They had moved only about forty feet into the cave when four muffled shots rang out. Instantly a heavy canvas curtain fell across the cave entrance about fifteen feet behind them. Slowly a light came up to the intensity of a normal room. Stamper and his three men lay on the floor. The men were bloody with bullet wounds to their heads. If not dead, they would soon be. Standing over them was Bob Rand, untouched.

CHAPTER SIXTY

May 28, 2013

Beneath Brimstone Hill, St. Kitts, 2:40 a.m.

Orrin Mattson was furious. He had taken the beating from Brees and was mad as hell. He wanted revenge even if it meant his own death. His face still hurt from Brees' attack. He lay in his bunk thinking of all of the ways to get back at Brees.

He could kill Brees. That would be the best thing since he would never have to see him again. But one of Brees' men would probably kill him. He didn't want that if he could avoid it. If he did anything else, he would have to leave the island and hide forever. Brees and his men would hunt him down like a dog. But he had to get back at that man, that miserable, poor excuse for a human being.

Then it came to him. The girls! They must be extremely important to him in some way. After all, his reaction to him trying to just let the girls get some air was very extreme. He didn't know the link but there evidently was a strong one there.

Orrin checked his watch. It was almost a quarter to three in the morning. He was sure Brees would be asleep along with ninety-nine percent of everyone else. He would have to hurry, though. He needed to begin his shift as a cook by five a.m.

Orrin liked the girls. They were very nice to him and treated him with respect. If he could throw a monkey wrench into the plans, it might get Brees in trouble with the captain. One thing Orrin knew, you do not want to get the captain mad at you. He may kill you. If the girls were as important to the captain as he thought, Brees losing them would not be good for the first officer.

So Orrin decided to help the girls escape. He jumped out of his bunk. His face still hurt from the kick from Brees' boot. The teeth he lost hurt even more. His anger increased.

Orrin dressed silently in the bunk room and checked on the others asleep in their bunks. All of them were asleep, snoring away. He crept toward the door and opened it slightly. If he was caught out in the hall, he would say he was going to work early. Thankfully there was no one there as he stepped out and closed the door quietly behind him; now to get to the girls.

Orrin walked quietly down the halls until he came to the area that was once the old mine. De Terr and Brees had modified the old mine tunnels to create a near escape-proof group of cells where their prisoners were housed. That is if they brought back any prisoners at all. They rarely did except for a few women that the men used for "entertainment" or a young, beautiful girl that was worth a small fortune in the white slave market.

Thankfully at this hour there were very few men awake. Orrin only expected to encounter the night guards. As he came down the tunnel to the girls' cell, he heard a series of muffled bangs. It must be someone moving cargo, he thought.

He stopped at the corner and peeked around. There was a guard sitting in a chair outside the girls' cell. That concerned him. He was not expecting a guard. But then he thought the guard was there to keep them in. That he could understand. Hopefully he was not expecting someone trying to get in.

He watched the guard for a minute. Curiously he was not moving at all. Was this idiot asleep? If the captain or Brees saw this, the man would be severely punished. Orrin made a shuffling noise to test the guard's attention. He didn't move.

Orrin stepped back from the corner. He needed something to knock out the guard. He backtracked to the first open door he found and peered in. He knew it was a storeroom and no one should be in there. He opened the door wide to get some light in the small closet-like room and found a hefty pipe wrench on a shelf among other maintenance tools. That would definitely do the trick, he thought. Taking the wrench, he exited the closet and walked back to the corner.

Again he looked down the hall toward the girls' cell. The guard was still asleep. How lucky, he thought. Methodically Orrin crept up to the guard and slammed the pipe wrench down on the guard's head. There was a sickening crunch and the man fell to the floor like a sack of potatoes. Blood streamed from his head. Oh, no, thought Orrin, I hit him too hard. I think I killed him!

He reached down and riffled through the guard's pockets until he found the key to the cell. He unlocked the door and stepped into the cell. It was dark and quiet. The girls were asleep. He smiled to himself. How very different it was in a room with sleeping girls. Men snored like bulls. This room was silent.

CHAPTER SIXTY-ONE

May 28, 2013

Beneath Brimstone Hill, St. Kitts, 3:00 a.m.

Sherrie and Erin were sleeping soundly when Orrin shook them awake.

"Get up, ladies. Get up quickly!" he said in a subdued but frantic voice. "I'm going to get you out of here."

Sherrie wiped her eyes and looked up at him. "Orrin, what are you doing here?"

"I have come to get you out. But we have to be quiet and we must hurry. Get her ready to go," he said, looking over at Erin.

"That won't take but a second," answered Erin, jumping to her feet. "Let's go!"

Sherrie stood up and the two followed Orrin to the door. That's when they saw the guard.

"Oh, God!" cried Sherrie. "Is he dead?"

"I'm afraid I hit him harder than I thought," said Orrin almost apologetically. "I didn't mean to kill him, Missy."

"Serves the bastard right," added Erin. She was pissed and was showing her anger. "I'm happy to kill every last one of them."

"Should we pull his body in here?" asked Sherrie.

"No. We don't have the time. They will find him anyway. Look at all of the blood on the floor."

"He's right," blurted Erin. "We don't have the time. Let's move!"

The group scurried down the tunnel to the corner. Both girls were barefoot, their feet making a slight slapping noise as they ran.

"Please be quiet. Try to run softly."

Orrin looked around. There was no one in sight. The group paused for a moment.

"Can you swim?" he asked Sherrie and Erin.

"Hell, yes, we can swim," answered Sherrie. "Just get us to the water and we will be gone."

"Okay," smiled Orrin. "There are two ways out. One is the main tunnel out the back of the mountain. It connects with a dirt road that leads to the main road back to Basseterre. But that is where most of those who are awake at this time of day will be. So we can't go out there. But there is a way out to the docks and out to the sea by the sea cave."

"Sea cave?" said Erin confused. "What sea cave?"

Orrin grinned. "The one you will use to get out of this hell hole!"

"Works for me," added Sherrie. "Which way do we go?"

"Follow me. Be very, very quiet. We have to pass the officers' quarters where the captain and Mr. Brees' cabins are located. If they find us, we are all dead."

"Sounds like a good safety tip," joked Sherrie. Erin smiled. Just like Sherrie to make a joke at a time like this.

Stealthily they moved down the hall. Suddenly Orrin froze. Voices! Someone was coming down the hall ahead. He spun around and looked for a door. About four feet away was the door to the kitchen. It looked like their only escape, but was anyone in there?

Orrin cracked open the door. The light was on! Someone was working. He looked closer and saw another cook mixing what looked like bread dough at the far end of the room. He turned to the girls and motioned for them to follow.

They entered the kitchen without a sound. It did help, however, that the other cook was singing. As the cook belted out some local song, Orrin led the girls behind some storage shelving and told them to hide. Then he returned to the door and stepped out.

Two men were walking down the hall toward the main dining mess around the corner. Orrin stepped across in front of them and reached for the doorknob on the closet in front of him.

"Good morning!" Orrin said in a bright voice. "Are you up early or are you coming off your shift?"

"We are getting an early start," answered one of the men smiling. "Looks like you are too."

"We cooks are always up early," replied Orrin. "Somebody has to cook for you."

"Make it good, Orrin," said the other man. "I'm hungry as hell this morning. We have a big day today."

"Oh, really?" Orrin asked. "What's up?"

"We have guests arriving today. We have to make certain everything is in fine order for them."

"Okay then. Go on in to the mess and I will get some breakfast very soon," said Orrin as he watched the men continue down the hall, disappearing around the corner.

Quickly he ducked back into the kitchen to find the girls quietly waiting.

"I think the way is clear now. Follow me. And be very quiet," whispered Orrin as he led them back into the hall. They were getting closer and closer to freedom.

CHAPTER SIXTY-TWO

May 28, 2013

Beneath Brimstone Hill, St. Kitts, 3:00 a.m.

Team One had control of the dock area. Dane spread his men about in defensive positions waiting for a counterattack. But there was none.

"So we get shot at in a cave and no one comes running?" questioned Hugo.

"Yeah, we have a problem," replied Dane. "This is a trap, pure and simple. They gave up the two guys out here hoping that we will blindly enter the building and then they will kill us all."

"I don't know about you, Boss, but I ain't playing that game," Hugo said sharply.

"Me neither," added Dane. "We are going to screw up their world and take them all down."

"That's my man!" Hugo gave Dane a huge grin. "I'm thinking we can cause a diversion out here and see if we can draw these bastards out into the open. If we set it up right, we should be able to pin them down and try to get inside to see if the girls are there. What do you think?"

Dane sat stoically for a second or two. "Not a bad idea. Position Greg and the men around the dock here. Put one in the boat over there so he has a clear view of the main door. You and I will go up a level and get into the building from there. If we work it right, we can end up behind them with these guys in front. That should do it."

"Agreed," said Hugo, keeping a watchful eye for movement inside the building. He motioned to everyone to do a quick huddle-up and explained the plan.

"Greg, you are in charge here. You have to hold this position or else we may not have an escape route. Understand?"

"I do," said Greg quietly. "We will stand our ground here. Don't worry about us. We will be okay. You and Dane go see if the girls are here."

Hugo smiled and tapped Greg on the shoulder. "I have all the confidence in the world you will."

Each man took his place. They were ready.

Dane and Hugo went over to the far left side of the dock and climbed up the rope from the makeshift crane above. Once in place, Dane signaled the men below. They began firing into the building and the area around it more to make noise than cause damage. Within seconds they were under heavy return fire from the inside. Three men burst from the door and attempted to shoot the team members. The problem was they couldn't see Greg and the guys. Dane's forces mowed the pirates down in a hail of gunfire.

By this time, those inside the building and back into the caves were swarming like bees. They grabbed their guns and other weapons and prepared to wreak havoc on the intruders. Led by Brees, they felt they could repel any invaders no matter how many there were. But Brees quickly found he was up against well-trained and well-armed professionals who had good cover and were not about to leave it. Not a good equation.

As the firefight ensued, Dane and Hugo made their way back into one of the upper caves and deeper into the mountain. There seemed to be no one in the cave. As they continued further into the cave, they reached a heavy iron door which blocked further access.

"End of the line here," cried Hugo over the echoing sounds of gunfire below.

"Yeah, we need to double back and take that right turn back there. Hurry before we get trapped here."

As they turned, two armed men came around the corner running. They were no match for both Hugo and Dane. They were shredded in two seconds of fire.

"Like I said, let's get out of here now!" screamed Dane, breaking into a trot. "We can't get caught down this dead end."

Hugo followed. They slowed slightly to round the corner just before they came to the passage to the left Dane spoke of before.

"Quick. Down here!" he yelled.

Hugo checked their six and then followed Dane into the other tunnel. This cave was much newer than the other. It still held fresh pickaxe and chisel marks on the walls. About twenty feet back they could see faint light. Dane signaled Hugo to be alert.

The light was coming from the lower level. There was a stairway leading down to a well-lit area below.

"Looks like we found the gopher hole," said Dane, pointing down.

"Let's flush 'em out," added Hugo.

"Careful. We don't know what is down there."

"I do...bad guys," said Hugo with a smirk. "I'm going to get me some."

"Damn," said Dane under his breath. "Hell-bent Hugo."

Hugo led the way down the steps, his automatic weapon leveled for instant use. He took a few steps down and crouched to see more. The stairway led to an open area that looked like the entrance area in a house. There was a nice leather chair on one side and a large piece of mahogany furniture, a huge bookshelf on the opposite wall. Doorways flanked each end. With the room empty, Hugo jumped to the floor below and took a position beside the bookcase so he could cover both ends of the room. He looked up at Dane and signaled the all clear.

Dane rushed down the stairs and crouched on the opposite wall beside the chair. Now they had complete control of both accesses to the room. Suddenly a pirate ran in. Hugo nailed him instantly. He was dead before he hit the floor. The man sprawled across the middle of the room.

"We need to find a quieter place," said Hugo.

"We need to find the girls," said Dane. Hugo nodded in agreement.

"That way has to be out so let's go this way," he said, pointing to the opposite way than they had entered. "If the girls are here, they are back there," said Dane over the sound of gunfire down the hall to his right.

"Go!" cried Hugo. The two men moved quickly down the hall. They were amazed that the pirates were not swarming them. Everyone seemed to be either deeper in the cave or back at the dock. They continued down hall after hall, checking each room that they encountered. No girls so far.

CHAPTER SIXTY-THREE

De Terr stepped over and stood beside Stamper. The inspector moaned and opened his eyes.

"Damn, man, I bet that hurts," said deTerr smiling. "What are you trying to do coming in here, my house? You knew we would kill you all." Stamper grimaced with pain; two bullets had ripped into his abdomen and one had smashed his leg. He was slowly dying.

"You piece of ..." groaned Stamper.

"Now, now," said someone to Stamper's left. "We cannot have language like that. It's not very nice."

Inspector Stamper knew that voice. He turned his head to see Bob Rand standing there smiling.

"You were right to think this was a trap. Too bad you didn't follow your own advice. It got you shot and all of your men killed. Yeah, even the poor guy we left outside for cover. We took good care of him too."

"You son-of-a-bitch," barked Stamper. "You were in on this all the time!"

Rand bellowed. "Damn, man, what did you expect? I had to protect my own people."

Stamper let out a long sigh and slowly closed his eyes. For him the fight was over.

"He's no worry to us now," said de Terr. "You men get him out of here. We will dispose of all the bodies at sea. Take them in and get some chains and concrete block ready. The fish will eat tomorrow."

Three men pulled the bodies further back into the tunnel.

Bob checked his watch. It was almost dawn outside. But where were Dane and Hugo?

"What about the other entrance? What's the status?" he asked.

DeTerr turned quickly as two men ran from deeper in the cave.

"They killed most of our men," one man said, trying to catch his breath. "They are everywhere."

"Wait a minute," said de Terr. "What do you mean they are everywhere?"

"They have many men attacking at the dock. We lost most of the crew within a minute. Now there are more men inside the compound. They are in the caves and the building. We have to leave here now!"

The first sign of fear rolled onto de Terr's face. Not as much from the report of the intruders but from what he thought Hawk would do.

"Where's Brees?" he demanded.

"He is back there with Smith," he screamed, pointing back toward the dock. "They are trying to keep the men fighting. But they are all going to die."

De Terr decided to take matters into his own hands.

"Get off your asses and get back there," bellowed de Terr. "Get everyone else and rid the cave of all attackers. If you don't succeed, I will kill you myself. Do you understand?"

The two men looked at each other, scared to death. What were they to do? If they refused, they would be killed. If they returned to the battle, they would surely die as well. "Yes, sir! We will get them out of here. I promise." That was their only chance to live. So they took it.

"If you succeed, I will make certain that you get paid well for your service," added Rand. "Now go!"

The men turned and ran back into the cave, screaming for all of the men to follow them. De Terr smiled.

"They will get the job done. Brees will not fail."

Rand returned the smile. "I'm sure he will succeed. And I liked the rah-rah of kill them or die." Rand stepped back and began walking into the cave. "Oh, by the way, the same encouragement goes for you too, Captain."

De Terr simply stood there thinking he could gun him down now. His fingers ran across the grips of his pistol. Then the thought of being a very wealthy man returned. De Terr checked each door he came to for others to join the fight, anyone, cooks and maids, anyone who could shoot. They had to win.

CHAPTER SIXTY-FOUR

May 28, 2013

Beneath Brimstone Hill, St. Kitts, 4:35 a.m.

The battle at the dock raged on. Greg and the rest of the team were pounding the pirates. They were totally dominating Brees and his men regardless of what was thrown at them. When the pirates tried to take the offensive, Team One scoured them with withering fire, driving them back. Meanwhile Dane and Hugo were nowhere to be seen. There was no word from them since they had climbed to the upper level and disappeared into the tunnels.

Greg checked his watch. Dane and Hugo had been gone for nearly an hour and a half. He hoped that meant that they had found Sherrie and Erin and were on their way back. Maybe no news was good news. Meanwhile he kept to his job of holding back the pirate hordes on the sea side of the cave.

Brees knew his men were losing the battle. Of the two dozen or so men they had thrown against Team One, only eight remained. That included Brees. In a few more minutes those eight would be toast.

Brees was in trouble. Their dead lay all about the dock and inside the building. Their resolve to fight was waning. Three of the eight stopped shooting, turned and began running back through the house. They were met by de Terr at the door to the next room.

"Get back there and fight!" screamed de Terr. "Now!"

One man tried to explain but de Terr pulled his gun and pointed it directly at the man's head.

"Go back or die here," yelled de Terr. The men glanced quickly at each other and returned to the fight. De Terr followed at a crouch and moved over beside Brees. Smith was crouched across the room, his pistol drawn at the ready.

"We must drive them back," said de Terr.

"We have been trying mightily," answered Brees. "As fast as we attack, they cut us down like dogs. They are hidden around the docks out there and we can't get a good shot at them."

De Terr thought for a minute.

"Do we still have some hand grenades in the armory?" asked de Terr.

"We may have one or two. I'll get a man to get them," said Brees. He turned and motioned a man to his side.

"Go to the armory and bring me hand grenades. Hurry!"

"Yes, sir," the man replied and he was off.

De Terr looked around the room. "How many men do you have left?"

"Too few. We lost most of the crew within two minutes."

De Terr shook his head slowly. He knew this was bad. He thought for a minute. "We have to attack them again and drive them from the dock," he said matter-of-factly.

Brees turned to him and stared.

"Sir, they will kill us all!" he cried. "We must retreat back into the cave, regroup and methodically search out the attackers and kill all of them."

De Terr glared at Brees. "You do that and Hawk will shoot both of us. I have just left him. He is gathering more men. Stay here and fight. I must go back and check the status of the land entrance. Finish this job and meet me in the main conference room. Oh, and Smith does not make it out alive. Do you understand?"

Brees glanced over at Smith. "Right...."

With that de Terr vanished down one of the corridors behind them leading back into the mountain. "Finish this job and meet me in the conference room." What the hell did de Terr think they were trying to do? The attackers were winning and he did not see a way to change that. But maybe the grenades would help gain a leg-up. Brees sat there waiting for his man to bring the grenades.

CHAPTER SIXTY-FIVE

May 28, 2013

Beneath Brimstone Hill, St. Kitts, 4:35 a.m.

Orrin and the girls were methodically making their way toward the dock, hearing all of the gunfire and starting to worry if there really would be a way out.

The group stopped. Thinking about an escape route, Orrin hurried them into a small room to their left until he could figure out how to get the girls out to the dock. He quickly closed the door behind them. He tried to lock the door but was unable to from the inside. He turned and pushed the girls back to the rear of the closet-like room. They all sat with their feet against the door. Even that small amount of resistance might deter the pirates from entering.

"Sounds like somebody's attacking the building on the dock," said Orrin, looking very distraught. "That is our only way out. We can't go back now. We have to find a way to the docks that is not blocked by gunmen."

The gunfire continued. He was on the spot and he was scared. Someone was attacking. Sherrie figured she knew who it was, Dane. She hoped he would find them and get them all out safely, including Orrin.

"That's Dane and Hugo, you know," Sherrie said quietly to Erin. "They are fighting their way to us."

"Really?" asked Erin, looking astonished. "How do you…?" But Orrin cut her off.

"Who do you say that is?" asked Orrin, looking very worried now.

"Those are very good friends of mine that are coming to help us get out," explained Sherrie.

"Me too?" asked Orrin meekly. "They won't kill me, will they? Make me go to jail?"

Sherrie smiled and placed her hand on Orrin's shoulder.

"Orrin, after what you have done to help us, they will be happy to take you with us and keep you safe."

"She is right," added Erin. "You are the best!"

Orrin smiled and sat back, clearly relieved. It was one thing to have Brees and his guys after him, but to have the other side after him as well was too much to bear.

"That's very good, very good," sighed Orrin. "Maybe we have a chance now. I sure would like to see my family and kids again."

"You will," said Sherrie. "You definitely will."

Suddenly loud shots rang out just outside the door. The sound and concussion was deafening. Next they heard several heavy footsteps. It sounded like men were running past them.

"Quiet," whispered Orrin. "It's them, the pirates. They are running away."

In seconds there were more footsteps and more shots. The battle now seemed to be in the hall outside. There were several 'thwacks' on the wall across from where the trio sat as a series of bullets sliced through the wall. Dozens of shots were fired, some automatic, some single shots. The three cowered in the room, praying that no one would open the door.

As their eyes grew accustomed to the low light, they found the room to be slightly larger than a broom closet. It seemed to be a storeroom for radio equipment and computers. The walls were lined with heavy wire shelving and looked as though they would hold a ton of equipment.

The chaos outside seemed to subside as the immediate battle passed down the hall. They wondered if the danger had passed. They did not know the pirates were in full retreat. Greg, Jones and the rest of Team One were still on the docks.

What the girls heard were reinforcements moving forward to aid in the battle against the attackers. With the lull of gunfire, some pirates went from room to room checking for anyone hiding that may be pressed into battle. So far they found none. Their search continued.

There was a noise at the door. Someone was trying to enter. The foursome pressed their feet hard against the door. From outside the pirate attempted to open the door but found it tightly closed.

"Quit wasting time and come on," said another pirate. "If the door won't open, move on." And they did. There was silence.

Five minutes passed. Erin decided to ask the question everyone was thinking. "Think we can leave now?" She listened intently to the silence out in the hall.

"I vote to sit here a few more minutes until we can be more certain the pirates are gone," Sherrie said quietly.

"Me too," interjected Orrin. He was still shaking with fear.

First they heard nothing. Then they began to hear slow footsteps, almost imperceptible but footsteps none the less. Sherrie sat up straight. It must be Dane or Hugo working their way down the hall. Her hand rose toward the door handle.

She was scared. What if it were the pirates? They would kill them there on the spot. Orrin grasped her hand and tried to pull it back. He was gesturing frantically for Sherrie to not open the door.

But she felt confident the footsteps were from a careful survey of the hall outside. That could only mean Dane or Hugo. Her shaking hand reached the doorknob and began to turn it. Orrin hid his face in his hands. The door slowly opened and a man dressed in black spun around pointing his gun.

Sherrie screamed, "Don't shoot! Don't shoot!"

The man immediately raised his gun; it was Dane!

"Damn, Sherrie, that was close," he said excitedly. He checked up and down the hall. Hugo heard the commotion and darted back down the hall toward Dane.

"I found the girls," said Dane quietly. "Both are all right. Step in here out of the hall." Sherrie, Erin and Orrin moved further back in the storeroom. Dane and Hugo ducked in and closed the door. It was a tight squeeze. Five people in a small storeroom built for maybe three at the most. Dane released his weapon so it would hang down his back and reached for Sherrie, picking her up from the floor and embracing her.

"Dane, you have no idea how happy we are to see you," beamed Sherrie in the darkened room.

"Same here, sweetheart, same here!"

There was a slight click as Hugo turned on the light. He saw a group of scared folks wincing at the brightness of the light.

"Good evening, ladies. Sorry we are late for our dates but we had a slight run-in with the locals."

"Same old Hugo," beamed Sherrie.

Dane glanced over at Orrin at the same time Hugo leveled his weapon on the meek man in the corner.

"Don't kill me, please! I helped them, I did," he cried.

"No," said Sherrie, reaching out and pressing Hugo's weapon away from Orrin. "He's with us. He was leading us out when the other pirates came. We hid in here until you came along," she explained. "He's our friend."

Dane looked at him and extended a hand. "I don't know who you are, brother, but I do thank you."

"Yes, yes. I am your friend too. We have to get out now before the captain or Mr. Brees comes back. They will kill us all," said Orrin excitedly.

"Not if we have anything to say about it," smiled Dane, trying to soothe the fears of the old man.

Hugo was at the door. Erin stood behind him. "Let's get moving," whispered Hugo. He turned out the light and cracked open the door. He could hear gunfire back down to his left, the way back to the water. No one was in the hall.

"The party seems to be back with Greg and the others," said Hugo. "I say we go back to the right and make our way out the back entrance. Surely Bob and Stamper have that open for us."

"You mean Greg is here?" asked Sherrie.

"Yes. He's leading the frontal attack out by the docks," said Dane. "From the sound of it, he's doing a damn good job." Before Sherrie could react further Orrin spoke.

"No... You can't go that way," cried Orrin. "The captain and Brees are back there. That's where most of their men are. We can't get out that way."

Hugo thought a second. Maybe Orrin was right. The only gunfire he could hear was to his left. There was only silence to the right, deeper into the pirates' lair.

"What do you think?" asked Hugo, still focused on the hall outside. "Bob and Stamper must have taken control since there we can't hear any gunfire."

"Or, and I hate to say this, but the pirates may have them," said Dane quietly.

"Surely not," answered Hugo without a smile.

"Now that we have the girls, I say try the back way. At least there is no shooting back there," explained Dane. "If we try to make the water, we already know we must shoot our way out. That's too dangerous for the girls."

"Don't worry about us," said Erin. "Just give me a gun and I'll be happy to help fight."

"Me too," added Sherrie.

Dane grinned. "I hope it won't get to that but if it does, I can't think of any better help than you guys. Hugo, go to the right."

"Yes, sir, Boss," answered Hugo as he made a final check of the hall. Seeing it still clear, he darted out, covering the way deeper into the mountain. The girls and Orrin followed with Dane covering the rear.

"No, no, no," whined Orrin. "This is bad..."

At the first corner Hugo paused. The hall opened into another large room with shelving all around. The center of the room was open. What bothered him was there was no cover at all. He listened. He heard only the gunfire behind them.

The group moved into the large room. Their footsteps crunched given the amount of debris on the floor. It sounded much louder than it was. The walls were lined with shelves full of a vast array of supplies, military goods, and general merchandise. Hugo looked over at about ten cases of Gentleman Jack Bourbon whiskey. Beside those boxes were boxes of what looked like Cuban cigars. Hugo silently pointed the boxes out to Dane and smiled. They moved on. They heard nothing but their own footsteps.

As they reached the other side of the room, a voice rang out.

"Freeze! Do not move or you will die!" There was a heavy island accent.

Orrin's hands shot up over his head. "It's the Captain!" he shouted.

Both Hugo and Dane froze, more for the protection of the girls than anything else.

"Drop your guns now!" bellowed the voice again.

From behind and from a pair of doors to their right came several heavily armed men. None were in any kind of uniform. They looked like normal country folks. Their group was moving toward the front of the building to reinforce the pirates at the dock. They were entering the room when they heard Dane's group coming. They merely stepped back into the shadows and waited. When they saw them move into the room, they pounced.

"I will not speak again... Drop your guns, NOW!" commanded the voice, screaming now.

Dane nodded to Hugo and the two lowered their weapons to the floor, rising back up with their hands held at their shoulders. Out of the shadows in front of them stepped the voice and two more armed men.

"It's Captain de Terr!" cried Orrin.

"Shut up, you little welp," snarled de Terr. "I will deal with you very soon."

"You like picking on little guys, huh?" asked Hugo, looking for a fight.

De Terr grinned. "I like killing little guys, especially ones that betray me and bring mercenaries like you into my home. He will die for this. And so will you. But all of this after we enjoy the ladies' company."

"My good captain," boomed another voice from the darkness behind de Terr, "I would not want to make our guests feel not welcome." A large man with an Indiana Jones type hat stepped into the room. "Welcome!"

Dane and Hugo stood there stunned.

"Daddy?" cried Erin. "Is that you?"

"Hello, you two," the man said, grinning at Dane and Hugo. "You may have heard of me. Hawk's the name..."

Hugo gritted his teeth. "You son-of-a-b..."

"Now, now, Hugo, that's no way to greet a trusted friend, is it? Oh, and how are you, Dane?"

"What in God's name is going on here?" asked Dane in a quiet but firm voice.

"What does it look like, Dane? You have broken into my home and killed several of my family. I'm afraid you two will have to pay dearly for that." Hawk stepped slightly to the side, raised his Glock 9mm and fired one shot point blank into Hugo.

"No!" screamed Erin as she rushed to help Hugo, who immediately slumped to the floor.

"Damn, it's only a slight wound," smiled Hawk. "But that should shut him up for a while. I'll let de Terr and his men finish the job later."

Erin stared at her father with tears in her eyes. "How could you do this?" she cried. "How could you?"

"It's easy," said Dane in a calm voice, stepping in front of Sherrie. "The bastard's gone crazy. Money has rotted his mind."

"Oooo… that sounds bad," laughed Hawk.

"Bad but true."

"You have a nice way of putting that," said Hawk, surveying Hugo's condition. "But this time you have bitten off way too much more than you can chew, my friend."

"Friend? No way. Just a piece of garbage ready to be taken out and tossed in the dumpster," said Dane seething. He was already thinking of how to kill this traitor.

CHAPTER SIXTY-SIX

May 28, 2013

Beneath Brimstone Hill, St. Kitts, 5:10 a.m.

The shooting had stopped. Miraculously, Greg and his original force still held the dock area, which was riddled with bullet holes. Through the dim light they could see the dock and railings. They looked as though a swarm of woodpeckers had decided to hold a food convention. Wood chips and broken rails were strewn everywhere. For a moment he worried about the dock collapsing. Greg looked over to Captain Jones.

"Why did they stop firing?" he asked.

"I don't know," answered Jones as he ejected a magazine and checked his bandolier for another. "But they will counter attack again. Maybe they are rounding up more men."

"I hope not. We are getting low on ammo. I don't think we can hang on much longer," moaned Greg. "How many more magazines you got?"

"Just five," said Jones, keeping one eye on the door.

"I've got only three. Where the devil are Dane and Hugo? If they don't get back here soon, they won't have an escape route. Not good for any of us."

Jones handed Greg a full magazine for his submachine gun. He raised his head cautiously. The captain motioned to the police officers in their team to their right and left. Their hand waved replies denoted they were okay. He returned his attention to Greg.

"I have an idea. We could move over to the left side there and create crossfire when they come out again. They will think we are still in our places as before and we can take them down before they discover we have moved. They will never see it coming."

"Not a bad idea," said Greg in a low voice. "We can move over to the boats." It only took a second for him to decide. "Let's do it!"

Jones motioned to the others to move to the right side of the dock. Silently, they proceeded from boat to boat tied to the dock in order to stay out of the water and off the dock. In less than two minutes, they moved fifteen yards into the new position flanking the bullet riddled front of the building.

"We have them now," grinned Jones. "We have the cave wall on our left and these boxes on our right and in front. We are well hidden and have good cover. They will never see us."

They didn't have to wait long. About two minutes later there was a large thud as someone tossed a small heavy object straight out from the building's open door onto the dock. The object rolled over to edge of the dock beside the boat where Greg had been previously positioned.

A second later the grenade exploded with a deafening explosion. The large cave seemed to roar along with the blast causing Greg and his men to grasp their ears in pain. They were totally surprised by the blast.

"What the hell was that?" cried Greg. He turned to Jones, who was shaking his head trying to clear his thoughts.

"That was a grenade!" he cried, unable to hear himself talk. "This is getting bad!"

Before Greg could answer, about a dozen men spilled from the building and raced toward the boats where Greg's men once were. One was Brees. Their weapons were trained on the remnants of the boat and the splintered edge of the dock. The men began firing into the boats indiscriminately. Splinters from the boat and rooster tails from the water flew all about. They must have fired a hundred rounds of ammunition all together. Smith was there too, firing his small pistol. As the dust and smoke cleared, they all stepped forward to admire their kills. Looking into the remains of the now sinking boats, Brees realized there were no bodies. Fear filled his face. Smith stood there smiling. He had no clue as to what had happened.

Brees never heard the shot that killed him. He went from standing on the dock bewildered to lying dead on the dock as Greg's first bullet entered Brees' brain by way of his right temple, exploding out the other side, taking much of his brain with it. Jones and the other men joined in, killing all twelve men and Smith in less than ten seconds.

There was complete silence. Greg thought, was it over? Jones was wary. He motioned for everyone to stay under cover. He did not want to fall into the same trap that Brees and his men did. So they waited.

After a full two minutes of continued silence and inactivity, Greg motioned for one of Jones' men to go up to the door and survey the area. The man stepped from his safe hiding place and stepped out into the open on the dock. As he stepped carefully, his boots crunched through the wood shards spread everywhere. He crept closer and closer until he was leaning directly against the bullet-ridden door frame. Jones' man took a deep breath and snapped his head in the door and immediately back out. He saw nothing.

The dim light inside showed no one in the outer room. The man slowly stepped into the door and entered. The room was a mess. Riddled with bullets from the earlier battles, shards of wood, glass and other items filled the floor, along with numerous dead pirate bodies. The floor seemed as if it were painted red with blood. Quickly he checked the short hallway into the next room and returned to the door, waving an all clear sign.

"It's clear," said Jones to Greg. "Let's move in."

The three remaining men raced in a crouch to the door and stepped inside.

"My, my," said Jones. "Looks like the housekeeper has a big job to do." He said something quietly to one of his men, who started counting the bodies.

Greg surveyed the room. He had seen dead people before but nothing like this. He figured there were two dozen dead in this room alone.

"Sir, I count forty-two dead with the twelve outside," reported Jones' man.

"Good God," said Greg. "We killed forty-two pirates?"

"It certainly looks that way," grinned Jones. "Always remember… better them than us." With that Jones resumed looking around the room.

"Over here," said one man. "I found a box of hand grenades."

Jones strode over, smiling. "Now we have some superior weaponry. Everyone take a couple and let's move on."

The men also found several hundred rounds of 5.56mm ammo for their guns. Jones posted a lookout as the men began to open a second box of ammunition. After reloading their weapons and stocking up on ammo, they were ready to continue.

"Fully loaded and armed to the teeth," smiled Greg. Looking up the hall, Greg surveyed their next move. "This looks like the way in."

"Lead on, my brother," said Captain Jones. The two other men followed in the rear.

CHAPTER SIXTY-SEVEN

May 28, 2013

Beneath Brimstone Hill, St. Kitts, 5:10 a.m.

"So YOU are the Hawk!" said Dane, glaring at Bob Rand. "You bastard! You set us up from the beginning." Dane felt totally betrayed by one of his oldest and most trusted comrades in arms. He was heartbroken but massively pissed off.

"Aww, come on now, Dane. You set yourself up. All I had to do was follow and let my folks know what our next move was to be," said Rand, gloating. "Hell, you did everything for me. I didn't do a thing!"

"And you used your own daughter as bait," Dane continued. "What a poor excuse for a human being."

"Well, that part was a bit of a mistake. We didn't count on the girls getting involved so we had to change our plans just a wee bit. But now we are back on track, albeit short on manpower. But that can be addressed very quickly," gloated Rand.

Sherrie and Erin were tending to Hugo's wound under the close, watchful eyes of de Terr's gunmen. The shot hit him in the left shoulder, breaking his shoulder blade before exiting nastily from his back. Miraculously he was not bleeding too badly.

"Daddy, how could you do this?" cried Erin, tears flowing down her face. "I just can't believe this!"

"Don't be a cry baby," scolded Rand. "This is a cut-throat world and you knew that. Put on your big girl panties and get over here." He motioned with his hand for her to stand beside him. Erin glared at her father. For the first time in her life she hated the man.

"So you are the one behind this nerve gas plot," said Dane calmly, trying to feel out Rand's intentions.

"Yeah," answered Rand looking down, almost embarrassed. "Pretty damn good, huh? I came up with that one with my friends over a few drinks. We will be kicking that plan off next week. Too bad you folks won't be around to enjoy the show. Imagine the entire Dutch side of St. Maarten out like a light. We'll just waltz in and take everything in sight and disappear back here. It will be the biggest crime of all time! Hey, that sounded good, 'The Biggest Crime of all Time'. I should get t-shirts made; don't you think?"

Dane and his group stared at Rand. They could not believe what he was saying, much less what he had just admitted to everyone.

"You are sick, Bob," sighed Dane. "You will never get away with it."

Rand stepped closer to Dane and smiled, aiming his Glock at Dane's head.

"Hell, Dane. I already have."

Rand turned to de Terr. "Send someone to check on the nerve gas. Here's the key to the room." He reached into his pocket and retrieved a brass key ring with a single key.

"Yes, Hawk." De Terr turned to one of his lieutenants. "Check the gas. Make sure it is safe and come back and report here quickly. Now go!"

The man motioned for two more men to follow him. They cocked their weapons and set off out of the door. That left de Terr, his lieutenant and two pirate men to back up Rand.

"So now, what to do with you," smiled Rand, surveying the group. "You." he said, pointing at Orrin, "We will bury at sea... before we kill you. I want you to know you are dying as you plummet to the sea bottom with weights around your legs. I hear drowning is so pleasant."

"No, please don't," pleaded Orrin. "I have a family and kids to take care of."

"You should have considered them before you sold us out," snarled de Terr. "Besides, we will kill them all as well. I will personally rape your wife and daughter before we slice their throats."

Orrin collapsed on the floor.

"Damn you!" cried Sherrie. "I will kill you myself!" She was furious at Rand's taunting of Orrin.

"Ha ha," laughed de Terr, throwing his head back. "Missy, you are not going to kill anyone. You are going to be sold to the white slavers in the Middle East. A pretty young thing like you will fetch a commanding price. They will love those pretty painted toes of yours."

Sherrie sat there stunned. She was ready to die with Dane but not be a slave to some stinking fool who would buy her for his own pleasure.

"Oh, by the way, Dane, if you are counting on being rescued by Inspector Stamper, let's just say don't. He will not be coming over the hill like the cavalry. We took care of him and his men an hour ago," said de Terr laughing. "They all died like dogs."

"Okay, enough fun," interjected Rand. "It's time to wrap this up. De Terr, we have work to do."

De Terr grinned widely. "Yes, we do. And our first job is to get rid of the two Mercs." He turned to his lieutenant. "Take these men to a cell and keep them under heavy guard until I come get them."

The lieutenant moved over beside Dane and reached for his arm. That is when Dane sprang into action. In an instant Dane spun around, grabbed a small combat knife from his waistband and slit the man's throat. A second later several shots rang out. The remainder of Rand's men along with de Terr fell.

"Freeze!" bellowed a command from behind Dane. It was Jones and Greg, gun leveled for action.

Rand grabbed Sherrie and held her in front of him, his pistol aimed at her head.

"No, you freeze, you young buck, unless you want to see Dane's sweet girlfriend's brains all over the wall," screamed Rand.

Dane froze. So did Greg and Jones. What now, wondered Dane, he had to protect Sherrie at all costs and fast. He slowly stepped to his right.

"Uh-huh," said Rand. "You move and I kill her. Right here in front of your eyes."

"Look, Bob, we can work this out, can't we? She's done nothing to you, for God's sake. Just lock us all up and call it quits. No use in killing all of us," said Dane in a monotone while locking eyes with Sherrie. He hoped she got what he was thinking.

Rand laughed. "Are you serious, bro? Hell, I might as well just kill you now." Bob aimed his pistol at Dane, who winked. Sherrie went limp and dropped to the floor right out of Rand's grasp. Bob's reaction was swift.

As Bob pulled the trigger, Erin rushed her father. There was a loud single shot. The bullet struck Erin in the right side of her chest, spinning her around as she fell to the floor. Another burst of gunfire roared as Bob Rand took about twenty rounds to the head and torso. The shots literally tore him apart. His lifeless corpse lay in two pieces, sprawled across the floor in a massive, growing pool of blood.

When silence ruled again, Dane and Sherrie stood together, unhurt. Greg and Captain Jones had unloaded on Rand. So had Hugo, who had feigned being unconscious, waiting for the time to strike. But Erin was gravely wounded, lying in a pool of blood, a high price to pay. And it did not look good.

CHAPTER SIXTY-EIGHT

May 28, 2013

Beneath Brimstone Hill, St. Kitts, 5:30 a.m.

"Erin!" screamed Sherrie, dropping to the floor beside her. "Oh, my God, she's dying! Dane!" Instantly Dane and Greg leapt forward, Greg tearing at his first–aid kit on his web belt. He handed a large bandage to Dane, who slid it inside Erin's shirt over the bleeding wound. Sherrie knelt at her side, cradling her near lifeless head. Orrin sat over beside a chair, terrified.

"Oh, Dane, this is bad, really bad. She's bleeding too much. You have to help her," cried Sherrie, quivering with fear. Her new best friend was laying here, a huge hole in her chest and bleeding to death.

"Greg, hold this bandage here. Push down hard. You have to stop the bleeding," said Dane with an unnatural calm. "We can't move her back to the dock. She'll never survive a boat ride out of here." He turned to Hugo, now up on one knee.

"Ready when you are, Boss," said Hugo. Sherrie had stuffed part of her shirt over Hugo's wound. He wasn't going to let a single shot to the shoulder stop him.

Dane stood up and retrieved his weapon. He knew the only chance Erin had was to leave via the cave and back to town by truck.

"Let's go," said Dane, reaching down to help Hugo to his feet. "Time to pay the piper." He turned to Greg and Sherrie. "You two stay here with Jones and Orrin. We will come back to get you as fast as we can. Greg, keep pressure on the wound or else she will bleed to death. Just pray there is not a lot of internal damage. How's she breathing?"

"Not good," answered Sherrie. "She's really having problems."

"Looks like her lung is hit," added Greg. "Dane, you have to hurry. We can't lose her."

Dane nodded and checked with Jones. "We will get out through the back entrance of the cave. Protect these girls with your life. Do you understand?"

"Don't worry about them," said Captain Jones sternly. "You get moving. I have control here."

"I can help too," cried Orrin, moving over beside Erin. Dane smiled.

"You do that."

Dane tapped Jones on the shoulder, smiled and immediately disappeared down the hall with Hugo.

The two hurriedly stalked down the now dark hall. Most of the lighting had been shot out but they could still see. After about twenty feet and passing several doors, the corridor turned right and widened significantly.

"Main hall," Dane said quietly, still leading, Hugo covering the rear. Dane pointed forward. They moved swiftly, briefly checking each door they came upon. Most were locked. Those that were not were dark. They moved on.

Soon they heard voices. It must be de Terr's men guarding the back entrance. The two stopped.

"You take the right side and I will take the left. Move swiftly. At this point, kill anything that moves. We know our guys are already dead," said Dane quietly and deliberately.

By moving on both sides, Dane and Hugo set up a killing crossfire to hopefully confuse and overwhelm the pirates before they could get off a shot. They moved forward, using the many doorways along the hall for cover. Twenty feet forward Dane could now see a dim glow from the brightening sky outside. They were close to the mouth of the cave. Hugo stepped up to the doorway across from Dane and nodded his readiness. Both took a deep breath, shouldered their arms and struck.

The men at the entrance did not expect the two. After all, Hawk told them to merely stay there and watch the outside. He would take care of the last of the enemy inside. So when Dane and Hugo came running out of the darkness of the inside of the cave, they were upon the guards in seconds. De Terr's five guards were caught totally off guard. Dane and Hugo cut them down mercilessly.

It took only five seconds for five more souls to end their time on this earth. As Hugo checked the bodies, Dane saw Inspector Stamper's body thrown in the back of a truck near the entrance. The four policemen's bodies were lying on the ground beside the truck. Dane walked over and checked for vitals. When he touched Stamper's neck he knew the answer. His cold skin announced his demise.

Hugo stepped over. "They are all dead. Let's head back in."

"Lead on."

Running at full speed, it took less than a minute to return to the girls and prepare for their extraction.

CHAPTER SIXTY-NINE

May 28, 2013

Beneath Brimstone Hill, St. Kitts, 5:48 a.m.

"Someone's coming," said Jones, bringing his weapon up to the ready. "Stay down."

The footsteps became louder and louder.

"Jones! It's us. Don't shoot!"

Jones let out a sigh of relief as Dane and Hugo emerged from the darkness.

"Great to have you back," smiled Captain Jones. "All clear back there?"

"Clear, but I'm afraid Inspector Stamper and your men did not make it," said Hugo quietly. Jones pursed his lips and then took a deep breath.

"He was a good man, Stamper. He hired me and took me under his wing when I was starting on the police force in St. Maarten. When I moved to St. Kitts, I credited it all to him. I will miss the man."

"I'm sorry," said Dane, turning his attention to the girls. "How's Erin?"

"We have slowed the bleeding big time but we need to get her to a hospital as quickly as we can," said Greg with a sincere sense of urgency.

"Dane, she's in serious condition," added Greg. "We gotta get her to the hospital now. We can't lose her, man." It was becoming clear that Greg was more than casually involved.

"Don't worry. We've come this far. I refuse to end this on a bad note." Dane turned his attention to Sherrie. "How you doin', Sher?" he asked.

"Fine. Erin opened her eyes a few minutes ago but went right back out. But she's hanging in there."

"Good!" smiled Dane. "The way out is clear but even so Hugo will lead and Cap, you have our tail. Greg, can you carry Erin?"

"Got her," answered Greg, scooping her up into his arms. "Sherrie, hold that bandage for me, please." Greg did not want the bandage to come loose from Erin's wound. The bleeding had stopped and much of the blood coagulated, creating a natural plug to the hole in her chest.

"I have it," said Sherrie. She turned to Dane. "Let's get the hell out of here."

"Your wish is my command," grinned Hugo weakly. His wound was bleeding a bit from the recoil of the shots he had fired. And it hurt. Putting all of the pain aside like his SEAL training had taught him, he ducked off down the hall. The rest of the group followed.

"Captain Jones, I'll tell Nelson to get up here jiffy quick," Dane yelled back as he trotted away.

"Not a problem. We need the rest."

At the cave mouth the morning was breaking. The rays of the warm sun were beginning to trickle through the trees from the east. Sherrie stopped to get the first breath of fresh air in days.

Orrin stuck to Sherrie like glue. He was still unsure as to how he would be treated once the police arrived. He saw safety with Sherrie.

While the group rested for a minute, Dane procured one of the unmarked vans parked under the trees to the right and pulled over to the group.

Once Erin was loaded into the van, the remaining group piled in and left the clearing, only slowing slightly to tell Commissioner Nelson to go on in. Now they sped toward Basseterre and the hospital.

CHAPTER SEVENTY

May 28, 2013

Beneath Brimstone Hill, St. Kitts, 6:15 a.m.

"Captain Jones!"

"In here," answered Jones, his hand on his weapon just in case.

"Nelson here!" came the response from down the hall.

"Come on in!"

Jones and his men were still resting and taking a count of all of the dead men left after the fighting ended. Still there was a sigh of relief as Commissioner Nelson and his men emerged from the darkness.

"It is great to see you, sir," smiled Captain Jones, standing. "It's all clear here."

Nelson raised his hand. "Please do not stand on my account. Looks like you and your men had it pretty bad." He looked around at the tired but smiling men. "Is this all that survived?"

"Yes sir."

"Where's Stamper?"

Jones looked down for a second and then back at Nelson. There was silence for a second. "You passed his body when you came in."

"Oh…I see," said Nelson, his hand to his mouth. "My God…" He paused for a second. "I am sorry," said Nelson. "I can't believe it."

Jones turned to Nelson. "How's Erin?"

"I don't know. Dane is racing back to the hospital. He should be there by now. We should know soon."

Commissioner Nelson looked around the room. "What the hell is this place?"

Jones smiled meekly. "Let me show you, Commissioner. You are not going to believe your eyes."

Captain Jones led Nelson across the rubble and bodies, through the myriad of rooms and finally out onto the dock. Commissioner Nelson was stunned.

"Oh, my God, it does exist! Just like Mr. Skoglund said. This is amazing!"

"Yes, sir, he was right. This is the pirates' base. They hid here and raided boats all around this region. This will close several of our open cases of missing boats and crews."

"Yes, I imagine you are right, Captain. But this is absolutely incredible!"

By now several of Nelson's men had joined them on the dock. They too were awestruck.

Nelson turned to one of his officers. "Help Captain Jones and his men back to my car. Also call headquarters and ask for a full forensics team to get out here now. And bring several photographers. And tell the coroner that he is going to be very busy."

"Captain, gather your men. You and your men will be riding back to town with me." With that, Nelson slapped his hands together. "Wow!"

CHAPTER SEVENTY-ONE

June 4, 2013

Aboard the Sweet Texas, Basseterre Harbor, St. Kitts, 2:35 p.m.

Two weeks passed since the raid on the Brimstone cave. During that time the local authorities took control of the cave and the nerve gas hidden inside. The St. Kitts Police Force called in the United States Government, who provided the expertise to safely remove the gas and take it from the island.

The locals provided heroes' funerals for Inspector Stamper and his men back in St. Maarten. The pirates were buried in pauper's graves on the other side of St. Kitts.

The St. Maarten and Netherlands authorities joined with the St. Kitts and U.S Government to discuss the situation. While some extra safeguards were put into place, the primary goal was to ferret out the source of the nerve gas and bring those responsible to justice. That undertaking was continuing with several U.S. covert services and Homeland Security heavily involved. Most of the work was classified. The results would never reach the public.

The trail led directly back to Winston Danson and Hamza Al-Bari. Undisclosed forces later arrested Al-Bari in Damascus. He mysteriously died within days.

C.I. A. operatives and a U.S. elite force were clandestinely sent to Damascus. Very early one morning Danson was plucked from his opulent home. He was the recipient of a very quick and secure trip back to the U.S. for trial. His assets were absorbed by the Syrian government as payment for looking the other way during the operation. Danson's world was crushed. His arms dealings in the region were erased.

Many say that the actual capture of Danson was done by the Israelis but details of the multiple operations were never released. Such is the outcome of most of these types of heinous plots against the world. They are quietly but effectively dispatched.

Even Dane and his group would likely never hear of the final outcome.

Bob Rand's cohort, James Doss, upon learning of Hawk's death, disappeared. The authorities in St. Kitts swore out numerous warrants against Doss and he was on the most wanted list of INTERPOL. The U.S. and Syrian governments were also on his trail. His running days would soon be over.

Orrin Mattson was pardoned by the court in St. Kitts after Dane, Hugo and Nelson testified as to the immeasurable assistance he had rendered. He received a generous reward from the St. Kitts government and settled into a quiet life with his family. Dane and Hugo made certain Orrin's family enjoyed a nice new home and two vehicles.

Hugo, Dane, Sherrie, Greg and Captain Jones sat around the main salon table aboard the *Sweet Texas*. Jones was granted a one-month leave to recuperate from the stress of the assault. Hugo and Dane insisted he do so with them aboard the big cat.

Erin was recovering well in the hospital. Her wounds were much more severe than first thought. The bullet had traveled through her right lung and narrowly missed her spine. It also caused damage to her spleen and liver. Add to that the loss of blood and she was extremely lucky to have survived. Doctors told them that if they had not applied constant pressure on her wound, she would most certainly have died before reaching the hospital.

Greg visited her each day, sometimes more than once. Erin and Greg were becoming an item. They had a mutual fondness that spread from nearly losing each other. Everyone was thrilled, especially Sherrie. She kept at Greg constantly. "Erin would make a great sister-in-law!" Greg's response was always a red-faced grin.

The entire Rand Corporation now fell to her. She was able to get Dane to help appoint a general manager while she was in the hospital. Her employees rallied around her like family. In actuality, they were the only family she had now. And the business moved on. That was the good part. The bad part was Erin felt totally betrayed by her father and was still carrying his death like a weight around her neck. While she certainly regretted his death, she had come to realize that he was not the man she had thought. She yearned to be able to speak to him one more time and ask him one last question again...Why? Dane and Hugo had similar thoughts about their old friend, Bob Rand. Why would Bob succumb to the greed and power he sought to amass? The two had thought they knew Rand better. And they too were crushed to find out the opposite.

"So what are your plans when you leave our fair island paradise?" asked Captain Jones, his bare feet propped up on the outer edge of the cat, holding a nearly empty Corona.

"Plans?" mocked Hugo. "What plans? We don't need no stinking plans!"

The group laughed heartily. Humor replaced the stress of the past few weeks.

Dane took a drink of cold bottled water. "I can't see us staying around here, especially with hurricane season just coming on."

"Hurricanes... no way! I don't do hurricanes," quipped Sherrie.

"We could sail down the South American coast," added Hugo. "When is carnival in Rio? Now, that would be a riot!"

"Ahhh, we missed it this year, Hugo. It goes on before Lent," said Sherrie, devouring the last bite of a plate of fresh cooked lobster. "Besides, haven't you had enough of Brazil?"

"Hmmm. Yeah, you got a point there, Sher." They all laughed, recalling their run-in with the Neo-Nazis last year. "Don't want to go back there. Got that t-shirt and one was too many," chortled Hugo.

"We could return triumphantly to Miami," said Dane, half joking.

Both Hugo and Sherrie looked at each other for just a second before chiming in together, "No way!"

"You want to leave all this?" asked Sherrie. "Hell, I don't. I want to sail away with Dane forever." Dane grinned. That's my girl, he thought.

Hugo turned to Dane and Greg. "Well, I do have a surprise for all of you. I mixed up a mighty fine concoction for our libation period this afternoon."

With that, Hugo strode off into the galley.

"Oh, Lord, what's he come up with now," groaned Greg.

"Remember, he's from Texas. It might be steer meat and vodka," laughed Sherrie.

"Sounds terrible," said Dane.

Hugo returned with a tray of glasses and a very large pitcher of a beautiful red, orange and blue liquid. Each glass was festooned with a pineapple slice, an orange slice, a cherry and one of little umbrellas.

The eyes of the group widened. Captain Jones took his last gulp of beer and set the empty bottle aside. He was so ready for Hugo's mixture. It looked wonderful! Hugo poured a generous glass for each person and passed the glasses around.

"To the best damn bunch of folks in the world," cried Hugo loudly. With that, they all tasted their drinks. They tasted even better than they looked.

"Hugo, you have outdone yourself," said Greg.

"Yes, you have," added Jones. "I could drink these all day long."

"Hugo, this really is very good. What are they?" asked Sherrie.

Hugo raised his glass and grinned. "This, dear friends, is my own mixture, my own creation. Ladies and gentlemen, I bring you the Caribbean Chill!"

"Here, here!" shouted Dane. "A winner."

"*Absolument!*" said Captain Jones.

EPILOGUE

July 4, 2013

At Sea, Aboard the Sweet Texas, Headed South, 7:30 p.m.

The *Sweet Texas* ripped through the two-foot waves, spraying what looked like thousands of orange diamonds across her bow. The sun was low on the horizon as they sailed due west across the Caribbean Sea. Their destination was the Yucatan coast of Mexico, down near Belize. The group had been invited to help out on an archeological dig run by Dane's sister, Dana, and her husband, Randall Finley.

  The Finleys were fully recovered from their ordeal in the Amazon but yearned to get back to their work. Randall was hand-picked to lead an interesting Mayan dig. The duo jumped at the chance, especially since it was fully funded by a very wealthy but eccentric benefactor. Money was no object. So they asked Dane and the group to stop by and visit. They also needed the extra manpower. While the trip did not get them out of the track of most hurricanes, Dane was able to deter Sherrie's fears. So off they went.

  Greg and Erin were side by side on the upper couch at the helm. Her wounds had healed and the group talked her into leaving the business to those that were running it well and take a long-deserved vacation. The fact that Greg was aboard made Erin's answer an automatic and resounding yes. Everyone was thrilled to have her aboard.

  Hugo was in the galley cooking up what he called a Texas feast, tacos and burritos with all the trimmings, chased with ice cold Tecate. Dane and Sherrie sat arm in arm on the back lounge watching the sun's last appearance of the day.

The group had dropped Captain Jones off back in Basseterre a few days before to rejoin the police force. In fact, rejoin was not exactly accurate. Jones was promoted to Inspector Jones and was named the natural replacement for Commissioner Nelson, who had recently announced his retirement at the end of the year. The group had tried their best to talk Jones into coming with them, but as he said, duty calls.

"Isn't this just gorgeous?" asked Sherrie.

"What a way to live," added Dane. "Looks like Greg and Erin have, as Hugo would say, *'taken a likin' to each other'*. That's Texan for love."

"He really does like her. And she likes him. They are nearly inseparable."

"Sounds like someone else I know," added Dane coyly.

"Well, I hope there's more than like…"

"Hmmm, ya think I may have gotten myself in a wee bit of trouble?"

Sherrie poked Dane in the side. "Yeah…" Dane turned and gave her a kiss. Sherrie seemed to melt in his arms. "Wonder when dinner will be ready. You think we have time to…"

"Later Sher, we have plenty of time. We are on the way to Mexico!"

Sherrie grinned. "Yeah, I have you for a long, long time."

"Yes, that's definitely true. Just think of the time we can have in Cozumel and Cancun."

"Hey, just think of the time we can have down in our cabin."

Dane began to blush. "Lord, let's don't start something now we can't finish."

"Oh, I can finish it," smiled Sherrie.

"Hey, let's eat!" Hugo cried from the salon. "Greg, put her on auto and bring Erin down and eat some real Texas chow."

As Erin and Greg came down from the helm, Dane whispered to Sherrie,

"Tonight…" and smiled. Sherrie smiled and gave him a peck on the cheek.

"You betcha."

ABOUT THE AUTHOR

This is Ron Smoak's second novel. Born and raised in South Carolina, he graduated from Clemson University and began his career in banking. He later worked in the textile industry and spent twenty years at the Atlanta Journal/Constitution. He also formed and ran an IT consulting business. Now a retired Information Technology professional, he lives in Canton, Georgia outside of Atlanta with his wife Lee and cat Hobie. He is an avid reader and traveler who especially loves cruising the Caribbean. His love of adventure novels led him to write his own.

Ron plans to continue this series with more adventures of Dane Skoglund and Hugo Winsor with book number three, their biggest and most thrilling adventure yet. Keep on reading!